THE MISTS OF FEAR

THE MISTS OF FEAR

JOHN CREASEY

WALKER AND COMPANY
New York

First published in the United States of America
in 1977 by the Walker Publishing Company, Inc.

ISBN: 0-8027-5381-7

Library of Congress Catalog Card Number: 77-80203

Printed in the United States of America

10   9   8   7   6   5   4   3   2   1

CONTENTS

PART ONE

JIM FORRESTER

1

FORRESTER sat at the window of the hotel room, and looked out into the wind-rocked street. So many things were moving that it gave the impression that the street, even the whole town, was being thrown about by an earthquake. He had first experienced the fury of the storm when he had been down by the sea, alone; and was frightened by Nature's violence. The wind had swept down on him, his easel, paints and folding stool. It had hissed among the grey pebbles—which in normal times looked as if a plague of gulls had swept in from the sea and laid millions of grey eggs—then whipped the sea into venomous fury. The sea had answered back and come pounding down on pebbles and the dunes, driving him away in swift alarm.

He could remember it now.

He had saved himself; everything else had been blown away or swept out to sea.

He had been a stranger to Estafillo then, and the Spaniards had watched his solitary return with courteous curiosity, but no one had talked to him about it until that night, at the wine shop.

The wine shop was just across the road from the hotel.

In the wine shop he had met Saturnino; plump, ruddy, jolly, red-haired Saturnino with the light-brown eyes and brave command of English. It was not a full command, although in the past eight weeks it had improved considerably. To the delight of the twenty or thirty regular patrons of the wine shop, Saturnino had translated everything Forrester had said into Spanish. And of course, Saturnino and everyone else had been delighted with the Englishman's attempts to learn Spanish, and to get his tongue round consonants which were not really there.

Now, Saturnino was out with the fishing-fleet. No one would say so, but Forrester had been in Estafillo long enough to know that many anxious eyes were turned towards the sea; as many anxious ears were alert, hating the howling, whining wind because of what it might do to the fishermen. There had been a wind ten days ago, and——

"Now we live six week, eight week, no wind-o," Saturnino had said with the downrightness of a weather prophet who was never wrong; or else forgetful of his errors. "No wind-o, the weather shall be the goods."

At dawn that morning, the fleet had set out, fifty wooden vessels which looked no different from the vessels pictured by the historians of centuries ago. Heavy brown sails, thick masts, high prows and long oars, all manned with tough-looking jerseyed fishermen wearing scarves wound tightly round their heads, like skull-caps with wide pigtails. The morning had been calm, warm, serene; the fleet had sailed out of sight across the sapphire sea, each boat mirrored on the blue water, and no one had thought twice about it. Tomorrow it should return, with all nets filled.

At midday the first spurts of dust in the narrow streets had been followed by the same short, spiteful gusts of wind, slamming doors, rattling windows, making the electric lamps in the middle of the narrow streets sway like pendulums as they hung from the covered cables. By the middle of the afternoon even Forrester had known that Saturnino's prophecy had gone awry.

He smoked and watched.

It was nearly five o'clock. In some ways, five o'clock was the worst time of the day. At five o'clock he was always in a mood to jump to his feet, stride to the small table, snatch up pen and paper and write to Palfrey. He had pictured the message time and time again, something like:

> Dear Sap,
>   This is a goddawful waste of time. I can't stand it any longer. Please send someone who likes doing nothing or call the whole thing off. I'm serious.
>
>   Jim.

He hadn't sent it yet.

He did not think so seriously about getting away today, because he was worried about the fleet. No one had told him there was cause for worry, but looking out he could see the people, the old women dressed in thick black shawls and long black skirts, hurry out of their narrow doorways and go to a street corner, look towards the sea, anxiety in their bearing. The young and the old were there together.

Saturnino and others had told Forrester of the deadliness of being caught at sea in the wind. It would last two or even three days. The tales Saturnino had told were legendary, going back into ages almost forgotten, but among them was one of the whole fleet which had been caught in a storm, and never come back.

"Feefty-nine boats, Señor Forrester, and how many return? No, sir, not one."

Now, all Estafillo had an anxious, nervous look—both the people and the town, or that part of it that Forrester could see. The electric lamps were jigging and jumping, doors slamming, bits of paper, orange peel, donkey droppings and dust swept along the street until they reached a corner where wind hurtled down from other directions, too, and made little whirlwinds which rose to roof height.

The straw, the pieces of wood and paper, the donkey droppings and all the things one saw daily in the gutter, seemed to take on life. It was as if the whole town were swinging in a nervous dance, to try to forget the fleet and the absent fishermen.

Inside the hotel doors were continually banging, windows rattling, and outside there was constant movement, too.

A little group was at every corner, peering out to sea.

Especially on mornings like this, Forrester wished that he had paid the forty pesetas a day for a room with a view of the Mediterranean, but he hadn't. It was false economy, but the thing he always remembered was that he wasn't spending his own money. Sometimes he wondered whose money it was. Sap Palfrey's? Possibly. The Government's? Oh, forget it, he was saving someone 280 pesetas, nearly three pounds, a week, and had been here eight weeks already. This room was all right, wasn't it? It was spacious, with a very high ceiling, a tiled floor doubly welcome on the hot days, a big bed and a bathroom. There was the biggest bath and the most handsome marble wash-basin Forrester had ever seen in his life; ample room for a family to bath in together.

He hadn't any family.

He hadn't a wife, either. Not now.

He jumped up with his hands clenched, shook them at the cherubims moulded on the ceiling, clenched his teeth, closed his eyes, held his whole body as if pain racked it. Slowly, very slowly, he relaxed, dropped his arms, opened his eyes and moved back towards the window. He didn't sit down again. He looked pale, in spite of his tan, and was trembling. It was a long time, nearly three weeks, since he had been taken with a fit like that.

Sorrow for himself and mourning for his wife were equally to blame. After the weeks of numbed shock, when he had come to realise that he would never see Alice again, that she was dead and he was alive, Forrester had known those paroxysms. Grief? Shock? The diagnosis didn't really matter. He was sure that Palfrey had sent him to this little corner of Spain, where the wind sometimes came from the Atlantic, over the hills and then hurtling on towards the Mediterranean, to help him get over it. It was a kind of enforced rest; yet he had a little to do, and he realised that a day might come when that little would become both much and significant.

And he could indulge his one hobby: painting water-colours.

He leaned against the window, with an unlit cigarette between his lips. A gust of wind which seemed at least eighty miles an hour strong smashed at the window and set it shivering and banging. Outside everything danced a wild fandango. Something hard cracked against the small window of the wine shop, where a few dozen dusty bottles of red wine lay by the side of a sign for *Sandeman's Port* and an advertisement picture of Jerez.

The night of his first wind and the loss of his things, he had told Saturnino about it, in halting Spanish; he had been understood, and been answered in English. Nothing would satisfy Saturnino, after that, except to go into the greatest detail about the nearest spot where Forrester could replace his losses at low cost. For an artist, Saturnino had said in hushed tones, what greater suffering could there be than to lack the tools of his art? La Lineas, yes, perhaps; Gibraltar, certainly, but it took time to get there, and he had been to

Gibraltar once, why should he wish to go again? Malaga, now, the beautiful city on the beautiful hill which almost fell into the sea, and beyond, through the mountains to Granada——

The next day Forrester had driven to Malaga, and enjoyed it. He'd bought everything he needed, and been back before dark. He had to have an ostensible reason for holidaying in the South of Spain, but all except the cynical or the sceptical were satisfied by his sketches. They weren't bad, either; to the untutored eye, almost good. He had grown used to painting with a crowd of people behind him; children as well as their grandparents, silent as if they feared that the slightest sound would disturb the mood of the painter. At first they had irritated him; now he felt lonely if he were by himself. He was accepted as a guest by them all. Estafillo made him welcome, from old Father Juan to young Father Aristides, from the kindly old *madame*—only the French had the right word and the right inflection—to the girls whom she fussed over. All very illegal, of course, and very wrong. Wasn't it?

Now the fleet had been caught at sea when a wind had come down, and probably the minds of all the townsfolk were carried back to the day of the legend when not a single boat or a single fisherman had returned to dry land.

And perhaps the thought of death had suddenly spurred Forrester to that moment of physical revolt against the bitter past—against the acceptance of death as final. He realised an odd thing as he looked out: the picture of Alice's face had not been as clear as it had even weeks ago. It was blurring.

Well, twelve months was a long time.

Perhaps the two he had spent here were really doing him good. But he simply couldn't stay much longer. He was beginning to doubt whether there was really any point in waiting and watching in case Botticelli came. Palfrey had acted on the slimmest possible evidence; had the quarry been anyone else it would have been ludicrous to have a man spending all his time lurking—and that was the one appropriate word—in the hope that a certain nasty piece of work would turn up.

Forrester knew the facts. A letter with the Estafillo

postmark had reached Botticelli in Chicago. When opened, the letter had been found to be in code. A copy had been made, the letter resealed and delivered. Cypher experts had been working on the letter ever since, and could not decode it. Using this as evidence, Palfrey had reasoned that someone with a place in Botticelli's scheme of evil had written to him from Estafillo. Evidence against Botticelli was so badly wanted, for he was suspected of such unspeakable villainies, that it had been worth sending an agent here.

Forrester had established only one fact.

An American had been staying at Estafillo, in this very hotel, on the date when the letter had been posted, and the envelope and airmail rice paper had been of American manufacture. By cautious, devious methods, Forrester had discovered a little about the American; that he had spent five days here, often visited Gibraltar and La Lineas, and had a woman with him.

"*Carra mia!*" Saturnino had often exclaimed, and rolled his amber eyes, "the señorita Americana, so bewt-iful! So luffley, so——" And he had made voluptuous shapes in the air with his hands, to the accompaniment of roars of laughter from the other men in the small, smoke-laden wine shop. The crammed tables had seemed likely to fall at any moment; each had a bottle, some small glasses and many resting elbows.

The Spaniards did not have a book-registration system in their hotels; all aliens had to fill up two cards, each with dozens of questions; then each was filed with elaborate care. So it had not been easy to find the name of the American. Forrester had come down in the early hours, sent the night clerk off on a fool's errand, and had a glimpse of the cards. He had sent the details to Palfrey long ago, but remembered them clearly. The main points were simple: the American, a man about fifty-five, had been Joseph Lennard ; the woman, in her twenties, was his wife Elenora. Lennard's birth-place and home town were given as Cincinnati, Ohio; his wife's birthplace as New York.

Joseph Lennard of Cincinnati had driven a bright-green Cadillac convertible, with an Ohio registration. Of course, there was no way of being sure that he had written to Botticelli, but as far as Forrester had been able to make out,

no other American had been at Estafillo at or about that time
—January 15th.

Forrester did not know what Palfrey had done about this.
When one was on the fringe of the Secret Service there were
many bewildering things, and much was unknown. Forrester
did not object to that. But he would soon need much more
convincing that he hadn't wasted his time.

But perhaps Palfrey had discovered more, and possibly
Forrester's careful work was not to be wasted. Forrester
wanted to know. He was beginning to feel buried alive. He
hated the wind, too, and the fears of the people.

A girl came out of one of the small houses near the wine
shop. These tiny houses were really sections of a long,
narrow, barn-like building, and the fronts looked like one
low wall dotted at intervals with squat doors and small square
windows. The outsides were painted white, and in sunlight
they were dazzling. The doors and windows were edged
with blue paint; perhaps that made this girl more noticeable.

She wore a red cotton dress which the wind clutched,
dragged up to her knees and pressed against her body. It
showed every curve, every provocative promise of a curve.
For a moment it was startling, and pulled Forrester's
thoughts away from everything else.

She turned into the wind, towards the wine shop. A
sudden gust made her stand still, to fight for her balance,
and her lovely figure was assaulted by the wind. Gradually
she fought back and, so as to save her eyes from the dust, she
pulled a scarf from her head, wound it about her forearm,
then held it up to make a kind of veil.

Before she did that she turned her face towards Forrester.

Then she walked into the wind, past the wine shop and to
a corner; next she turned down that street, towards the sea.

Forrester stared at the spot where she had been. She
stayed on the retina of his mind's eye like the filament of
an electric-lamp bulb on the physical retina, after one had
stared at a light; or like the image of the sun long after one
had looked inadvertently into it. Her body and her face
were both there; beauty that could hardly be real.

Forrester found himself wanting to see her again. He
did not say that this was the artist in him, although perhaps

the artist had caught that beauty and known that it was so free from blemish. He moved from the window and crossed to the door, taking a brown cloth cap from a peg behind the door as he opened it. This cap would stay on, in spite of the wind.

Two well-dressed women were at the reception desk talking to the clerk—about the wind and the fishing-fleet and their worry.

A door was banging.

A small boy in a puce-coloured uniform sprang to the swing doors leading to the street when he saw Forrester. He smiled into Forrester's face, his bright-brown eyes alive with a kind of secret merriment. Forrester winked at him, and went out. The wind struck hard, not cold but not warm, and grit flew into his eyes; then the wind got under the peak of his cap and lifted it off his head. He swung round, to rescue it. The boy had caught it, and was offering it back.

"*Gracias*," Forrester said, and smiled.

"*Si, señor!*"

Forrester turned away, clutching his cap this time, but that gust had gone; there was wind but not a squall. The distant howling and whining made a background to the nearer sounds—as if Estafillo had called on a thousand little demons, each carrying castanets, each clapping them with devilish vigour at the identical moment. Nothing was still, and everything that moved had its own particular tempo of sound, its own particular volume. Doors, windows, the wires, the lamps, the litter, even the long rows of houses seemed to be dancing.

Forrester reached the corner round which the girl in red had gone. She was some distance on, near the sea, still windswept but too far away for him to see her beauty. He ought not to follow. It had been an impulse which he would probably regret if he went on with it. It had not always been easy, but he had resisted the temptations inherent in the beauty of so many Spanish girls.

He stood and watched this one.

The wind must have drowned the sound of the approaching car, for the long, blaring note of a horn took him by surprise. He jumped to the narrow pavement, then turned round, realising that the warning blast had not been meant for him but for a boy and a herd of goats turning the corner. The car was passing the end of the road. It was vivid green. A middle-aged man sat at the wheel, a fair-haired woman, much younger than the man, sat beside him.

The car passed.

It was a Cadillac convertible.

2

FORRESTER knew this road well. There was only one place to which the man and woman in the green Cadillac would be going. To the harbour. Not far along, the road turned towards the sea and ended at the mass of grey pebbles and the jetties and the quay. Here was just a tiny harbour, and more beach. Above any spot likely to be reached by heavy waves, small row-boats were drawn up, and a few brown nets were hanging over wooden posts and railings, spares for the boats which were out at sea. A few lobster-pots, looking like rotting pieces of chestnut fencing, also stood about, and round marker floats, painted in many colours, festooned the nets.

Forrester could not see this from where he stood.

The girl had reached the end of this narrow road and turned left, so she was going towards the harbour.

Forrester followed her, not only because of her beauty or of the strange effect that the wind against her body had had on him. He wanted to see the man and the woman of the Cadillac, who might be Joseph Lennard and his wife. They would have to stop, or at least slow down, in order to turn. Unless they knew the town well, they had missed their road; if they knew the town at all—if, for instance, they were the Lennards—they would know exactly where the road led.

There was nothing near the little harbour except a few cottages; but the view of the rocky coast-line was magnificent, and on such a day, with the tideless sea whipped to wild fury, it would be worth anyone's time.

With the wind behind him, Forrester hurried.

He reached the end of the street, which was only a few yards from the bank of grey pebbles. The roar of the sea against them burst on him once he was in the open. As the water fell back to gather strength for another, tireless onslaught, it hissed and screamed through the pebbles, carrying countless numbers of them away.

The girl in red was now one of twenty or thirty women looking towards the sea.

The green Cadillac had pulled up, facing the sea. The driver and the woman next to him appeared to be watching the smashing waves and the turbulent blue. The sun reflected on the distant water, and the light was much brighter here than in the narrow streets.

All the women were looking for some sign of a sail, some reason to hope that their men were coming home. All, that was, except the girl in the red dress. She was at the back of the crowd, still struggling against the wind. She drew nearer the Cadillac. Forrester was fifty feet or so away, and had a clear view of the car driver's profile ; he hid his fair-haired companion, but it was certain that neither driver nor passenger was looking towards the girl. They did not seem to be aware that she was drawing nearer.

Suddenly she stopped.

The passenger leaned forward, as if to look at the girl in red. Forrester was startled by the contrast between fair beauty and dusky beauty; between blue eyes and eyes which had the dark glow of chestnuts fresh from their husk: here were two kinds of beauty, one facing him, one with her back towards him.

The woman in the car looked past the girl towards Forrester. She seemed to frown. Then she touched her companion's arm, and the man glanced round quickly. Forrester was aware of brief, tense scrutiny.

Then both man and girl turned away, and looked towards the sea.

Forrester went nearer the sea, his ears filled with the bluster of the waves and the shouting of the wind, with the hissing scream of water through the pebbles. Nothing was still, except the watching women. The shawls, the black skirts and the cotton blouses all shook and quivered in the wind, but the women stood quite still, keeping their tragic vigil.

Forrester drew closer to them, forcing himself not to

look at the car or the girl in red, although he began to doubt his wisdom; wouldn't curiosity be more natural than forced indifference? They could tell at a glance that he wasn't Spanish. By scanning the boisterous sea for some sign of a ship on the horizon, he might be doing the very thing he did not want to do.

So he looked towards them again.

The girl in red was disappearing; vanishing into thin air.

.   .   .   .   .

Until that moment Forrester had felt rising excitement because of the man in the car, the girl, the green convertible and the possibility that these were the Lennards. And he had still been under the influence of that startling beauty of the Spanish girl. Now, both things were driven out of his mind.

The girl in red *was* fading away.

It was as if some freak mist had drifted in from the sea, just one small cloud which enveloped her. One moment she was there in the vivid red-and-black scarf, looking at the car; the next she became a vague figure, enshrouded by that mist. The red was fading into pink, the black into grey.

The fishwives stared seawards.

The man and the girl in the car looked out to sea, also, until the man started the engine.

The girl in red simply was not there.

A few wispy traces of mist remained, but they were vanishing. The sun shone from a clear sky and the wind beat upon the earth on which the girl had been standing.

The Cadillac began to move, its wheels turning towards the harbour wall, then back towards Forrester. Neither the man nor the girl by his side appeared to pay any attention to Forrester, who was so bewildered that he took little notice of them. The car passed, with the girl passenger closer him. He saw her face, clearly.

It would not take much stretching of the imagination to believe that she was smiling at him.

Mockingly?

The man was looking ahead as he drove, and the engine's murmur was hardly a sound against the noises of the day.

The car gathered speed when it reached the road.

Then suddenly an ear-splitting whistle screamed through

the air, caused by a freakish gust of wind. The roof of a house crashed in. A hole yawned in a mud wall, revealing an iron bedstead, an old chest of drawers and a chair. Rubble and dust, more like fog than the dust of the dirty streets, blocked the road and hid the naked room.

People ran to help, others gaped at the scene, crossing themselves as they came out of their stupor. Forrester didn't blame them; the noise had been terrifying. A meteorite? He went closer to the hole in the house, and saw another in the ground, filled as with boiling mud—like lava. More Spaniards came and crossed themselves, an old woman was helped by a dozen thrusting or pulling hands from the ruined house.

It was a kind of molten metal, Forrester thought, and for the first time a new possibility crossed his mind—that there might be some connection between the disappearance of the girl in red and the explosion.

Nonsense?

He was badly shaken; and there, bubbling away, was the molten metal, like boiling, yellowish mud which gave off a thick vapour.

He almost forgot the Cadillac, the man and the fair-haired girl; but the disappearance of the Spanish girl haunted him.

.   .   .   .   .

Forrester went back to the harbour, and stared at the spot where he had last seen the girl in red. He shot quick, wary glances at the fishwives. Several had turned and were walking back towards the town, to the crowd about the "meteorite". Many more people were there now. A few wives, disheartened and fearful but with their work to be done, were moving on. Others, reluctant to admit the desolating truth, still stood on the beach or on the harbour, staring at the empty blue of sky and ocean.

Forrester walked towards the spot where the convertible had stood. He could see the mark of its tyres in the sandy soil near the harbour wall. He reached the spot, then turned and looked back to the corner of the street along which he had come. Now he had walked along the exact route which the girl in red had taken, and nothing had got in his way.

Of course it hadn't.

He had seen the girl and followed her; he could not have

made a mistake; but she had vanished into thin air just before that fearful "thing" had fallen from the heavens.

.　　.　　.　　.　　.

Two women, one young and one very old, stood on the unfriendly beach close to the huge slabs of rock which made the quay, and looked towards the distance which had no promise. Afar off, the sky was dark, and there were flashes of lightning, the rumbling of thunder. A girl child ran, alone, along the quayside and then began to climb down the slippery stone steps leading to the water, then to squat and dabble her hands.

The little flat-roofed houses, with their windows like square, sightless eyes, seemed to sway in the wind.

The traces of the car were vanishing beneath the force of the wind, which swept spray and sand up to this spot, settling about Forrester's feet. He had not moved from the place where the girl had been. He did not look in one direction all the time, but kept shifting his gaze. He had been scared by the wind once before; now he was frightened, and the wind alone wasn't to blame. Nor was the meteorite. He was frightened of himself. He had seen that girl, been quite sure that she had been there. Of course he had been sure! The old, familiar tension clutched his body, his nerves, his face; he had to clench his teeth to keep his mouth closed and so stop from screaming. First, he had felt the sudden stab of grief because of Alice. Then he had seen that girl, the thin dress pressed against her lovely body, her arm raised, with the shawl making a veil to keep her eyes free from sand. She had turned the corner, and he had followed her as if he had been drawn by a magnetic impulse. He could remember that so vividly in every detail. He had walked across the room, taken the cap off the door, put it on slowly, gone downstairs, winked at the bright-eyed bell-boy. He had seen the girl again at the end of the road—hadn't he, hadn't he, *hadn't he*?

But—she had vanished. She had gone gradually, as if—as if she had never been real, but a siren figure there to draw him from the hotel and out towards the sea and the car, and then to realise that she was not real.

She could never have been there.

She could not have disappeared; it was impossible.

So she could only have been the figment of his imagination. Those words were spoken into the tense hush of his mind. "So she could only have been a figment of his imagination." A Spanish girl he had seen for a few minutes had driven grief and thought of Alice away, had drawn him out of his room because the beauty of her face and body; and she sang the clear music of a siren's call, for she had never existed.

But he had *seen* her.

He swung round, heedless of the young wife and the old woman, who still watched. He avoided the street where hundreds surged agog about the damaged house and the boiling "mud". Two priests were hurrying to the spot, having learnt of the new fear in the minds of the people. The wind banged and clattered along the street, swept into the little shops with their dark, cave-like interiors and crammed shelves.

Men, women and children, some pale and scared, some eager and chattering, were hurrying towards the damaged house. Today the black clothes of the women seemed to take on some special significance. When Forrester saw their faces, it was as if they had been touched with a premonition which left them no hope.

He reached the hotel.

The Cadillac wasn't outside. Perhaps he had imagined that car, too—and the driver, the lovely fair-haired woman by his side, the shimmering green of the cellulose. Idiot. He moved past the old man who acted as night-watchman, and who touched his forehead in thanks for past and hopes of future backsheesh. The little boy opened the swing doors and beamed at him, eyes bright, teeth glistening.

"*Señor* come back." That was a painstaking linguistic triumph.

"Yes," said Forrester. He didn't smile, and the boy's expression lost its eagerness.

Forrester went across to the bar, which was between the dining-room and a large lounge with deep, comfortable chairs. There was concealed, subdued wall-lighting, rich carpets of blue and red; the lounge at least was a place of luxury.

Only Jacko was in the bar.

He graced it, in his short white coat and black cummer-
bund and wine-red trousers, olive-skinned face with its berry
bright eyes, olive hands with their long, nervous fingers.
Jacko was a live wire of activity day in and day out—but
never so much as when he danced, after the bar had closed or
when sufficient patrons demanded it. Then his heels clacked
and his fingers snapped with breathtaking, fabulous speed.

He wasn't Saturnino, who was out in the storm, but he had
some English, and would have had more if he had not been
so impatient to get his words out.

"Good evening, Señor Forrester!"

"Hallo, Jacko. Whisky-and-soda, please."

"At once, in a jiffy." Jacko bared his white teeth, and in a
series of movements which were almost sleight of hand,
produced the whisky bottle from Scotland and the soda water
from Malaga, and mixed them. The *pzzzz* of the squirting
soda was like the hiss of the water sliding back through the
stones.

"Very bad wind," Jacko announced. His eyes remained
bright, he was poised for speech and action, but obviously
sensed that there was something wrong with Señor Forrester,
who usually had a joke with him. Forrester kept his mood to
himself whenever black despair came upon him.

Words burst out of Jacko.

"Such bad storm, Señor! What you say, t'underbolt?
Yes?" He was elated at this triumph.

"That's right."

"Such big explode, I 'ear it!" exclaimed Jacko, and crossed
himself. "Two peoples die."

"Oh," said Forrester. "I'm sorry." Then he asked
absurdly: "Any news of the boats?"

Jacko became all distress.

"No, señor, we 'ave 'eard nothing." He could never
master his aitches, which led to an attractive mannerism.
"Everyone is so bad worry."

Forrester said: "Yes, naturally." He downed the drink
and pushed the glass back. "Another." He pretended not to
notice Jacko's look of surprise; Jacko slid into movement
again. "And I suppose it's bad for business?"

"*Señor?*"

"People won't travel in this wind, will they?"

"Some travel, some do not," Jacko said, and placed the glass close to Forrester's fingers.

Forrester drank half of his second at a go. That was how the girl in red had vanished: half at a time. He could see her now. She had been in bright red, lit up by the sun, with the black scarf making sharp contrasts. She had worn the little brown sandals which passed for shoes. Every line of her long, slender legs had been beautiful; a kind of promise. Then the red had misted and become pink, the black had turned grey, the picture had faded.

"Jacko!"

Jacko's smile had a sharper edge than usual.

"*Señor?*"

"Never mind," said Forrester. He had been going to ask Jacko about the girl, and then about the strangers in the Cadillac, but he must not. He must never ask direct questions about his job, had to find the answers without phrasing the question. Jacko hadn't risen to the bait about travelling, perhaps he didn't know of the couple in the Cadillac. Perhaps they had not come here. Perhaps they had never been in Estafillo except in his imagination. God, no!

He downed the rest of the drink. Jacko edged towards the far end of his small bar, and examined bottles of obscure liqueurs. Forrester went out, swinging his arms, long, lean body moving with jerky vigour. He did not go out of the front door, but along narrow passages, past the dining-room and the kitchen and into the great sandy yard at the back— a playground for children, park for ancients, field for donkeys, parking-place for cars. There were five, including his own red M.G.

There was no green Cadillac.

3

FORRESTER turned slowly away from the great square. The wind swept across it with the inevitable cloud of dust and sand, hissing and snarling. It struck the low, whitewashed houses on the far side with a crack, and set every door and every window rattling. One of the cars, a little Citroen, was shaking on its balding tyres.

Forrester went back past the kitchen, oblivious of the smell of garlic and of fish. He reached the hall, and hesitated near the reception desk. There Garcia, the little bellboy, smiled as brightly as if Forrester hadn't passed him without a word or look. Ramones, the manager, was behind the desk, portly and massive in a black, well-tailored coat, his big powdered face dark with tomorrow's stubble. He glanced up at Forrester over the edges of his rimless glasses. Forrester turned towards him, his breath coming in short, sharp gasps, his heart beginning to thud.

"Yes, Meester Forster?" For some reason the manager could never remember the middle syllable. He did not smile; he never smiled; he had too many worries. People coming and going, impudent inefficient staff, the problem of catering, a nagging, spreading wife, a precocious daughter, and now the wind. He was always in a kind of restrained hurry, hinting that his time was the hotel's, his courtesy the guest's, but please——

In front of him, Forrester did not know how to begin. Why create difficulties for himself? Until today, he had known exactly what he should do, had never worried about putting the direct question, provided there was a reasonable explanation of it. Why shouldn't he ask if there were new arrivals?

"Meester Forster?" The manager's patience grew plaintive.

"It's the damned wind!" Forrester blurted out, to excuse his pause. "It gets on my nerves. Have you had any new guests in today?"

The manager shook his head.

"No, Meester Forster, no ones. Tonight, three English ladies say to come, but perhaps the wind——" He shrugged, looked melancholy, and glanced down at his papers. He did not speak again.

Forrester walked up stone stairs, keeping to the strip of red carpet; along stone passages and into his room.

It wasn't hot, as it could be here, but he was sweating. The wind showed no sign of abating. Windows kept rattling, the howling sound along the street reminded him of shells

going up or bombs coming down; there was no escape. He
strode across and looked into the street, which was much
darker. A light glowed dimly in the wine shop. He closed
the wooden shutters, banging them with unnecessary
violence. When he had shot the small bolts, shutters and
window banged.

He said aloud: "There was a green Cadillac with a man at
the wheel, a man about fifty-five, dressed in a blue-grey
suit."

He turned towards the dressing-table and leaned down,
hands on the edge, face thrust towards the wide mirror.
"Understand? There was. He was dressed in blue-grey.
He had a sharp, pointed nose, not broad and rounded and
short, like mine. He had thin lips, not full and red, like mine.
He wore a hat with a wide brim, and a narrow band, but the
hair at his temple was silvery grey, although he didn't look
old. Fifty-five. Not thirty-five, like me. A girl was beside
him. She had a Rita Hayworth face with a long, square chin,
and she might have stepped out of a film, she was so made up.
Call her hair the colour of corn, and that's about it. Her eyes
were blue as the sea. Understand?" He raised a fist at his
reflection. *"Her eyes were as blue as the sea!"*

He glared at himself.

Then suddenly he drew back, and gave a choking laugh.
He lit a cigarette, unsteadily. The outburst had done him
good—like the paroxysms of grief about Alice. Whenever
he really let his self-control go for a few minutes, he felt
better; and usually he had himself under firm control soon
afterwards. The cigarette tasted good. He went to a suit-
case and opened it, then picked up what looked like a copy of
Life. Except for some inset pages it was. Here were photographs of girls or young women, all easy on the eye, all listed
as film starlets. They were nothing of the kind. They were
lovelies who had been "influenced" by Botticelli.

The girl of the Cadillac was there; but her name was given
as Elenora McCall.

Here was something for Palfrey to know.

Forrester didn't start writing a report; he wanted to think
first, to decide exactly what to put in. He put the copy of
Life back, went across to the bed, and sat down, hitching
the pillow into the small of his back and letting his feet hang

over the side. He was within reach of an ash-tray. He looked more rested, but his eyes were not free from fear.

He looked up at a chandelier made of gilt metal and porcelain with a flower pattern which hung from a stout metal chain.

"Let us take a leaf out of Palfrey's book," he said aloud. "The great Sap, the logical and dispassionate Great Man. There is an explanation for every situation, he would say. And in this case, of course, it is largely psychological. Either you imagined the girl in red, or else when you were at the harbour you had a brief mental blackout, which would explain a flesh-and-blood girl's apparent disappearance. It would also explain the peculiar way in which the Cadillac man and his passenger looked at you. There is nothing really remarkable about any of it, Jim, especially in a man who is tired, like you. The important factor is this Elenora McCall, or Lennard. But don't worry too much. You're a bit over-wrought.

"That's what Palfrey would say," Forrester declared when this soliloquy was over. "I've lolled about here for two months, haven't turned a hand to anything except some paints and a sliver of wood with a tuft of camel hair at the end of it. I've been well-fed, favoured and mollycoddled for nearly nine weeks, and I'm tired out. Exhausted."

He stopped this monotone, stubbed out his cigarette, and lay for a few minutes, without smoking. Then he took another cigarette.

"But there was a green Cadillac," he declared. "And remember that the Lennard who wrote to Botticelli had a green Cadillac. The girl is one of Botticelli's angels, too." He had heard that phrase in London when talking to Palfrey and others leaders of the group.

He thought of Saturnino, the wine shop, the friends he had acquired so skilfully and carefully, so that if the moment ever came when he needed help and information, he would be able to get it without obstruction from the locals. The wine shop was still there. Some of the older men would soon be there, too, and Pedro would be behind the bar, but—the young men and the middle aged would not show up tonight. Nor would Saturnino, the *only* one with any considerable knowledge of English.

Forrester went downstairs again.

The manager glanced over his glasses as he went, the two porters, now on duty because the one train of the day was in, looked at him and smiled. The boy Garcia had gone, but another was in his place, and opened the door.

The wind struck Forrester like a ravaged vixen, and made a cacaphony up and down the street. Before he had feared it; now he hated it. He looked up at the swaying electric lamps. It was dark enough for them to be on, but they were flickering as they missed contact because of the wind. The swaying white glow spread a ghostly light about the street, and filled it with shadows; but there were few real shadows. No men walked slowly and purposefully towards the wine shop, in twos and threes, but the wine-shop door was wide open, and inside was a thin haze of tobacco smoke.

The girl in red had disappeared in a haze.

"Listen," Forrester whispered into the wind, "get a hold on yourself. Go and find out if anyone has seen a green Cadillac."

He went in, and Pedro greeted him with a forced smile, showing his yellow teeth. The old men, waiting for the young, raised their heads and greeted him with friendly words, but the place seemed empty.

Saturnino, misnamed the Devil if anyone had ever been, was already a plump, red-haired ghost.

Forrester's Spanish now came in for testing. At first, all talk was about the storm and the lightning which had struck a little house, but at last Forrester was able to ask his questions.

No one had seen the green Cadillac.

.   .   .   .   .

The old man who kept a shop and a petrol pump at the extreme northern end of Estafillo had not seen an American car all day, except Saturnino's old one. That was in his garage, and likely to stay there until a spare part arrived from Malaga or Granada, or even Seville or perhaps Madrid. Possibly it would have to be sent for from America.

Papa Gino, who always sat in the main square all day, shifting from the shade of one spiky palm-tree to the shade of another, and who knew positively everything that happened and could name every man, woman and child who entered the square, had not seen a green American car.

No one could get into the town except by passing the petrol pump and coming into the square. True, the old man and Gino had been driven from their posts by the wind and by need once or twice, but not for long.

If any strange car came into the town, they would be told, anyway. Wife, son, daughter or grandchild would tell them, and as a last resort there was always some old crony in the square. No, there had been no green Cadillac.

Forrester drank a lot of red wine which was softer and more palatable than might have been expected. The others drank heavily, too; heavily, for them. Eyes were always turned towards the door, as if they all expected it to open and Saturnino to come in boisterously, laughing and clapping Forrester on the back, calling for his beloved white wine, setting the place alight.

The only thing that opened the door was the wind.

There had been a green Cadillac. Forrester had seen it. All these men were wrong. Gino had been dozing, he always dozed, it was nonsense to say that he knew every car that came into Estafillo, although there was Saturnino's word for it that he not only knew every car but also every donkey— even to the number of sores on each donkey's back.

There had been a green Cadillac.

Not today, Señor.

Forrester wanted to argue with them, but his Spanish simply wasn't good enough. Palfrey should never have sent a man who knew so little Spanish to this spot. Good God, no! And he was getting slow-witted as well as seeing visions; obviously he had no job to do. Palfrey had pretended there was one, so that he could come and have this rest. Would Palfrey, the Palfrey known to be a genius at his particular calling, send a man who knew little Spanish to keep watch in a Spanish town?

It was time to go back. Tomorrow. Tonight?

The wind made that impossible, and anyhow he would have to warn Palfrey. He could send a coded cable. He could telephone, if it came to that. He had to get away, but he did not want to go back to the hotel tonight. There he would be alone, here he had some kind of company, even if

every ear seemed to be listening for the excited shout of
wives whose faith had been sustained and justified; or if all
eyes were looking towards the door.

There had been a green Cadillac.

Hadn't—there?

And a girl in red.

Then he heard some of the men talking about a woman
who had disappeared. At first he didn't understand, and had
to concentrate so hard to distinguish the words, but gradually
the meaning came to him. A woman had "disappeared"
from Estafillo today; her name was Isabella, and she had
lived in the house which the lightning had struck.

Forrester put every nerve of concentration into trying to
understand.

She was a beauty, this Isabella Melado, but a bad one.
How often did she come to visit her poor old parents? Once,
twice perhaps, since she had left Estafillo for America. It
was a sad day for any pretty girl when she went there. Home
was the place, she should have settled down and married here
in Estafillo, and then this would never have happened. There
were many mysteries, and God had his own ways. Lightning
had struck, and misguided Isabella was no more.

.   .   .   .   .

Forrester prayed that his Spanish would suffice, when he
asked questions. The others were willing and patient.
There had been four people living in the house struck by
lightning, an old woman who had escaped, her daughter
Isabella, who had been killed—who must have been killed
because she had not been seen since—and Isabella's old
father and a sister. These had died also, but their bodies
could be seen.

.   .   .   .   .

Forrester left the wine shop just after ten. He was used
to the custom of late eating, and the dining-room would be
as full now as at any time. Only the visiting tourists, especially the English and Americans, liked to eat early, and chafed
if they were kept later than half-past eight.

The wind was still blowing; he had to hug his clothes to
him. It was cooler, and there were clouds. He did not go
straight in, but round the side towards the car-park. A
single low-powered lamp outside the back door of the hotel

and a few yellow window squares at the houses gave the only
light. He was almost on top of the creaking cars before he
saw their dark shapes. He went from one to another, running
his hands over the wings; when he had finished he knew that
although there were now eight cars, none was a sleek
American beauty.

He went in, hurried upstairs, washed and walked down to
his corner table in the dining-room. Alfonso, the head waiter,
gave his customary grave smile. Two other waiters came up,
and the table was surrounded in the mighty ceremony.
Forrester ordered fish, followed by braised lamb, which he
knew would be deliciously tender; he did not need to order
wine; a bottle of *Fina*, from a valley near by, was already on
his table.

Among the diners were several locals who came here once
or twice a week, including a Mamma, Papa and two ample
daughters with rich black lace, fine mantillas and dark good
looks. They seldom spoke, but concentrated on the serious
business of eating. Tonight, as always, the women were
dressed in black, their dark hair relieved by white artificial
flowers. The three Englishwomen had arrived, and were in
the middle of the room, with coffee-cups in front of them,
cigarettes in their hands; a typical tourist trio.

And there was a man by himself.

The remarkable thing about this man was his size.

By ordinary standards, he was good-looking; he had a
chiselled profile, almost a subject for el Greco, and his
colouring was good and healthy, his complexion almost the
colour of honey. His hair, greying at the sides, was a rich
brown. Even sitting down, he looked a giant.

The big stranger was being watched by everyone, furtively
or openly. Every now and again, one of the English trio shot
a glance at him. Each señorita, as if in defiance of her
parents, would turn to stare. Two other Spanish couples
kept looking his way. No waiter moved without glancing at
him.

Forrester made himself look away.

No one else came in.

But there *had* been a green Cadillac—there must have
been. He'd seen it. He'd *heard* it.

A blaring noise seemed to sound in Forrester's ears as

he realised that; it had blared, he'd jumped and it had passed him.

The old men must have been dozing!

As for Isabella——

He finished his meal in a kind of frenzy of excitement. Whatever else he had imagined, it had not been the car. If he could find the driver and the Rita Hayworth type girl, he could also find someone who had seen the girl in red. The whole issue turned on the girl in red, whom he had *seen* disappearing. Fading.

He could peer at the rich red of the wine in his glass, and remember her; see her; and, moving slightly to one side or the other, he could see the figure fade. It was a trick of the light where it caught the side of the glass.

He needed just one witness to prove that the girl in red had been at the harbour, not in the ill-fated cottage. None of the other waiting women had seen her, so the couple from the green Cadillac were his only hope. Even if Elenora's name was Lennard, not McCall.

It was after eleven o'clock before he went upstairs, fighting against the call of the bar. Jacko would be unbearable tonight, conversation with strangers just as bad.

Gradually, the possible fate of Saturnino and the rest of the fishermen stole into Forrester's thoughts. It was easy to imagine those tiny ships being tossed about, taking in water as wave after wave smashed upon them. At best, they were being driven towards the north African coast, praying that the wind would drop before they were too far in. At worst, they had foundered. In the town, women were still waiting, praying and hoping.

He couldn't bring himself to start the report for Palfrey.

He undressed and got into bed.

Sleep sometimes came quickly and blessedly. When it did not, it meant a sleepless night. The probability of one now almost terrified him. He was soon turning from one side to the other, and the rattling windows and creaking door sawed at his nerves. On the night above all nights when he needed sleep and a clear head in the morning, he wasn't going to get off.

He lay on his back, eyes closed, body purposefully relaxed. At heart, he knew that it wouldn't work, but at least by trying

he could retain some self-respect. He did not doze, but for a
while his mind was empty of fears and strange imaginings.

Then he saw mist.

It was here, in this room.

Nonsense!

His eyes were closed, the hallucination was coming again.
Mist, a lovely figure clad in clinging red, fading, -vanishing.

He opened his eyes a fraction.

This room, which should have been in utter darkness, was
not dark. Light, dim yet quite unmistakable, came from the
open door.

He had closed the door.

Mist floated in, white like a cloud, pale in the soft light.
Gradually the door closed, as if an unseen hand had pulled it,
and as the light faded so the mist became darker. But it was
there, an amorphous cloud just inside the room.

4

FORRESTER'S lips were parted, his mouth was open, only the
paralysis of terror kept the scream from his lips. He stared
at the dark mist, into darkness itself, and tried to reason that
it was all imagination, that the door had never opened.
Something had happened to his mind, and this was part of
the hallucination.

Then he heard a new sound.

It came from the dressing-table, as something moved. It
was not the window or the noises from outside, but closer,
inside the room.

Forrester clenched his hands until they hurt, but the panic
was receding. His heart thudded, but he could think again.
He could think of ghosts and their human manifestation,
the eerie and the uncanny—and he could bring cold logic to
bear ; logic and disbelief and defiance.

He sat up, cautiously.

Another sound came, and he knew exactly what that was;
the opening of the top drawer in the dressing-table, the one
with his handkerchiefs, socks and oddments in it. It always

squeaked, in a moment it would jam, and would open only if it were eased to one side.

His heart hammered.

He stretched out his right hand towards the bedside table and a lamp. A glass ash-tray there might serve as a weapon. His automatic pistol was in a suit-case, there had been no need of a gun until now. But would a gun help to fight against this? The uncanny fears and his thudding heart fought logic and cold reason; you couldn't fight mist with a gun.

He touched the lamp.

He heard another sound—the sound that he made three or four times a day, when the drawer had come out as far as it could without being jammed. He even fancied that he heard the whisper of breathing, but the other noises made it difficult to be sure.

His fingers, cold and clammy, crept up the base of the lamp towards the little black switch. He touched it. He felt the smoothness. He heard the drawer yielding, knew the moment that it was open wide. He did not press the switch. He held his breath, fearful that any sound he made might be heard. There was darkness, the outline of the window but hardly any light beyond, and sounds from outside and inside.

He pressed the switch, and shouted: *"Don't move!"*

He leapt out of bed.

A man, or the shape of a man, turned swiftly from the dressing-table.

.   .   .   .

The face was hidden; the shape was definite, but seemed to be made of swirling mist.

Forrester could not move away from the bed, felt as if he were chained to it. And the creature stood by the dressing-table.

Forrester heard the rasping sound of his own breathing.

Then mist spread more thickly about the room, and the shape of the creature began to fade into it.

Forrester wanted to scream, to give way to terror. He did not know what held him back. A kind of blind courage came to him. The paralysis dropped away. He could see everything clearly—the mist, the fading creature, the dressing-table, the window. He snatched up the ash-tray and hurled it, then leapt forward.

He came up against some invisible barrier, simply smacked into it bodily, and fell back. His right hand, held out to strike, felt as if he had hit a stone wall; and he banged his forehead. He came up against the bed, but he actually felt better. Here was a physical barrier that could be moved. All he could see was mist, but——

The mist spread and thickened.

The door opened, light came in, the mist glowed like fog caught in the beam of a car's headlights; then the door closed sharply and all was dark again.

Forrester stood still for a length of time he could not measure; seconds or minutes. Then he forced himself to go forward, reached the door and pulled it open.

There was no mist in the passage.

A man so big that he seemed gigantic was coming swiftly towards the room.

.   .   .   .   .

Forrester was aware of his own fears, his thumping heart, the battle he had fought; and he knew that some indication of that must show in his face. He stood with the door open, clutching it tightly as the giant bore down—and if size were sufficient cause, the man was enough to frighten. But he did not add to Forrester's fears; rather he lessened them. His big face, handsome and with a smooth, honey-coloured complexion, was oddly reassuring. It was almost like looking upon the face of a saint.

Forrester felt something of his panic easing.

He said: "Did you—see anyone?"

"*Señor?*" asked the big man, politely.

Forrester made himself use Spanish. The big man followed his words closely, then smiled, shook his head, said "no" and asked if there were anything he could do.

"No," Forrester said. "No, thank you. *Gracias.*" He forced a smile painfully and turned back into the room. He heard the big man's footsteps stop some distance along the passage, and then looked out again. There was no mist; just the electric light, the stone floor with the single strip of carpet, tall, bare walls, shuttered windows.

Forrester went back into his room.

There was no trace of mist, but there were some of the visit. The drawer of the dressing-table was open. Nothing inside had been touched. The ash-tray lay on the stone floor close to the wall, where it had fallen. He could see that a piece was chipped out. He went slowly across to it, and picked both tray and chipping up. He was sweating freely, and his teeth were chattering, but he had fought back and knew that the thing had been real.

He turned the ash-tray over. It was heavy, made of a curiously smooth-looking glass, and quite a large piece had come off one corner, where there was a tinge of red. Blood? Forrester touched it, and a smear came off on to his thumb. It might be blood. He hoped it was.

He did not want to call the grotesque shape to mind, but it came—and he wondered if the ash-tray had cut the creature's flesh. He could only use the word "creature", could not make himself say "man"; yet surely it had been a kind of man.

He put the ash-tray down, and went to the bedside table, which had a cupboard beneath. He kept whisky and soda there. He poured himself a stiff one, and sat in an armchair. His teeth stopped chattering and he felt much calmer. He knew that he would soon be able to make himself think rationally, all emotion would be gone for the time being; he was more the man he had been before Alice's death.

He lit a cigarette.

Twice in the space of a few hours he had seen something with his own eyes which was unbelievable. It carried him back to Wells's *Invisible Man*, to imitative stories in boys' papers of his own period, but the important factor was that he had seen two people vanish into a mist.

He could think quite logically, now. The creature in this room had been able to open the door and go out—had needed to open the door, so he hadn't been able to vanish through it, as ectoplasm. That ruled out ghosts! Forrester could even think that and smile, and was grateful for this measure of self-control. All right, then, it had not been a ghost but a creature who had been able to create that concealing mist at will.

Mist had concealed the girl in red—Isabella.

Forrester felt very much better. He could even believe

that the girl in red had opened the door of the green Cadillac and, still concealed by the mist, sat in the back and been driven off. It might defy all known natural laws, but now he knew it could have happened. He hadn't seen the car door open, but the mist might have concealed that. He had not seen the door open in this room, but light shining on the mist had told him that it was opening.

He lit another cigarette.

He was here to do a specific job; to watch in case Botticelli or any of his "angels" came to Estafillo, and to report any incident that was not part of the everyday life of the village. Here was plenty! Palfrey had not talked of supernatural manifestations, but he would want to know about this, whether it had anything to do with Botticelli or not.

Forrester went across to the table which he used as a writing-desk. He decided not to try to use a code, for the story would be almost impossible to transcribe. He wrote slowly and with great deliberation, using a simple form of prose that was matter-of-fact and almost naïve. Now and again, he paused to get his facts marshalled in the right order. He made no comments, but simply stated the facts.

He had been writing for some time when he became aware of a faint mist in front of his eyes. He felt a sudden stab of fear, started back, then sat absolutely still. For the mist was about his right hand; now that his head was farther away it was not too close to his eyes.

His hand and the pen in it began to fade.

.   .   .   .   .

Forrester sat as if movement were impossible; almost without breathing. He was unaware of the sounds at the window and outside; oblivious of the wind, of the report he was writing. He stared down at the mist. It was as if his right hand had vaporised and was enveloped in a huge glove of mist which moved slowly, sluggishly, rather like steam coming out of a kettle which was gradually going off the boil.

He felt icy cold, and the coldness came from within. He could not move. At that first moment of realisation he did not think beyond the incredulous fact that his hand had vanished.

He began to breathe more heavily. He felt cold sweat on his forehead. Fear assaulted him, but he fended it off. This was really happening, it mattered, he had to watch and to be

quite sure of everything. He felt as if he were on the thresh-
hold of some great discovery, as if natural laws were being
defied, even being set aside. His mind began to work in
little, jerky movements. He saw that the mist was about the
same volume as it had been after the first few minutes of
starting; the size, perhaps, of a very large boxing-glove. He
could not see the bone in the wrist, but the sun-tanned flesh
above it was visible.

He moved his hand.

He could feel the movement, and was also aware of a
strange sensation—not pins and needles, but something akin
to it; like a very gentle electric shock. This filled his fingers,
the back and the palm of his hand, and the wrist; it stopped
where the mist stopped.

He raised his hand so that it was just in front of his face,
and all he could see was the mist.

He opened his fingers and let the pen go. It fell normally,
and appeared out of the mist, dropping on to Palfrey's letter
and spattering it with blue-black ink which looked bright and
fresh. The pen rolled to the edge of the desk; Forrester
shot out his right hand, instinctively, forgetting the mist;
he stopped the pen, but did not see his fingers.

He felt less chilled now; convinced that this was not part
of his imagination. His mind was all right, except that it
wasn't working fast enough.

How had this happened?

He glanced at the ash-tray, and saw the slight smear of red
on it, the red that might be blood. He had rubbed that with
his thumb.

Excitement began to pulse through him, almost suffocat-
ingly. It was fierce excitement at something revolutionary,
and it sent his mind reeling. Ideas of how it could be used
almost choked his brain; for good or for ill, the potential of
the mist was illimitable. *For good or for ill.*

He would not finish the letter to Palfrey, he would go to
see him. He could be there in a few hours, knew exactly
how to get in touch with Palfrey's agent near Malaga, and
lay on a plane. The excitement still coursed through him.

Then doubts came.

Why had that creature visited him? What had he wanted?
Was it safe to wait until the morning? Wouldn't it be better

to leave now, to take the car and drive towards Malaga and the airfield?

He was still looking at his hand.

Suddenly, he caught his breath.

The shape of the fingers came back gradually; the mist was thinning. He could see everything materialising, lines, nails, half-moons, small veins. The tingling sensation was almost gone. He began to work his fingers about; they had not changed in appearance. He wasn't sure how long they had been invisible, but it had been for at least five minutes.

Supposing that man came back.

Supposing he knew or guessed what had happened.

Forrester picked up the pen. He would finish the letter, and give a calm, factual account of what had just happened. He would post the letter on his way to Malaga. He would get away as soon as the last lights dimmed on the road outside; there were very few, now; quiet had fallen on Estafillo.

That startled him.

The wind had dropped.

He finished the letter, taking his time, pausing every now and again to make sure that he said exactly what he meant. He tried to guess what Palfrey would think when reading this. It would sound like the ravings of a lunatic, except that the prose was so simply couched that no one would call it raving. He did not over-emphasise anything; did not underline words, or fall for the temptation of saying: *This really happened.*

He sealed and stamped the letter, stuck on an airmail sticker, and put it on the desk. It wasn't addressed to Palfrey, but to a Mr. Courtney at an address in London which would mean nothing to people who might have some idea who Palfrey was.

At least this would shake Palfrey!

Forrester knew that he was smiling slightly. He caught a glimpse of his face in the mirror, and actually paused. He wasn't bad looking, especially now that the sun had bronzed him. He wasn't exactly an Apollo, but he knew that some people found his face attractive—with its grey eyes, well-marked eyebrows, squarish chin, full lips and short, broadish nose.

He dressed, and then packed a small hold-all. Now that

he had something to do, the years of training served him well. He had spent years in M.I.5 before joining Palfrey, and until Alice's death would have matched his self-possession with anyone's. It was not a case of being without fear, but of being able to work in spite of fear. And at times, he knew, one worked with a kind of unworldly elation; almost exultation. This was such a time. He alone of all the people in the world could do what he had to do.

He packed just enough oddments for one night, then wrapped up the ash-tray and put that in with his clothes. He left his easel, folding stool and paints in the corner, his clothes in the hanging cupboard; it would look as if he were coming back.

Palfrey might send him back, anyway.

Ready, he picked up the letter and the hold-all, then went to the door.

He opened it stealthily. A window rattled, then utter silence fell. He could have used the wind now, but it did not make much difference. There was no sign of anyone. He walked slowly towards the head of the stairs, down to the passage leading to the reception hall.

The night clerk and a night porter were on duty.

They did not see him put the letter in a post box.

He passed the kitchen again, and opened the door leading to the car-park. The stars were out, very bright and clear, and the heavens looked dark and velvety. The air was cool and pleasant, and there was only a gentle wind. The earth under his feet grated a little as he went towards the cars, but he did not think that anyone would hear him.

He passed all the cars there, stopped, and frowned. His wasn't there. Nonsense, he must have passed it in the darkness.

The bubble of his exultation pricked, he moved back along the line, counting each radiator, seeing the faint shimmer of starlight on windows and on chromium plating. He counted each one aloud but softly.

"... five ... six ... seven."

Seven.

When he had been out here to look for the green Cadillac, there had been eight. Now, his M.G. was gone.

•   •   •   •   •

Forrester stood quite still, watching the dark shape of the hotel, trying to persuade himself that this was just a casual theft, that it had nothing to do with his plan to leave. But he could not convince himself. Someone had suspected that he would want to get away and had taken the car.

Someone might be watching him.

He had always known that, it was one of the accepted things, but now the realisation was touched with a sense of horror. In the darkness there might be mist which he could not see. He heard no sound—but there might be no need for sound. Supposing one of those misty creatures were sitting in a car; or standing by the side of it, waiting.

A gentle breath of wind came again.

He looked at the hotel. A light showed, dim yellow and misty, at a window not far from the passage through which he had come. He hardly knew why he kept staring at it, but suddenly it was blotted out.

His teeth clamped down.

The light appeared again; someone, something, had passed between it and Forrester, and yet he had heard nothing.

He turned, and ran.

5

FORRESTER ran towards the road leading to the harbour, away from the shape which had cut that light away from him. He ran fast and smoothly, fighting back panic, not looking back.

He reached the road.

Two lights glowed, one at each corner in sight; and the girl in red had turned down one of those corners. He chose the other, nearer the harbour. The smooth surface of the road leading to the sea helped him to hurry without making much sound.

Now and again he paused, but all he could hear was the hiss of the water seething through the pebbles, and the measured, muted roar of waves against the beach. He turned a corner of the last house before the harbour, and saw the starlit sky, and the reflection of the stars on the sea, the shape of the harbour wall, everything he might expect. There were no lights anywhere in sight, no glow of a lighted ship.

But women were here, watching, waiting.

The eerie horror of what had happened at the hotel became less frightening when Forrester saw them. Some sat on boxes, and some stood and watched. He could not count their number. A few old men were among them, too, for he saw the flicker of light as one lit a pipe or cigarette.

Now and again, a word was spoken.

The people kept their vigil, and Forrester moved behind them. None turned to take notice of him. There was a kind of safety in the darkness and among the women, but he could not stay for long.

He wanted to hide somewhere until daylight; then he would be able to see if the clear air became misted, if danger threatened.

He remembered the light in the wine shop. Fishermen often sat there until the early hours, some until dawn, and while a customer remained the door was kept open. Forrester walked along the road he had taken that afternoon. Two people came towards him, talking in low-pitched voices. He sensed their curious gaze, but they did not speak as they passed. He reached the street near the hotel again, and the light still glowed in the wine shop.

He went in.

Several elderly men, one bearded, all unshaven, one completely bald, were playing an interminable game of cards in a corner. Two others sat with glasses and bottles in front of them, looking half-asleep. One raised a hand. Forrester greeted the shopkeeper in the hushed tone that the night seemed to demand, sat down, and waited for a small carafe and a thick, stumpy glass. They came.

He could eat here, if necessary.

He had company; and no one would attack him while he was in the snug little shop. The smell of the wine was pleasant and consoling, and he felt tired; more tired than he had all night. Why shouldn't he doze? The hold-all with the ash-tray was safely at his feet, and he might have a hard day tomorrow.

Why shouldn't he doze?

He closed his eyes. The dirge-like murmur of voices was

in the background. Twice, men came in and spoke to the wine-shop keeper, and his footsteps followed theirs as he took them their carafe or their bottle and glasses.

After that, there was a hazy kind of silence. Forrester was very near sleep, relaxed, resting, free from fear.

Then he felt something touch his leg.

He jerked his head up, but did not move his body. He felt the touch again, and in a moment, knew that someone was trying to get the hold-all away. The light was dim and the atmosphere smoky, but he could see nothing. Yet the gentle pressure continued, and the hold-all was being pulled away.

He kicked, savagely.

His foot caught something hard, there was a gasping sound, then the table rocked and the glass fell. Forrester stooped down, grabbed at the hold-all and found the handle. He lifted it, and jumped up. The table went sprawling. He could see the mist now, swirling about the doorway. The old men stared and gaped, the wine-shop owner stood with his lips parted and his elbows on the counter, looking as if he could not believe his eyes.

Forrester was holding the handle tightly.

The doorway was thick with the mist, and now he knew that the other men had seen it. Two were getting to their feet, crossing themselves. Forrester backed away. Creatures he couldn't see were coming towards him, and instinctively he knew that they wanted that ash-tray.

He did not know of a way out, except through the street door, but there was a narrow doorway leading to the back of the shop.

He turned and jumped towards it.

The mist was following!

He slammed the door, heard the bang as it closed, found himself in a small room. The walls were lined with bottles stacked in bins; a single candle, nearly out, flickered in the draught which the banging door had caused. He saw another door in a far corner, hugged close the hold-all to his body, went through. Here was a kitchen, reeking with garlic and the smell of sour wine, and only a glimmer of light. He opened the back door.

Mist was waiting there, and swirled about him.

He struck out with his left fist, and leapt forward, knowing that he was in the middle of a group of "men" who clutched at him and snatched at the bag. He struck again, kicked out, tried to force his way through. But it was hopeless. He doubled back, but men were behind him, the dimly-lighted kitchen was filled with writhing mist.

Hands touched the hold-all.

He had to have it, Palfrey needed it, Palfrey——

He felt a hand so strong and powerful that he had no defence against it. It gripped his right wrist and pulled his arm away from the side of his body; he felt the hold-all plucked away. He hadn't a chance, but as it went he was filled with fury which turned him into a fighting machine, he struck wildly into the blinding mist, felt some punches land, heard sounds as of breathing.

But that soon stopped.

The mist moved away as if wind had driven it, and vanished into the darkness. Faint sounds faded into silence, too.

Soon, Forrester was surrounded by the scared old men of the wine shop, all asking questions which he could not understand. They led him back. There was no doubt about their sympathy. They had seen that mist, so there was more than sympathy, there was fear of the uncanny. Some talked in furtive whispers.

Never before had Forrester needed the reassuring voice of Saturnino as he did now.

The wine-shop keeper insisted on bathing a cut in his cheek. When that was done, in solemn tones he advised Forrester to go back to the hotel. He had been robbed, it was a very bad thing, in the morning he could tell the police, also the Civil Guard. Tonight, sleep. Forget this talk of the Devil!

Tonight? It was already three o'clock.

"All right," Forrester said. "I'll go."

The man accompanied him across the road, and would not leave him until they reached the hotel, where the Spaniard talked volubly to the porter and the night clerk; and they talked as volubly back. Almost against his will, Forrester was escorted up to his own room. The clerk switched on the light, looked round, smiled, and bowed as Forrester went in.

The door closed.

Forrester felt stupid with fatigue, with disappointment, with anxiety; and superimposed upon all these was fear of the unseen. But he no longer had the ash-tray, so "they" would not worry him again about that. "They" had been to search his room before——

He quickened his pace as he went to the dressing-table. He had only to open the top drawer to find that it had been searched; everything was out of position. The other drawers were also disturbed, although his clothes had been carefully replaced. He went to the wardrobe; it was the same there. His suit-cases had been opened, too, and the few oddments of clothing left in them had been tossed about.

If anything were certain, it was that he had nothing more to fear; yet.

He kicked off his shoes, took off his coat and trousers, and pushed back the bedclothes. He felt stupid from want of sleep, and decided not to worry to pull on his pyjamas. But they were folded in the middle of the bed; and he hadn't folded them.

He picked them up.

Inside the jacket there was something hard and bulky. He lifted the jacket and let the thing fall.

It was the ash-tray, just as he had wrapped it.

.　　.　　.　　.　　.

He was past thought.

He put the thing beneath his mattress, and an automatic pistol, loaded, by his side. The night was beyond reason, and he had to rest.

.　　.　　.　　.　　.

He woke at eight o'clock.

It was a perfect morning, the kind Forrester had come to expect at Estafillo. The sky was a soft blue, not yet made harsh by the fierce heat of the sun; and the sun itself was hidden behind the hills to the east, its heat as yet only promise or threat. Forrester made sure that the ash-tray was there, then ran his bath. He had only one thought and purpose—to get away. The morning, in its way, was as unreal as the night had been.

At half-past nine, with the ash-tray in his pocket, he went down to breakfast of coffee, rolls and jam. The three

English tourists were there; no one else. The manager was looking powdered, darker-jowled and aloof. No one took any particular notice of Forrester. His usual waiter brought his breakfast with a double allowance of butter, and the coffee really hot; it had taken him weeks to get hot coffee instead of lukewarm.

It might all have been a nightmare.

Finished, he went out to the car-park. He was not really surprised to see his red M.G. standing where he had left it the previous morning; or about the same place. He went towards it and looked inside. Nothing indicated that it had been used by anyone else.

No one except two old men watched him.

He got into the car, and drove slowly towards the harbour. As he turned seawards, he saw women and children hurrying towards the beach on the other side of the town, half a mile away—they looked like little black dots. All were hurrying; and some were running from the back streets, too.

Forrester was touched with the excitement which lay upon them all, as he drove back, then in the wake of the crowds.

Soon he was near enough to see and understand.

Three boats had been thrown up on to the beach during the night; and three bodies were now laid out on the grey pebbles. Weather-darkened faces were turned towards the sky and its blue promise, dark eyes closed, dark clothes sodden. There were pieces of wreckage, too, and a little group of people standing together. In their midst was one woman staring at the youngest of the men; at a handsome dead lover.

Saturnino was not there.

Forrester drove away, passing others who were hurrying to the beach. He doubted if they saw him, they were so intent.

He drove out of Estafillo.

Hatless, without any luggage, without his paints and brushes, he might be going for a morning drive, as he often did. There was only one way to go from the town—northwards through the square with those spreading, spiky palms, then over the narrow bridge, which had room for only one car at a time; the general shop with the petrol pump stood there.

He saw old Gino nodding on a seat beneath a decaying palm, undisturbed by several dogs, one so thin that its ribs stuck out, all snapping and snarling around a tiny carcase lying in the dust with a cloud of flies humming about it. The shop seemed deserted. Forrester went past, putting his foot down harder.

"They" no longer seemed to worry about him.

He did not think beyond that. The secret of the ash-tray could wait. Everything could wait, except escape. He had to reach Malaga, find Palfrey's man, get an aircraft, and arrive in England that very day.

Soon, he was on the narrow dirt road going towards the main road between Gibraltar and Malaga. Dust spewed out behind the car, like writhing brown mist. Forget it. The road twisted and turned through low, rocky hills. Very little grew except grass, thick and parched-looking, as it would be until the summer rains. There was no wind now. Occasionally he caught sight of the sea, a pure blue; sometimes he believed that he could make out the shape of the North African coast-line.

Suddenly he saw the great rock of Gibraltar standing out like a black sentinel against the sky.

He turned a corner.

The huge man who had been at the hotel stood in his path.

. . . . .

Forrester could drive on, and force the man to move; or else drive over him. He could swerve right or left; or he could stop. His foot was already over the brake, his hands tight on the wheel. He had little time, but enough to see the giant's face, and to be reminded of that strange look—of goodness.

Forrester braked, the tyres squealed in the hard dirt, more dust flew. The giant, who might have been expected to jump right or left, simply waited; the car pulled up a foot in front of him.

Forrester already had his gun in his hand.

"What's this, a hold-up?" His voice was rough.

"No, Jim," the giant said, in excellent but very careful English; and he smiled faintly. "Sap wouldn't like that, would he?" He didn't pause, didn't give Forrester a chance to recover from that "Sap". He meant Palfrey; Sap was

Palfrey's nickname, coined from his initials: Stanislaus Alexander Palfrey. "I haven't much time to spare, they'll soon be after me," the giant went on. "They've been watching me closely, that's why I ignored you when we first met, and pretended not to speak English when we met again. They think I still have the vital ash-tray, but instead I have one like it. Get yours, the original one, to Sap. Make absolutely sure he gets it."

There could be plenty of room for doubt about this man's implicit claim to be one of Palfrey's men. Yet Forrester, who should have been alive with suspicion, did not doubt at all. He accepted it as a fact, and already he felt the driving need for haste.

"It's easy to talk," he said, trying to be rational. "What do you know about the ash-tray? How——?"

"They were obviously after a packet of yours last night, and whatever was in it would be at the heart of the trouble," the giant said, "so I took it instead. I opened it, found the ash-tray, and returned it when you were out. They won't be likely to come after you, because they think I still have it."

Forrester asked jerkily: "Do you know—why they want it?"

"I think it has a bloodstain of one of these creatures," the giant said, and somehow that seemed reasonable, almost convincing. "If it has, we may find out how they can disappear in the mist. Sap *will* find out. Oh—tell him quickly that McCall's daughter has been here, she was the girl in the American car. Did you see her?"

"Yes," Forrester said, with an effort. His mouth was parched.

"Watch her if you see her again, and tell Pirando in Malaga about it—if he doesn't know already. But don't let anything stop you from delivering that ash-tray to Sap Palfrey."

"No," Forrester said. "No, I won't. But what is all this? Where do the creatures come from? This mist——"

The big man said softly: "We don't know much, Jim, we are trying to find out. They can produce the mist at will, and sometimes induce it in others." He gripped Forrester's arm. "Now I must go. They will soon be after me, and I want to lure them away from you."

"I don't even know who you are!"

The giant smiled, as if at a mild joke.

"I am Stefan Andromovitch," he said simply. His great hand moved and closed round Forrester's wrist; it was the hand which had plucked away the case last night. "God be with you," went on the giant who called himself Stefan Andromovitch. "Always."

He turned and walked away, off the road and heading for a crevice in the rock hills. Forrester did not start the engine until he had disappeared. He drove slowly at first, trying to grasp it all. The morning air was crystal clear, the hum of the tyres was a kind of music, he was getting farther and farther away from Estafillo, from the mist that could swallow a man up; from the illusions of the night before. But the big Andromovitch wasn't getting away; he was leading the creatures away from Forrester.

A turn in the road led to a steep hill; the road Forrester was on swung to the right, another, narrow and very steep, went to the left.

Forrester kept seeing the giant in his mind's eye, and knew that he must be somewhere in a valley beyond the hill on the left. He drove on to the narrow dirt road, dust billowing behind him, then reached an old, derelict house built into the hillside.

The roof was falling in, the windows were like square, blank eyes. No one was near, it was doubtful whether anyone had lived here for years.

Forrester looked down over the valley.

He saw a few grey patches of clouds, merging together to make a very dark patch. The formation was so unusual that at first he didn't look for Andromovitch, only at the patch which made a blot against the blue sky. A mist spread from this centre, until even the sky and the sun were dulled. Fascinated, almost overawed, Forrester watched the fog patch moving towards the earth.

Down in the valley was a small olive grove, and the everlasting dusty, barren soil.

Suddenly, the fog patch seemed to split. Wind smashed at the olive trees and the earth, a great spiral of sand rose up. Forrester remembered the storm at Estafillo, could imagine its turning the sea to great turbulence, as it now turned the sand.

He was horror-struck.

Then he saw the giant.

The man, far away and tiny now, was standing quite still. Forrester forced himself to move, and snatched for a pair of field-glasses in a door pocket. The giant stood looking upwards, as the wind and the storm raged about him. Then lightning struck.

Forrester was blinded.

He let the glasses fall from his eyes, and kept his eyes tightly closed. He remembered the explosion in the narrow street, the flash and the ruined house.

This struck terror in the same way.

Teeth clenched, hands clenched, Forrester made himself look again, although he was afraid. He saw that the giant was still moving as if quite unperturbed. The storm cloud had risen much higher, and was less black, as if it had spent the worst of its fury.

To Forrester, it seemed as if the storm had deliberately attacked Palfrey's friend, the fabulous Stefan Andromovitch.

Nonsense?

The disappearance of Isabella had been nonsense, hadn't it?

Suddenly Andromovitch turned round, scanning these distant hills. He could not possibly see Forrester, but seemed to be signalling to him, saying: "Go quickly, go quickly, deliver that to Palfrey."

Forrester turned back to the car. He sat at the wheel for several minutes, feeling physically sick. Then he started the engine and drove back to the proper road, sending the little car rattling over the uneven surface. The sun grew hotter. Now and again he glimpsed movement ahead, and knew that he was drawing near the main road. Twice he passed big herds of goats, with a boy goatherd guarding them, wearing his goatskin coat and Tyrolean-shaped hat, one hand half-raised in shy greeting. Forrester smiled at each one, absently, bleakly.

He turned on to the main road.

The fog or cloud had dispersed.

There was less likelihood of trouble here, wasn't there? No southern Spanish roads carried very much traffic, but this, connecting the main cities, had more than most. He would seldom go more than five minutes without seeing a car or truck, and there would always be the peasants working in the fields. He was within sight of the sea most of the time, too; and the only mist showed against the horizon, concealing the wreckage of other fishing-boats, probably hiding the bodies of men—and of Saturnino.

He wasn't thinking much of the Spaniard; mostly of the giant's big, handsome, almost saintly face. Saintly? The kind of face that would turn away the Devil? Forrester began to realise how often he had pictured the old men of the wine shop in his mind's eye, several of them crossing themselves fearfully, and he remembered the wine-shop man's brusque: "Forget this talk of the Devil!"

The giant's face had held a great serenity. It had reminded Forrester of Palfrey. No one would look at Palfrey and think that he was saintly, but they might think of him as "good". He had something of the serenity of the giant with the familiar Russian name.

What had happened in the valley?

Forget it!

It dawned on Forrester that the only agents of Palfrey whom he knew had the same sort of qualities. Calmness—he himself had been almost a placid type before Alice's death—and, don't blush, a kind of goodness. Palfrey's men had to be able to rub shoulders with the seamy side without getting too soiled. They weren't saints, but there was a quality common to them all. Forrester had met Frenchmen, Englishmen, Italians and Americans who served Palfrey, and that common factor had been in each.

Thinking of Andromovitch had made Forrester forget his urgent anxiety about the mist. It came back like a blanket. He drove for miles, thinking only of the mist and storms and what they meant.

Near the coast the land was flat. Little whitewashed cottages boasted tiny gardens ablaze with the startling red of geraniums. The farmers were all working, their wives and children too.

There was no suspicion of mist or cloud anywhere.

Forrester saw the outskirts of Malaga straight in front of him; long, wide roads, with tramlines crossed time and time by big, high-walled carts which looked like moving hurdle fences drawn by slow-stepping oxen; and donkey carts, or donkey caravans, modern cars, ancient cars which looked as if they would fall to bits, big lorries, tiny vans, bicycles—everything in a heterogeneous mixture of old and new, of East and West.

He knew Malaga well by now.

Palfrey's agent was at the Luxor Hotel, on the sea-front; Forrester had to go and ask for him by name—Pirando. That was easy enough. The hotel was at the far side of the town, a huge building in its own grounds, with the little beach railway running just outside its walls. Forrester turned into the hotel, and a brown-clad porter pointed to a parking-place, but he almost ran the alarmed man down.

He was to park close to a glittering green Cadillac.

6

FORRESTER parked, apologised to the porter, and went inside. He'd been in the hotel several times; receptionists smiled a suave welcome. He did not ask for Pirando at once, but went into the huge central room. The ceiling must have been a hundred feet high. He sat near a little fountain which streamed water into the pool where goldfish swam with perpetual laziness. Few people were here. Forrester ordered a drink, and shifted his chair so that he could see the two main entrances. There was an undertone of conversation; he heard English, American and French voices. A waiter brought him his *aperitif*. He sipped, while watching the hall; anyone leaving would have to pass within twenty yards of him.

Yet it was someone coming from the entrance to the garden and the swimming-pool who made him turn his head—and he felt as if he had turned into stone.

Isabella, the girl in red, came towards him.

She walked with a natural grace which he would never forget. She was dressed in red, but this dress might have come from the most exclusive *salon* in Paris, not from a cheap stall in the open village market. It was narrow at the hem, had flounces at the waist, and narrowed again at the shoulders. Her dark hair was covered with a red lace cap, and she wore two magnificent, jewelled combs. Her shoes were white; so were the gloves and her handbag.

Half a dozen people stared at her; she must be used to being stared at, and took no more notice than she would had she been a mannequin. She glanced at Forrester; he dared even imagine that she looked at him more closely than at the others; but she was soon past.

Breathlessly, he watched her go.

He had seen her hurrying round the corner towards the harbour, seen her approach the green Cadillac, seen her vanish in that patch of mist.

Then she had looked like the wife of a poor fisherman.

She went out of sight, near the stairs leading to the bedroom floors.

Forrester waited for five minutes, his heart pounding. He finished his drink, paid, and went into the reception hall. There were several armchairs; he could sit and watch the wide staircase, and also see the Cadillac when he glanced out of the window. He lit a cigarette, and beckoned one of the smartly uniformed bell-boys.

"*Si, señor?*"

"Is Señor Pirando here?"

"*Si, señor!*"

"I'd like to speak to him."

The boy bowed and hurried off. Two couples came down the stairs, dressed for the beach, legs and arms browned to the colour of old bronze. They sauntered towards the garden.

Then two women came down, one in red, unchanged, beautiful enough to startle. The other was the fair-haired woman of the Cadillac, Elenora Lennard, or McCall. Forrester's face was hidden by a travel brochure, but neither of the women glanced at him as they went out.

He heard the fair-haired woman speak in an American voice.

Forrester stood up.

A short, dark-haired man with a swarthy skin and remarkably fine black eyes came up, smiled, and said:

"All is well, Mr. Forrester, they will be followed."

This was Pirando; dressed in a black coat and striped trousers, he was the perfect hotel manager, quiet-voiced, suave, courteous; and with that peculiar ability to read or to guess one's thoughts, like Palfrey, like Andromovitch. Forrester found himself liking the man.

"That's fine," Forrester said heavily.

"How can I help you, Mr. Forrester?" Pirando went on. He must have spoken in that low-pitched voice to a thousand hotel guests; and he looked and sounded as if he really wanted to help.

"I want to get to England tonight," Forrester said. "I've an urgent message for Palfrey."

"There should be no difficulty about that," observed Pirando. "It will take a little time, and I hope you will have lunch here, because you will not be able to leave until early this afternoon."

"I'd like to, thanks," Forester said. "Pirando, that woman in red——"

"I can guess what you think about the woman in red," murmured Pirando, and a little smile played at his lips. "There are not many who do not feel the same way. She is magical, is she not? Magical. The face of an angel—perhaps a Botticelli angel."

His smile was gently mocking.

Forrester said gruffly: "Are you watching her closely?"

"We know that the man, Lennard, comes from Botticelli. We know that his companion, daughter of the American Senator Samuel McCall, was a convert to Botticelli." He did not try to explain "convert". "We know that this Spanish woman has appeared from nowhere to be with them," went on Pirando. "Anyone who serves Botticelli interests us. They are being followed, Mr. Forrester."

The Cadillac was already moving out of the grounds.

No one appeared to follow.

"Don't worry," Pirando said, with soft vehemence. "I will send messages as necessary."

"Don't take it too easy," Forrester warned.

He told Pirando what he knew of the woman in red; her name, her disappearance, the stories in Estafillo. Pirando took all this calmly; sceptically?

He went off.

Forrester could not keep away from the window. The green car was moving out of sight along the road into Malaga. He did not know who was driving. He kept seeing the face of the woman in red, and remembering what Pirando had said: "The face of an angel—perhaps of a Botticelli angel."

The Botticelli he meant was believed to be the most evil man in the world.

.   .   .   .   .

Forrester had lunch, and soon afterwards was called by a bell-boy, who escorted him to a taxi. He didn't glance at his M.G. Half an hour afterwards he was in a twin-engined Dakota aeroplane, with the engines roaring and the machine quivering, and a few disinterested airfield ground staff watching him, believing that he was heading for Barcelona.

On the way he had time to think; and reason. The mist could conceal his own hand; so it could have concealed the Cadillac, when coming in to Estafillo; could have concealed his own car, so as to keep him prisoner in the town.

Why?

He believed in the mist, for he knew it existed.

He looked at his right hand, as if expecting to see it vanish again.

It didn't.

.   .   .   .

By evening, Forrester was over the coast of England.

The weather had been perfect, they hadn't felt a bump, and although the sun was sinking low as they approached London, there was no sign of mist. They were actually circling to land, and Forrester was looking down at the tiny patchwork of fields and gardens, the criss-cross of streets and roads and the tiny boxes which were actually houses, when he saw the mist.

At first, he didn't associate it with the mystery. Patches over the airport seemed to be rising, rather like a patch of morning mist over a valley.

Then, with a stab of horror, he saw little clouds of pale mist about the aircraft; following it.

Horror imprisoned him.

He could see the blue sky beyond the patches; the green of the airfield and the grey of the runways—but everywhere were those little patches of mist. Some hovered about other aircraft on the ground, one was close to two fire trailers.

The mist did not seem to touch any part of the surrounding land.

Forrester felt his jaws hurting, because his teeth were clenched so hard.

The engineer came out of the flight-deck door.

"Patchy bit of fog down there," he announced. "Haven't seen anything like it before." He was young, red-faced, earnest yet mildly amused. "Bob's going up a bit, to have a look round again before he lands."

Forrester said: "Is he? Thanks."

"Okay?"

"I'm all right," said Forrester. He knew that he didn't look it, and knew that the other man would assume that was because he was scared of landing in the mist. Well, wasn't he?

The flight-deck door closed slowly on its hydraulic hinges. Forrester stood up. Mist brushed against his window; he seemed to see a man's shape, but it was only mist. There were dozens of patches within sight, some keeping pace as the aircraft climbed and began to circle the airfield.

Down below, the mist now almost covered the field.

The flight-deck door remained closed, and Forrester was the only passenger, there were just the three of them on board. Mist seemed to bump against several windows. He went forward, and pushed the door open. The roar of the engines struck at him. The engineer had a pair of earphones on, and was sitting in front of the radio. The pilot's back was towards Forrester.

The engineer leaned back, and shouted:

"They say they don't understand the mist, but it's clear enough to land on runway three."

"Okay," the pilot called.

Forrester said: "Listen, we're under attack. We aren't going to be allowed to land, they'll crash us first. I'm going to jump for it."

He stood by the open door staring at two startled faces. He knew what they thought; that he was mad. They couldn't think anything else. But he knew in his bones that he was right. His heart was pounding, and his nerves weren't steady, but he knew what he had to do, and he meant to do it.

He went out, and hurried along the gangway. He wasn't surprised when the flight-deck door opened and the engineer called sharply:

"Don't be a fool! It's only a bit of fog, we'll be down——"

"I've warned you," Forrester said. The words came out slowly, clearly. He was already hitching a parachute harness over his shoulders; he was near the exit, and knew how to open it. "You'll be fools if you don't jump. I——"

The aircraft shuddered.

There was a funny little popping sound, only it wasn't so funny. The red-faced youth in navy-blue uniform looked round, startled. The windows were dense with mist.

The aircraft steadied, but there was a noticeable difference in the sound of the engines.

Only one was turning.

"Now perhaps you'll believe me," Forrester growled.

He pulled the lever, and the door opened. Air swept in, cold, vicious. A trail of mist passed the open door, and disappeared; there was blue sky and, in the distance, the green of the land and the roofs of tiny houses.

The engineer yelled: *"Don't!"*

Forrester jumped out, feet first, looking through eight thousand feet of space. They were several miles away from the airfield, and there was no mist at all immediately beneath him. He could see it, mushrooming more like smoke than mist, over the airport itself; it hid runways, buildings, aircraft, approach roads, everything.

He went down, fast as a bullet. One or two wisps of mist appeared below him, so small that he didn't think twice about them. He pulled the cord. A moment later he felt the tug at his harness and, looking up involuntarily, saw the great envelope open.

Above it, a long way above, were patches of mist. And above them, the clear, blue sky.

He was floating down, now.

He lost sight of the aircraft, but it appeared in his line of vision again. Smoke was billowing back from both engines. It was still under control, but only a couple of thousand feet up and almost certainly going too fast to land without disaster.

He felt astonishingly cool.

He did not know what would happen if he were seen; for the misty shapes had eyes.

Men from another planet?

When the thought came, he knew that he had been thinking about that possibility subconsciously for hours. This was not like the work of humans.

He floated down, carried gently by the slight wind, thinking of those idiot things. Creatures from another planet? —here was a joke for Palfrey! He was suffering from a form of D.T.'s, of course; he had been all the time.

The ground was very near; some playing-fields, where little dots of people stood watching. Some started to run, a few still kicked a ball about. Forrester looked up. The envelope billowed gently, giving him a drunken feeling. No mist was near, but some distant patches seemed miles above him. The airfield was still covered with the only patch of mist anywhere below him; it must be two miles away.

Immediately below, people were streaming out of houses into streets leading to the playing-fields, more and more were craning their necks. Some were at windows and doors, a few on roofs. Cars were pulling into the side of the road, and stopping, but red buses went on as if nothing in the world could make them stop.

Forrester heard a distant roar.

He saw a great cloud of smoke, split with red, rising from a spot about a mile away. Pieces of wreckage were flying through and above the smoke; he thought that houses were crumbling. It all seemed remote and impersonal. He had a job to do: take this ash-tray to Palfrey. Get down to earth and get a car—the police would help. He couldn't tell them who he was, but if they took him to a telephone he could talk to Palfrey.

He was now much nearer the ground, a matter of a few hundred feet. Would he reach the park or the little gardens beyond it? In the gardens, trees and fences might do a lot of harm. He began to fear for himself.

Suddenly, Forrester's feet touched the ground. He was dragged along for a few yards, bumped his head, sprawled full length on grass, then slowly came to a standstill. He was twenty yards from the nearest fence.

He heard people running, but only one thing mattered: mist.

None was near.

There were patches up in the sky, and they might have seen the white envelope of the parachute, and be after him. Could they swoop down? *Had* they seen him? Suddenly it became desperately urgent to get that parachute folded up, to hide the evidence that he had escaped.

Then the people baulked him.

Excited voices, shouts on the perimeter of the crowd, curious, eager hands, the hands and faces of men and women, boys and girls, were all part of the moving medley. And cleaving the crowd in two came two policemen, massive in navy blue.

Forrester stood up.

"I'm all right," he said roughly. "I'm all right. I must get to a telephone." He stared up. There were twenty or thirty little patches of mist, and he thought they were nearer. "Urgently," he added, and licked his lips. The big patch of mist was out of sight, but he had no idea how fast it could move—except that it had kept pace with the aircraft.

He shuddered.

"We'll soon fix you up, sir," said a police-sergeant, as if he were an elderly parent talking to a worried son. "We'll make sure you're not hurt, and——"

"I'm not hurt," Forrester said sharply. "I must get to a telephone! It——"

He stopped.

Not far away, above the heads of the cloud, was a little patch of mist. It wasn't as big as those he had seen up by the aircraft, only about the size of a large umbrella. It seemed to be rolling aimlessly over the heads of the crowd.

The police-sergeant and a hundred people looked in the same direction as Forrester.

"Everything's all right, sir," soothed the sergeant, "we'll get a doctor, and——"

"I must get to a telephone!"

"There's one in my house," a man said in a high-pitched voice. "Glad for him to use it. Just there." The gate of his garden fence led into the playing-fields, and he was on the fringe of the crowd.

"Thanks very much," said Forrester. "Thanks! Let me through, officer, please."

The sergeant waved his arms, and the crowd parted. Forrester glanced up again at that patch of mist. It was only a few hundred yards away, perhaps two hundred feet above the ground. It floated just like mist on an autumn morning.

"There's nothing up there, sir," the sergeant soothed.

Forrester licked his lips.

"No," he muttered. "No." But at the gate, in the garden, from the window of the house, he watched the patch of mist. It was hovering. He dialled the number of Palfrey's London house, the headquarters of the organisation which, for the sake of a better name, was called Z 5. That was in Brierly Square, Mayfair.

If Palfrey wasn't in, someone would be, someone who could be trusted.

The ash-tray was in his pocket.

The patch of mist was coming farther down, a few feet above the crowd, now, and at the end of the garden. Mist with eyes? Forrester began to shiver, uncontrollably. The householder and the sergeant exchanged glances, and there was no doubt what was in their minds. The shock had affected this man's head, he would collapse at any minute.

"Hot cup o' tea," the sergeant suggested.

"Spot of whisky'll do him more good," said the householder. "I'll get it."

Forrester listened to the ringing sound. It went on and on. The mist still floated in the air, ten feet off the ground, as if it were searching for something—for someone. For him. He turned his back to the window, and damned the telephone. The householder drew near, with a finger of whisky in a small glass.

"This'll do you good." His voice still squeaked.

"Ah, thanks," said Forrester. He took it, as the ringing sound was interrupted. A woman said:

"Mrs. Paterson's house, who is that?"

Forrester almost choked on the whisky.

"They—they've given me a wrong number!" he said thinly. "I—Sorry." He tossed down the rest of the whisky, and dialled again, viciously. He kept his face averted, but there was a long mirror in the wall opposite the window, and

he could see the reflection of the gaping people and the crowd
—and the mist.

The mist seemed to be coming towards him.

"Listen," he said chokily to the sergeant. "Shut the doors,
shut the windows. Don't let——"

"Jim Kennedy here," a man said into the telephone, and
for a moment Forrester lost his dread, for Kennedy was
Palfrey's office chief. "Who's that?"

"Forrester," Forrester almost choked. He stared at the
window, which was open a foot at the top. "Jim, name a place
for me to meet you, anywhere, next hour. Name——"

"Lucy's Cake Shop, Bond Street," Kennedy said, without
a moment's hesitation. "Spare a minute to say——"

The mist was coming in at the window.

"The mist," choked Forrester. "Mist. Cloud. Watch
it."

He dropped the receiver.

The mist at the window was having difficulty in getting in,
seemed to have to squeeze itself flat. The householder was
gaping at it, the sergeant's face had turned pale, as if he
suddenly understood what was frightening Forrester.

The householder crossed himself.

Forrester turned and went blindly towards the door, into
a narrow hall, into the street where a crowd had gathered,
and as he looked up he saw two patches of mist at roof-top
level, floating calmly in the air.

Just outside was a smiling woman—Isabella Melado.

.   .   .   .

A storm cloud seemed to close on Forrester, terror filled
him, lightning flashed and an explosion roared in his ears,
driving away the vision of the woman.

"*No, no, no!*" he screamed.

He could still see the woman. Unexpectedly, she drew
nearer, touched him, and pulled him away.

The lightning flashed and the thunder roared and a fierce
wind blew. But somehow the woman's touch stilled his fear.

PART TWO
DR. PALFREY

7

DR. STANISLAUS ALEXANDER PALFREY stood at the french windows of his book-lined study at Brett Hall, which was listed in all good guide-books as one of the stately homes of England, and said inaccurately to be one of the few still in private hands. The hands of Dr. Palfrey, as he often liked it to be said, were by no means private. Occasionally, and this late afternoon on a day in March was one of the occasions, he would explain exactly what he meant.

He was smiling.

His elderly guest, a big and powerful man with a lock of iron-grey hair falling over a broad, high and lined forehead, looked at him appraisingly. The visitor, an American, was one of the most familiar figures in the United States, and television had added popularity to fame; that was the more remarkable because he was also a politician.

Senator Samuel McCall held a kind of roving commission, in that way which the Americans have made all their own; he had no executive powers, but his advisory influence was remarkable.

He had full lips, a nice smile, a curiously benign expression. He had a great reputation as a "do-gooder", an idealist whose head was always in the clouds, and he had many enemies among hard-headed materialists.

He also had many friends, in America and in many parts of the world.

People trusted him, and were never betrayed.

Compared with Samuel McCall, Dr. Palfrey was slender and unimpressive. His shoulders sloped, and consequently looked narrow; and were rounded, so that a little was taken deceptively off his height. His thinning hair was golden and silky, a little wavy, and his head was a good shape. In an unobtrusive way he was good-looking, although some said his nose was too arched and his chin a little too weak, although that was partly because of the way he tucked his chin in, as if he were all the time on guard against someone about to clip him hard.

His blue-grey eyes held a mild expression, his lashes and eyebrows were fair. His skin was golden brown, and he looked very fit. He used his slender hands a lot—more Gallic than English. While he talked, a tentative smile worried his lips, and he looked almost apologetic—or at least ready to apologise at the slightest need.

McCall knew Palfrey's reputation, but had never met him before. He was already recovering from a sense of disappointment. Palfrey's voice and manner helped that, for the voice which was completely under control and his manner, once one accepted the mannerisms, was one of very great self-confidence. He knew what he was saying and believed exactly what he said. That wasn't all that had made McCall feel happier about him, though. McCall just felt that he could trust him.

Palfrey was saying . . .

". . . and of course it's extremely difficult to believe, but I do believe it. If we accept the evidence—this man Botticelli is the most wicked man on earth. I use wicked, you understand, in the Hitlerian sense. Plus."

McCall's eyes became hard and bright.

"Yes, I understand," he said, "but before I believe it, I'd want a lot more evidence than you have, Dr. Palfrey. Sure, Botticelli's a bad hat. I have good reason to know that, as he chose to wreck the life of my only child. It was the Federal Bureau of Investigation which first suggested that your Department ought to look him over, but——"

"Oh, please," interrupted Palfrey. "Not my Department. I only serve." His smile was positively cherubic. "You, Washington, London—our Department, if we have to call it one. I prefer the word Service. Absurd, I know, but——" He shrugged. "Highly impersonal things, Departments, and there are too many persons in this one. I'm trying," he added, and his eyes positively glistened with good humour, "to give you some idea of what makes me tick."

McCall chuckled.

"I'm getting the idea!"

"That's splendid," cooed Palfrey. "I find it hard to believe that there is any—ah—service so misunderstood as this one. It's probably in the title, Z 5. Most apt for modern Mata Haris." He raised his right hand to his forehead, twisted a few strands of the silky hair round it, and pulled gently. "Even people who actually help to pay the bill get muddled. Not the F.B.I., though. They know what I'm supposed to try to do."

"And they've told me," said McCall. "You've an organisation of agents, men and women, moulded into the first world Secret Service. You came into being during the war, on the side of the Allies, and you've managed to hold the organisation together, with Russian and Chinese co-operation, too, although once you blotted your copybook with Russia. And now——"

McCall paused.

Palfrey proffered cigarettes from a slim gold case.

"Thanks," said McCall, and accepted a light. "Thanks, Palfrey. Well, the war was one thing. Now we're living in very different days. Now we're talking of taking trips to other planets, and perhaps other planets are talking of taking a look at us. And on this planet there are men, you've met some of them, who could make the weapons needed to hold the world to ransom." He made it all sound dry and factual; as it was. "Your job is to find them, and——"

"Sorry, no," Palfrey said, and patted down the strand of hair, making a ridiculous little curl on his forehead. "My job starts earlier. Seek and find the inexplicable, seek and find the men who see themselves as Hitler saw himself. After all, we've had quite a lot of them, one way and the other, haven't we? Tyrannical man's earliest ambition was to rule the whole earth, from Athens to Babylon, Rome to Cadiz, Paris to Berlin. Not to bring things too up-to-date to be mentioned. The odd and distressing thing about people and Governments, of course, is the shortness of their memory. There have been few centuries in world history which haven't seen at least one attempt to make world conquest. My history isn't strong, but it serves."

"Your history is all right," declared McCall. "And you seriously think that Botticelli is that mad?"

"I think it's probable. Hitlerian mad. Undoubtedly he sees himself as lord of all he surveys, and he surveys a lot. But I don't think he fancies himself as a twentieth-century Nero. His is simply the power to pull the strings, let the puppets be whom they may. Outwardly Botticelli is just a billionaire with a lot of influence, mostly financial and commercial, and why not, sir, why not? But it's much more than that," Palfrey went on, slowly, softly. "He has some peculiar influence, call it a magnetic power, which undoubtedly attracts people to him. As you know."

McCall said very slowly: "My own daughter fell victim to it, and Elenora was never just a good-time girl. To this day, I don't understand what happened to her. She went to a party at Botticelli's house in Chicago, and she never really belonged to me any more."

When he stopped, the American looked as a man might when thinking of the beloved dead.

"She's one of many," Palfrey murmured.

McCall made himself say:

"Yes, one of many. One of the Botticelli angels. The phrase is common talk, Palfrey. His house——"

He couldn't go on.

"Is called The House of the Angels," Palfrey finished for him. "Yes. But how much more do you know, sir?"

McCall was himself again now; hurt buried out of sight.

"That there are peculiar rumours about a form of *Yogi*; attempts to prove that mind can conquer mattter."

"That could be the core of all this." Palfrey agreed. "I've never been able to get an agent inside Botticelli's own house. I've had them very close, but something always keeps them out. Still, rumour is very strong. It's said that Botticelli can go into trances, during which he can be burnt, cut, kicked and beaten—and come out unscathed. There's certainly some truth in it. For years he has had small groups studying his 'methods of mind control'. One might say Yogi in twelve short lessons and twelve easy payments." Palfrey paused, but not for long, and he was not as flippant as the words sounded. "Some of the members of these groups have acquired remarkable powers. I have actually seen one, a young girl, walk on red-hot coals without being even slightly burnt."

McCall asked sharply:

"With your own eyes?"

"Yes."

"Where?"

"In Belgium, last month."

"I don't want to believe you, but I guess I have to. How many of these Botticelli study groups are there?"

"We've always known there were a lot, but only in the past few weeks have we discovered how many," Palfrey said. "There are hundreds of them, all over the world. The students go to Botticelli's Chicago home, stay for several weeks, then leave and start groups of converts—converts, that is, to Botticelli's method of training the mind so as to overcome matter. If it weren't for his known history, we might wonder if he were just a crank, even a kind of prophet, but—well, you know about him. Eight years or so ago Botticelli was a kid-glove Al Capone with far too much influence in your country. He had so many interests overseas, too, that the F.B.I.—thanks to you—thought it better to pass the inquiries on to us. Now we work hand-in-hand on the job." Palfrey's little smile lingered, was almost speculative; but there was no smile in his eyes. "In the old days, Botticelli was believed to have done many ugly things. Wherever he met opposition, he crushed it—financially, commercially, every way he came face to face with it. He is ruthless, and has always had remarkable power. He always knows when to stop, and he covers his own guilt brilliantly. He knows that national, state and city Governments will take just so much, and no more—and he never drives them too far. Tell me, sir, if Botticelli were known to be working hand-in-hand with Moscow, would you be happy?"

"I'd hate it, I guess," McCall said. There was apprehension in his eyes. "I'd be scared, too. Don't tell me——"

"I don't think he's doing that," Palfrey assured him crisply. "We haven't a tittle of evidence to say so. But like the Communists—and like the Nazis and like all political parties, if it comes to that—he has these agents everywhere. Rub shoulders with Ned Kelly and he might be a Botticelli man. Or woman. But the women do the training. They are often of great beauty, and they influence the most unlikely men. In the Senate, in Congress, in the House of Commons and in the House of Lords. In both hemispheres, and in all countries where money talks. A thousand lines from influential people lead back to Botticelli, most of them through the women he has taught at The House of the Angels."

Palfrey was looking very straightly into McCall's eyes.

"Palfrey," McCall said, "I know exactly what you have been doing. You know how deeply my daughter's going has hurt me. You've talked bluntly, and I'm grateful. I think you know that I had hopes that my daughter would——"

He broke off.

Palfrey said gently: "I know, Senator."

"Yes," McCall said. "Yes. I guess you do. I repeat, I'm grateful for the way you have made me face unpalatable facts. Now I'd like an answer to a very important personal question. Do you know where my daughter is?"

"A few days ago she was safe and well, in Spain," Palfrey told him. "She has since been to London, and is now believed to be on her way back to America."

McCall almost whispered. "Back home. Palfrey, my house on the Lakeside Drive is opposite Botticelli's. She used to watch him, as a child. He's a very handsome man, and when she was young Elenora worshipped him. I thought I'd cured her. If I'd moved her away——"

"I doubt if it would have made any difference," Palfrey said, briskly. "He'd have found her. Think of the hundreds who have gone to his home, to train themselves, then returned to their own countries to start a group."

"Has Elenora——?"

"She has no group, but seems to work as a kind of travelling missionary, often with a man named Lennard. Do you know him?"

"No. What is he?"

"We don't know much about him," Palfrey said. "But Elenora certainly travels widely and visits many Botticelli groups."

McCall made a quick movement with his hands.

"Thank you again, Palfrey. Will you go on, please?"

Palfrey moved away from the desk, glancing out into the garden. It was a clear evening, and as he looked towards the east the sky was a beautiful dark blue with a hint of purple behind it, and a shadowy ghost of a moon was already glowing. Nearer, there were a few little patches of mist, unusual near the house, which was on high ground. Still, mist often came up from the lake, two miles away, and from some of the farms and the river which ran through the park of Brett Hall.

Palfrey did not look twice at these patches of mist.

"And here's a summary of most of the activities," he said, lifting a heavy book, bound in black leather, from the top of a small table. He needed both hands to carry it in comfort. "The Book of Botticelli's Doom! We've been a long time getting this. There's enough evidence in here to hang, draw, quarter, guillotine, fry and behead him, and there are a lot of copies of that dossier, because once he knows it exists, he'll do a lot to destroy it. You can read it at your leisure, but the evidence is so conclusive that no panel of legal experts, High Court or Queen's Bench, could even think of a way out for Botticelli. But we daren't take action because there's one thing we don't know." Palfrey spread his hands, and smiled faintly. "I take that back, there's one thing we *know* we don't know. I'd hate to say how many we don't even suspect."

McCall touched the book.

"I'll take your word for it, and read it later for the sake of my conscience," he said dryly. "What stops you from having him pulled in?"

"We know too little about him," Palfrey said. "We don't know what his power is or how far it stretches. We must learn more about him before we make any arrest."

McCall looked at Palfrey with narrowed, almost scared eyes.

He was facing the window, the lovely lawns and flower-gardens and the gentle sky, and saw the patches of mist; it did not even occur to him to be surprised. The patches were so soft and white; fleecy.

"What are you trying to tell me, Palfrey?"

Palfrey pulled up a chair. He didn't glance out of the window this time, although the mist was very close. He spread his hands and gave a little shrug; his face had a strange, pale tautness.

"I don't quite know, unless it is that I'm frightened."

McCall didn't speak.

"I've talked to several people in Whitehall," Palfrey went

on slowly, "and I can't blame them for being sceptical. But Botticelli scares me, because of the things he can do—rather, the way he can do them. One particularly unpleasing story illustrates what I mean best, I think. We know that he believes himself to be irresistible to women, to—quite young girls. And he has one pride—one pride he boasts about, anyway—that of being a supreme judge of beauty. He's not by any means illiterate, you know——"

"Oh, I know," McCall said, "his father was a rich *restaurateur*. Botticelli had everything, including a University course —until he was politely sent away."

"He likes his name, and dotes on his namesake of a few centuries ago," Palfrey went on. "He has more Botticelli paintings than any private collector in the world. Some of his groups are said to be even more wonderful than the Adoration of the Magi and the Madonna and Child, but Botticelli's collection is mostly of the mythological groups. He's said to have cut up some canvasses, so as to separate the faces of the women—the 'angels'." Palfrey paused. "He buys wherever he can, and is known to have arranged for the theft of several paintings. He has bought up every good copy of a Botticelli that he can lay his hands on. He knows the masterpieces off by heart—almost as some people know a poem. If a girl has the face of a Botticelli angel, Botticelli wants to know all about it, and most of these girls work for him. Sometimes they vanish."

Palfrey paused, and glanced over his shoulder involuntarily. The mist was a white blanket against the glass. He shivered, without knowing why.

Something drew McCall's eye past Palfrey, towards the window. It was more than a mist, now, it was thick, white fog, which had come up amazingly fast. In spite of Palfrey's story and the Book of Botticelli's Doom, McCall paused to stare.

And he shivered, too.

"I'll put on a fire," Palfrey said. "It's getting chilly."

"Maybe that's a good idea," McCall said. He watched Palfrey move towards the fireplace, where an electric fire stood, quite dead until Palfrey switched it on. This house had central heating, though, the fire was only an *aide*; and it wasn't really cold. "Pretty girls have disappeared before."

"One of them vanished into thin air," said Palfrey.

McCall just looked his disbelief.

"I can show you how it happened," Palfrey went on, deliberately.

McCall said: "Now, Palfrey——"

Palfrey smiled, yet it wasn't quite the free smile that he'd shown before; it was as if he were preoccupied, almost worried. Now and again he glanced round.

"And later I will," he said. "Other people who served Botticelli have just disappeared. Reports have come in from different parts of the world about the same kind of phenomenon."

Palfrey paused, and looked at the window. The lower half was smothered by a blanket of mist. He took a step towards it.

"I've got the creeps tonight!" he said, abruptly. "It's the mist, I suppose, it's going to be thick later on. I ought to tell you that no one else except my Chief in England has heard about this."

McCall said: "I quite understand." He stubbed out his cigarette, watching Palfrey as if he were beginning to believe this story of vanishing people.

"Then we heard that Botticelli had influenced the twenty-year-old daughter of a French industrialist," Palfrey went on. "I won't go into details about how we found out that Botticelli was anxious to 'convert' her, but we did. She was never left alone. We had a woman agent sleeping in a room leading off hers. The girl herself was a little fey, and unworldly in some ways. She laughed at the precautions, but raised no objections."

Palfrey paused. McCall was intent and watchful and the mist was forgotten.

"She lived in Paris, a nice house on the left bank," Palfrey declared. "There was a small garden or courtyard in the French style. The only approach to the garden was by big wooden doors which fitted flush to the floor and ceiling, or over the roof. If the girl was safe anywhere, she was safe there. It was a lovely afternoon, a week ago. The whole family was in the garden, with my agent. The girl's father brought out a ciné camera, and took some pictures. He took some of his Octavie while she was cutting some flowers, not knowing what he was doing."

Palfrey paused, and studied McCall's face; the unbelievable truth affected him almost as much now as it had when he had first heard of it.

McCall said harshly: "Go on."

"She vanished," said Palfrey abruptly. "Her father thought she had moved behind some shrubs. Instead, she'd disappeared. It was early afternoon, but all the doors were closed, it was impossible for anyone to get in or out of the garden, but—she vanished. And the film her father took shows her vanishing. Shows her there one moment, gone the next—the film blurs quite suddenly, and next moment she is gone. Afterwards the garden and the flowers, and the wall and window of the house appear, but Octavie Delacroix isn't seen again."

Palfrey's voice faded into a whisper.

McCall wiped the perspiration from his forehead. The two bars of the electric fire were glowing, and the American felt hot, but it wasn't from the fire.

"That sounds to me like a piece of trick photography," he said with difficulty. "Are you sure you can trust the witnesses?"

"One of my own agents was there. I am as sure as if I had seen it myself," Palfrey told him. "The girl is bending down, holding a pair of scissors. Her father took the picture. The exposure was perfect, the lighting good. Suddenly something white blurred the screen, and next moment——"

He stopped abruptly.

He didn't turn, didn't move; McCall might not have suspected what had sprung into his mind but for the swift, startled movement of his eyes towards the window and the mist pressing against it.

"Something *white*," McCall breathed.

8

PALFREY moved to his desk swiftly, almost without a sound. McCall glanced at him, then back at the mist, which was five or six feet from the ground, tight against the window and swirling wildly. He could see the movement, it wasn't just mist that rose from damp ground at the end of a day of warm sun.

Palfrey flicked a switch, leaned forward and spoke into an inter-office telephone:

"You there, Ronnie?"

A man's voice came into the room and made McCall look round sharply.

"Yes."

"Send to every part of the house, at once, and have all outside doors and windows locked."

"Okay," said Ronnie, as if that were the most normal request. "Right away."

"Just a minute," Palfrey went on. "If anyone sees smoke, mist, vapour of any kind in a room, lock the door, make sure it can't get into any other part of the house."

Ronnie's voice wasn't quite so matter-of-fact.

"What is this, Sap?"

"I'll be telling you," Palfrey said. He switched off, and to McCall's surprise, his right hand went to his forehead and he started to twist a few strands of hair round his forefinger. "I'm going to have a look from upstairs. Care to come?"

"I will, certainly."

"Odd business, isn't it?" remarked Palfrey, as if it were a trifle. "We'll keep it out of this room, anyhow." He smiled faintly. "Or I hope we will!" He pressed a button in his desk, there was a sharp click and then a faint hissing sound; dark doors began to slide over the window, shutting out the evening light and blotting out the mist. They were like modern lift doors, closing tightly. "Now we'll get out, and shut this door," Palfrey added. "Steel, quite fireproof." He gave McCall the impression that he wasn't as sure as he wanted to be that the steel doors would keep the mist out.

They went into the big spacious hall; a baronial hall.

Two youngish men in lounge suits came hurrying along wide passages which led off it. They didn't look round. An elderly man was closing and bolting the huge, massive front doors. The four-hundred-year-old flooring was of oak darkened by centuries of polishing and rubbing. Two suits of mediæval armour stood on silent sentry-go at the foot of the wide, circular staircase. Portraits in oils, covering the centuries in modes of dress, were on the walls in the hall and up the staircase. There was a marked likeness among many of the faces, but none was like Palfrey.

"Could sell the place to Hollywood as it stands, couldn't I?" Palfrey said, but it was for the sake of something to say, McCall sensed his tension; his fear.

Palfrey led the way. When walking, he proved to be as tall as McCall, and nearly as broad. Palfrey wasn't so round-shouldered as he had seemed, either, it was almost as if he were bracing himself to withstand some onslaught. At the first landing there was a semicircular gallery, overlooking the great hall. There were skin rugs, oak flooring, more portraits, one enormous tapestry of a battle scene. McCall saw all of these things but noticed none of them.

"More stairs, sorry," Palfrey said mechanically. "We don't work on an elevator economy."

He was moving so swiftly that McCall had difficulty in keeping up. They passed two wide windows, and although McCall glanced out, he couldn't see anything; Palfrey didn't pause. The next flight of stairs was very narrow, obviously leading to a turret. There was a half-landing, and above that a spiral staircase, with steps of worn stone. McCall felt brushed by something of the history and the tradition of the place as he followed Palfrey, holding the smooth wooden railing firmly. Hands long dead had helped to polish it.

They reached a small room with windows on all sides.

McCall cried: "*Look at it!*" and nearly choked.

"Yes," said Palfrey, in a voice which was hardly more than a whisper. "Look at it."

.   .   .   .   .

The parkland, undulating, grass- and tree-clad, had the cold beauty of the English landscape in the early spring. A few larches and a copse of pines were green against the lowering sky, but the branches of the oaks, the beech and the birch, the elm and the ash, were bared and dark, a skeleton promise soon to be clothed, buds tight and showing no sign of bursting. There was an ornamental pool, and, farther away, a boating-lake. In the distance were two farms and a village, all part of the estate.

And everywhere, were tiny patches of mist.

Some were high against the sky, some as high as the

window, most were close to the ground. All were moving towards the house. None was really near this room, but there was a fear that one might appear at any moment. It was not like ordinary mist; there were hundreds of tiny patches, thin and wispy, almost human in shape.

Palfrey picked up a telephone, and with his other hand pushed cigarettes towards McCall. Then he took a cigarette himself. McCall struck a match with icy fingers.

"Ronnie?" Palfrey said into the telephone. "Get all the upstairs windows closed, will you? Take especial care with the entrances to the vaults."

"All right," Ronnie said. It didn't sound the same voice, no one could mistake the edge of fear in it. "Hold on, will you?" Palfrey drew at his cigarette and smiled tautly into McCall's face; and McCall turned and looked at those odd little patches of mist, which appeared to be so innocuous. Neither of them spoke.

Ronnie said: "Sap?"

"Yes?"

"There was mist in two rooms—the kitchen and the morning-room. We've locked them both. The kitchen boy——"
He broke off.

Palfrey said very softly: "Go on."

"Dead," choked Ronnie. "Str-strangled."

Palfrey's cigarette burned red half-way down its length. He didn't speak. Ronnie held on, and McCall, who had not heard this, felt that shudder again, and began to understand and to share Palfrey's dread.

"All right," Palfrey said. "Make as sure as you can that the mist doesn't get out of either room, we might learn a lot from it." His voice was free from outward evidence of fear. "Look after yourself."

Ronnie grunted.

Palfrey said to McCall: "We'd better get downstairs. You won't mind waiting in the vaults for a while, will you? I don't think there's anything to worry about there."

"Palfrey, what is this?"

"As I stand here," Palfrey said, "I don't know." He looked out of the window again; the tiny patches of mist were everywhere. One floated close to the window, went past, then turned back and pressed against the window.

Just outside the door was a smaller, narrow one which McCall hadn't seen.

"Used for emergency only," Palfrey said, "sorry I misled you." It was a lift, large enough for four people. The light came on and they stepped inside; the door closed as Palfrey pressed the bottom of four buttons. "One of the reasons why we use Brett Hall as headquarters these days is that the vaults are so big. Run under practically the whole house. Wine cellars originally, of course, but more than that—they were extended at the time of the Civil War, when some of the Stuart fans turned the place into a storehouse of weapons and ammunition. It's written that at one time twenty-seven cavaliers with a price on their heads were living in the vaults at the same time, and even the servants didn't know."

They were going down, slowly.

"What didn't you tell me about that telephone message?" McCall demanded. He was massive, as calm as Palfrey, but with a shadow in his eyes.

"A kitchen boy was strangled," Palfrey said. "Man or mist we don't yet know."

The lift stopped, the doors opened automatically, and they stepped into a wide passage, lit by fluorescent lighting which was very like daylight. It was much cooler here than it had been in the study. They walked briskly.

A man appeared out of a room on the right of the passage.

"Everything all right?" Palfrey asked.

"No alarms my side," the man answered. He was short, had curly brown hair, and the empty left sleeve of his jacket was tucked carelessly into the pocket. "What's this about fighting shadows?"

"Mist."

"You should know," the one-armed man said.

Palfrey smiled faintly. "Keep a close watch, Howard, and it isn't a joke. If you see any mist—smoke, vapour or steam for that matter—close the compartment doors and lock it in. You get out," he added. "Don't go near it, and don't let it get near you."

"So it's gas," Howard said. "Masks?"

"I don't think so."

Palfrey put a hand on McCall's arm, and they went on. It was like walking along the different passages and tunnels of London's underground railway; the lighting was uniform, the air clear. "He won't be long," Palfrey said. "Bit bewildering down here, isn't it? Some sections are still as they were, stone walls, damp and frowsty but pretty safe. We had this part reinforced with concrete. Keep a lot of records and other things down here that we wouldn't want anyone else to get hold of. The doors are hermetically sealed and operated, we can shut off sections, as in a ship if a part of it's holed. The whole job was done scientifically, all known methods of breaking in were guarded against."

"Known methods," McCall echoed. He tossed the hair back from his forehead. "Have you ever heard of this mist before?"

"No. But think what it would answer. Disappearances like Octavie's wouldn't be so mysterious after all. Under cover of stuff like this——"

"You could be wrong." McCall sounded harsh.

"Well, yes," said Palfrey, and looked at the American with an almost humorous expression, matching the drollness which McCall tried to hold but couldn't quite manage. "Of course I could. Could be harmless stuff. Still, there's some in the kitchen, and a boy was strangled."

He stopped, and thrust open a door.

The room beyond might have been the entrance hall of any small, good-class hotel. There were easy-chairs, couches, tables, stacks of newspapers and magazines, all the usual oddments; but no one was in here. Palfrey let the door close behind him, and then went to a telephone, He motioned to another, near McCall. The American picked it up.

"You there, Ronnie?" Palfrey asked.

There was no answer.

Palfrey began to twist strands of hair round his forefinger.

"Ronnie, are you there?"

McCall's grip on his telephone tightened until the knuckles of his powerful hands showed very white. He didn't look away from Palfrey's face. The only sound in this room was of his own breathing; he couldn't hear Palfrey's.

"I don't like——" began Palfrey.

A man spoke into the telephone. "Who's that?" It was a shrill, breathless voice, as if the speaker had been running.

"Palfrey. What's doing?"

"I don't—don't quite know. Heard a hell of a scream and came running. Ronnie's—dead. I don't see anyone, but he's been strangled. The bruises on his neck——"

The man at the other end of the wire broke off, as if he couldn't bare to finish.

Palfrey asked urgently: "Can you see any mist, vapour, smoke——"

"I know what we're looking for," the man said reedily. "None in sight, but the ruddy stuff creeps up on you. I——"

He broke off.

Along the wires came a new sound, a frightening scream, like a woman's voice. It drew nearer. It was as if a terrified woman were running towards them, screaming all the time, unable to stop.

"One of the maids," the man said. "I—oh, my God!" His voice rose to a wild scream. "Oh, God, she's gone," he cried, "she's gone, swallowed up in mist, she's——"

He stopped.

There was a clattering sound, as if he had dropped the instrument, then a gasping, thudding noise, the kind a man might make if he were fighting. Then the gasps became less loud, were little more than tiny panting sounds.

Then—silence.

McCall stood with the receiver close to his ear, as white as the mist which had pressed against the window. His grey eyes had a strange, starry brilliance. He shuddered involuntarily, but when he spoke his voice was almost normal.

"So it's everywhere in the house, Palfrey."

"That could have happened," Palfrey agreed. "I hope to heaven we manage to hold on to a patch or two." He pulled the hair straight out from his forehead, then tapped it down into a tiny ringlet. "This is no place for you, sir. Better get you away." He pressed down another switch, and went on: "We've several lodge gates, and we can get out of the vaults in half a dozen places. I shouldn't think there'll be any difficulty."

"I'd prefer to stay here," McCall said, abruptly.

"Don't doubt that for a moment," Palfrey said, and his smile was more free, it was almost as if he had managed to forget that scream and those dying sounds on the telephone.

"But you're precious cargo and safer out than in—hallo, that North Lodge? . . . How are things? . . . Good, bring a car along to the ornamental lake, will you? and collect Senator McCall. I won't be there. Get him back to London and don't lose any time. . . . No sign of the stuff about you, is there?"

There was a pause; then he rang off.

"It seems to be concentrated on and in the Hall," he observed. "No difficulty in you getting away, as far as I can judge. I wish I could guarantee it."

"I have never felt so powerless in all my life," McCall said.

Palfrey's lips puckered.

"I know how you feel. Helpless and frightened. As I told you, I've been scared of this for some time. Botticelli's been able to do things which no man should be able to do. But that doesn't mean we can't stop him." He paused. "I wish they hadn't arrived here in force. I wonder what brought them." He eyed McCall speculatively. "Could be you, could be me." He gave the impression that he wasn't really thinking about what he said. "I'll take you to the car."

McCall snapped: "I told you I want to stay!"

"Oh, no," said Palfrey. "My responsibility to Whitehall and the State Department is greater than that, and your present job is to stay alive. You might telephone Washington about this when you get back to London, they'll believe you before they'll believe me."

McCall didn't answer.

Palfrey led the way across the big lounge, and thrust open a glass door. This led into a wide passage, still lit by the strip lighting. They looked up and down, but there was no sign of mist. A man was sitting in a small car, rather like the kind used in amusement parks the world over. He jumped up.

"All clear?" asked Palfrey.

"So far."

"Good. Take Mr. McCall to the ornamental pool, will you? and see him into a car which they're sending out from North Lodge. If there's any sign of the mist near the pool, come back. He's precious." Palfrey smiled at McCall, and put out his hand. "I'll see you in London."

McCall growled: "I hope to heaven I do."

.   .   .   .   .

Palfrey watched the little car, with its electric motor humming, as it disappeared along the tunnel. He felt the deadliness of the danger here, hoped desperately that he was right in thinking that McCall was safer outside. Then he turned slowly back to the big hall. He looked pale, and there was no longer a hint of a smile in his eyes. He walked past the telephone, then pressed a button in the wall close to another doorway. It was a lift.

He stepped in, and the door closed.

He said to the four walls which pressed upon him: "Thank God Drusilla's not here." As he spoke, he felt as if his wife were as close to him as the whisper of his own voice. When he closed his eyes, he could see her face. She had been gravely ill that winter, and had gone with their small daughter to the South of France; they were due to stay for another three weeks. If this job wasn't finished by then, she must stay longer.

Their only son was at school.

The lift stopped. Palfrey hesitated, before pressing the button which opened the sliding doors. Now he was in the great hall of the house, and two chandeliers, each with a hundred tiny lights flickering and scintillating on the Waterford glass of the pendants and the drop-pieces, gave a brightness very different from the light below.

He saw nothing but the paintings, the two suits of armour, all the things he would expect to see.

He stepped out.

There was no sign of mist to the right or to the left; in fact, there was no sign of anyone. In emergency, two men were under orders to come to the hall, the pivotal point of all activity at Brett Hall. And they would not have disobeyed, had they been able to get here.

There was no sound.

The telephone exchange, where Ronnie had been, was in a small room off the hall. The door was closed. Palfrey went slowly towards it—slowly, because he had a feeling that he was being watched. He had to force himself to go on. He touched the handle of the door, but didn't turn it at first. He looked over his shoulder, towards the staircase.

Nothing moved.

The unseen eyes seemed to be closer.

He shivered uncontrollably, and gritted his teeth, not knowing that he felt just as Forrester had felt so often in the past two days. To overcome his own silent, gripping terror, he thrust the door open.

There was Ronnie, on the floor, face and neck swollen and discoloured, the tip of his tongue showing against his lips; and there was the other man who had spoken to Palfrey, still sitting on the chair in front of the telephone exchange, leaning forward; and there were dark bruises at the back of his neck.

That was all.

Palfrey turned and opened the door slowly, thinking less of what might be outside than of the death of those two men. He took a step forward.

Mist was swirling about wildly, half-way down the stairs.

9

PALFREY couldn't move.

His hand seemed to be forced tightly against the door, his feet stuck to the floor. Even the desire to move had gone. He stood with his mouth open, eyes rounded and wide with horror such as he had never known before.

The mist seemed to be billowing towards him, great wispy tentacles spread out, he felt as if they were touching him, or stretching out to grip his neck and to throttle the life out of him.

There came a flash.

It was sudden and binding. Lightning itself could not have filled the hall with such awful light. Pain flashed across Palfrey's eyes, and he could not see.

He could picture the mist, and he seemed to be standing in the middle of it, with those tentacles, half-unseen, clutching at his hands, his arms, his legs, his waist, his face. There was no pressure at his neck, and that was where he had expected it to be tight, throttling pressure, of the kind that had killed the others.

There was none.

He knew that he was still standing there, alive, held fast
to floor and door.

There was a pressure against his eyes, like a hot iron bar.
He could not open them. He heard the rushing of the blood
through his ears and the thumping of his heart, felt the
pounding beat of his pulse.

These noises and the thudding and the pulsing gradually
quietened. The pressure against his eyes became easier. He
tried to open them. It was not easy, but he managed to get
the lids up slightly, and could see through his lashes. Every
time he blinked, blinding light flashed across his eyes again,
but soon he could see the hall—and one suit of armour lying
on its side near a gaping hole in the marble staircase.

Soon, he was able to keep his eyes open.

The thing which most astounded him was that he was alive.
This was not some ante-chamber to another world, but Brett
Hall. The breach in the wall of the staircase was large enough
for a man to sit in, and the marble and masonry was on the
floor immediately beneath it. Dust floated about the great
hall and hovered near the chandeliers, almost like the mist;
but it was not mist, it was only the dust.

There was no other sound.

Palfrey moistened his lips. His jaws hurt when he moved
them. He went forward slowly, and his joints seemed to
creak; but he could move, and he had to remind himself
that he was still alive.

He went nearer the staircase, and doing so, he shivered
again, as if the mist were still swirling, threatening, billowing,
shooting out the tentacles that were soon to strangle him.
But there was no mist; wherever he looked there was only
the pale, floating dust.

He stopped at the foot of the stairs.

Half-way down, where he had last seen the mist itself,
there was a patch of reddish stain, as if someone had dropped
a cloth, heavy with pale dye, and dropped it there. He went
nearer. There was more of the same stain at the side of the
stairs, and when he looked at the rubble he saw a few more
patches there.

He stood staring.

Then footsteps sounded, a man came hurrying, and Palfrey
spun round. In spite of all that had happened, his right hand

flashed to his pocket—as if a gun could protect him against the evil which had been here.

But this was a friend; a short, wiry-looking man with iron-grey hair, a young face belying the iron grey, dark-blue eyes deep set and with a myriad crowsfeet etched in the mahogany skin. He walked briskly but did not run, and when he saw Palfrey he slowed down but didn't stop .

He said very slowly: "So they can't kill you."

Palfrey didn't speak.

"What's the matter, deaf?" growled the smaller man, his voice unmistakably American, yet lacking the drawling casualness of McCall's. He drew nearer, gripped Palfrey's forearms, and said with fierce intensity: "Sap, don't look like that!"

Palfrey closed his eyes.

"What do I look like?" he muttered. "Sorry. Shock. Er —be careful. Might be——"

He stopped and looked round, and he could not keep the new fear out of his eyes.

"If you mean the mist," said Cornelius. Bruton, in that tight, hard voice and in a manner which suggested that he almost feared that he was fighting for Palfrey's reason, "it's gone."

Palfrey straightened up.

"What?"

"Yes, it's gone. I saw it going," Bruton went on abruptly. He still gripped Palfrey's forearms. "Like a cloud, swifter than the wind, a billowing cloud going"—he cocked a thumb towards the ceiling—"back up there." His own tension showed in his clipped, explosive words. "To join the clouds it came from. You hurt?"

"No," said Palfrey, slowly, painfully. "I don't think so. Ronnie and Arthur are in there. Strangled."

"I saw two more, on the way in. A kid and a woman," said Bruton, in the same hard, clipped voice. "Otherwise the place seems deserted." He dropped Palfrey's arms. "I want a drink. A big drink. Come on." He led the way to a small room, in the corner of which was a cocktail bar. He lifted the flap and went through. Palfrey, looking and feeling almost stupid, as if there were no strength left in his body, leaned against the counter, then sat heavily on a leather-topped stool. Nothing in this small room was affected, but the curtains were drawn and, through a gap, Palfrey saw that the wooden shutters—with which every window in Brett Hall was fitted—were in position.

Bruton put a small glass of brandy into Palfrey's hand.

"Just sip," he said roughly. "Want to know something? I was driving in. I'd picked up a message on the radio from Kennedy, and that made me step on it. Then I reached North Lodge, and Smith was talking gibberish. Something about an attack by patches of mist, and a lot of messages coming from the house. He'd just seen McCall off, by the way—you send him?"

Palfrey was savouring the brandy; fighting against collapse. "Yes."

"He ought to be all right, I passed him outside the ground, on the main road," said Bruton. He didn't savour, he gulped. "So I came here as fast as I know how, and the domestic garden is nearer from North Lodge." He gulped again. "There were a few patches of mist about, I could just see them—it was getting dark. Then more of the stuff came out of the doorways. I thought the place was on fire. It came out like a squall, and before I knew it it was up out of sight. Up *there*." This time he stabbed a forefinger at the ceiling.

Palfrey said with great deliberation:

"My head's a bit better, I think. We ought to look for the others. Twenty odd men were here. Have you been in the kitchen?"

"Yes."

"Door open?" Palfrey spoke with the concentrated deliberation of a drunken man. "Sure about that?"

"Yes."

"Should have been locked," said Palfrey, still carefully. "Told them to lock it. Ought to have captured some." He blinked at the American, then moved towards the door, still holding his glass. "I know, I look stupid. I feel stupid. I feel as if something's been drawn out of me. Pints and pints of blood, perhaps. Or will-power. Or guts. But we must find the others. We must——"

They were in the hall again.

Along a passage leading off it, pressed close to the wall, a gun in his right hand pointing towards Palfrey, was one of the Z 5 men who had been on duty. He had been closing the windows and locking the doors. He looked like Palfrey had declared that he felt—as if the blood and life had been drawn out of him. Palfrey had never seen a face so devoid of all colour—except for the eyes. This man's eyes were hazel brown in that ghostly pallor. They reflected shock, fear and a kind of desperate courage.

Palfrey said in a cracked voice: "It's all right, Tony."

The man stiffened, for a moment it looked as if he were going to shoot, and the gun still pointed at Palfrey, but the hand holding it began to shake. Without warning, he collapsed. The gun dropped, struck the floor and slithered almost to Palfrey's feet. The man fell, struck his head against a chair and rolled over, arms held wide, knees bent. His mouth was open, and it looked as if he were dead.

. . . . .

Palfrey said: "Yes, he's dead. Not a mark on him. But no mystery about this one. He died of shock."

. . . . .

Compelling himself to examine the dead man, calling on his store of professional knowledge, which he seldom needed as the Chief of Z 5, did Palfrey good. Having Bruton here, self-possessed and confident in spite of what had happened, also helped. He couldn't be positive that he was right about the diagnosis; he felt sure that he was.

His forefinger was at his hair.

"Let's look for the others," he said. "They've sent for help at North Lodge, I take it."

"Yes, telephoning Kennedy."

"Good. Let's go," Palfrey said. "Eerie when this place is empty, isn't it? As if filled with ghosts. Say you saw the mist going heavenwards."

"At hell's pace."

Palfrey found himself smiling.

"I think I know what you mean."

They were trying door after door and, whenever one yielded, thrusting it open. They looked into seven rooms before they came upon a large chamber, once used as the armoury, now a games room with billiards, darts, jokari, squash—everything for the eagle of eye or the trim of muscle. In here they found most of the men who worked at Brett Hall, and all the servants except the one girl who had been found dead.

These were alive—shocked and badly shaken, but alive.

All they could remember was being enveloped in mist, running in a desperate effort to get through it, collapsing—and waking up here.

They had all felt much as Palfrey had when the tentacles had spread out from the stairs, before the blinding flash and the blackout.

Men began to arrive from London, agents who usually worked in the Brierly Place house, others who had been called from other duties or from leave. Few of those who had been at Brett Hall would be much use for the next few days, although, like Palfrey, two or three threw off the effect of the experience and insisted on staying on duty.

A strange quiet lay upon the house, and Palfrey and Bruton were almost coldly matter-of-fact. The damaged staircase was roped off, secondary staircases and lifts were used to go upstairs. Experts from the National Research Board's Laboratories arrived within two hours, and began their inspection. Statements were taken from everyone in condition to make them. The bodies of the four strangled people, including the girl, were taken into a room which was turned into a morgue; doctors from a nearby Research Group came to do the *post mortems*. A search was made for the slightest trace of mist, but none was found. The only pinkish stain, undoubtedly from an oily liquid according to the expert, was on the stairs and the rubble.

Palfrey was closely questioned by one of his own men and by one of the experts, to make sure that he had omitted nothing from his statement.

McCall, who telephoned twice from London, was also cross examined before he made his report to Washington.

.   .   .   .   .

One of the first things that Kennedy had told Palfrey when he had arrived from London was about the message from Jim Forrester, and Forrester's panic-stricken warning about mist. Forrester had not turned up at Lucy's Cake Shop in New Bond Street; the moment he did, a message would be flashed to Brett Hall. Z 5 men were active near the London airport, questioning the police, neighbours and passers-by who had seen Forrester's parachute come down. Every mention of mist or of small clouds was noted, the appearance of each patch was checked from every possible angle.

Gradually, the picture took on some shape.

Then a report arrived, in code, from Malaga. Pirando had sent this, explaining that most of it had been telephoned to him by Stefan Andromovitch on the afternoon of Forrester's departure for England. Pirando made no other comment. The story of the struggle with mysterious creatures enveloped in mist read simply, factually and, had they not seen it with their own eyes, would have been quite incredible.

Then Forrester's written report arrived, and Palfrey *had* to believe.

McCall had to believe, too.

The most stringent efforts were made to keep the story secret, but rumours reached the newspapers; in the interest of security, newspaper editors were asked not to publish any story about the mist, and none broke the voluntary censorship. A few people, including leading newspaper editors, were taken into Palfrey's confidence and faced with the situation. Disappearances had been reported from various parts of the world, but the only two major manifestations had been in Spain and in England. The obvious theory was that the "creatures" were men who were using a kind of gas which had never been known before. The marks on the throats of the strangled victims were undoubtedly those of fingers, the only comment from the doctors who did the *post mortems* being that all the pressure appeared to have been very powerful, in two cases necks had been broken; and the actual thickness of the fingers appeared to be very much less than that of the average man's.

At conferences which had taken place in London and Washington, the two capitals where most notice was taken of the manifestations, tentative suggestions were put forward about creatures from another planet. The suggestions were received politely but without enthusiasm.

Palfrey was asked to take his men off all other investigations, and to concentrate on this one. That was easy. Agents watching Botticelli sent regular reports, but the man appeared to live quietly in his lakeside home at Chicago. The man named Lennard was also there; so was McCall's daughter.

Although they sometimes travelled as man and wife, they were not married.

McCall now knew that; and also knew that his daughter was living at The House of the Angels.

Stefan Andromovitch, the Russian, was still missing.

So was Forrester.

No "clouds" were seen for several days, and on the fifth day Palfrey felt very nearly normal. Drusilla, his wife, knew that there had been some trouble at the Hall, but a chat by telephone had reassured her. She would be at Cap d'Antibes for the next two weeks. The weather was perfect, she reported, and she was feeling much better. She hoped that he could spend the last week-end with her.

Palfrey promised that he would try; but he had to fly to America, and might not be able to get back in time.

"Stay there until I can come and fetch you," he said, and Drusilla laughed, said that obviously he wanted her out of the way, and who was he going to see?

"Oh, just conferences," Palfrey said.

Actually, he was going to see Botticelli.

.   .   .   .   .

He sat in a strato-cruiser, half-way across the Atlantic, on a calm, cloudless day. It was a week since the raid on Brett Hall. Nothing else had been discovered, nothing else had happened. Researches had led to nowhere. Analysis of the red, oily substance had shown some trace of radio-active constituent, but it was believed that the quantity was too small to be of the slightest danger. There were red and white blood corpuscles, too.

He sat with his head resting on the back of a seat, his eyes half-closed. Bruton was across the gangway. The machine was on a trial flight and there were only two other passengers, both R.A.F. personnel. Another aircraft flew behind them on ordinary passenger service, with two Z 5 agents aboard. Other agents would be waiting at Idlewild; still more at Chicago.

Bruton stirred restlessly, flicked a lighter, lit a cigarette.
"Are you going to sleep all day?"

Palfrey widened his eyes and glanced sideways at him.
"Not quite," he said.

"You never say a word these days until someone prises it
out of you."

"Nice change," murmured Palfrey.

"What's on your mind all the time?"

Palfrey said: "Corny, if I talk too much, I'm going to
confess to you and everyone who knows me that I'm so
frightened I could jump out of my own skin." He turned his
head and looked out of the window. A wisp or two of cloud
—white, misty cloud—floated by some distance off. "I can't
look at a cloud without wondering what's in it. In a *cloud*,
understand."

"You're becoming neurotic."

"Probably. But I just don't follow. If Botticelli's converted a scientist who's found this gas, it might explain
part of it—but it wouldn't explain the thin finger-marks on
the throats of the dead, would it?"

Bruton growled: "Men can wear gloves with steel rods
fitted down the fingers."

"That's it," said Palfrey, softly. "Be rational. Explain
everything away in the proper dimensions, refuse to accept
the possibility of Dimension Number Four." He sat up. "If
only I could understand what drove the stuff away and what
happened on that staircase. I tell you it was coming for *me*. I
felt—I felt as if I were standing at the gateway of hell, looking
down." He paused, and then went on very deliberately—with
Bruton looking at him and believing every word he said. "At
that moment, Corny, I was absolutely convinced that it wasn't
a human agency—not human, as we know it. Now——" He
shrugged his shoulders. "I want to know what drove the
mist away, what frightened it out of the Hall."

Bruton echoed: "Frightened?"

"That's a possibility, anyhow."

Bruton brooded, before he said slowly: "I wish I could
believe that you were crazy." He turned away—and jumped
sharply, rearing back; and a moment later, grinned sheepishly. A little cloud had floated past the window. More
cloud lay ahead of them, thickening over the mid-Atlantic.

A few wisps broke away and were coming towards them, but none clung to the aircraft, and none followed.

"What do you expect to get out of Botticelli?" Bruton demanded, as if he hadn't asked the question before, and as if at all costs he wanted to change the subject.

"I just want to see the man," said Palfrey. "I'd like to know what I'm fighting. If I'm fighting him."

.   .   .   .

The cold hand of winter was loosening its grip on the middle western states. Lake Michigan was as calm as the lake in New York's Central Park, only the slightest ripples broke the surface, and a few hardy souls braved the beaches near Chicago, longing for the summer and warmth. The grass in the gardens along the lakeside was fresh and green, the trees were not yet in leaf, but gave promise. The sun shone out of a cloudless sky, and was quite warm.

Palfrey came out of the planetarium, and stood on the little isthmus on which it was built, looking at the city skyline. The tall buildings, thirty, forty, fifty stories high, seemed small from here; it was like looking at a picture drawn by an artist whose lines were always going straight across or straight up and down. There was little sign of the fierce, throbbing life of the city. Hidden behind that skyline were over three million people, a million homes, a thousand factories; the heart of the city throbbed, the poor and the rich rubbed shoulders in Clark Street and the Stevens, but in the tenements only the poor lived, and here, nearer Palfrey, were the homes of the wealthy.

They were some distance off, he knew; he could drive along the many-laned road towards it, or could go into the city and come out on another road; if he really felt inclined, he could take a boat. It wasn't the season for boats, but he could get one.

The lake lapped gently on the beach behind him.

Bruton was over by it, picking up pebbles and hurling them so that they ricocheted half a dozen times before dropping out of sight. A few children were playing on the steps leading into the water not far away. An aeroplane hummed above their heads, almost reminiscent of a different world.

Palfrey had sat with half a dozen others in the huge,

domed chamber, while the lecturer who held thousands en-
thralled when the planetarium was in public session, had
used the magic of his fantastic instrument to show the
known part of the universe, the swift movements of the stars,
the planets, mysteries which had hardly been suspected a
few years ago, others which were well known and yet not
solved.

There was the sun, possessing heat Man could not even
begin to comprehend, its writhing gases exploding and burning and blasting in constant movement, sending out that
fabulous heat, only to cool gently as it came through space
and finally to lay a benign, life-giving hand on the earth.

There was the moon, with its lifeless craters and harsh
mountains, its frigid coldness softened only by the reflected
light of the sun.

There were the planets——

Mars, with its reputation for fury, its canals, the long-held
belief that creatures lived upon it, the planet which Man
thought about most, to which it conceded a kind of life. Mars
with its seasons, its polar regions, its flat surface, its cloudless
atmosphere; cloud*less*, remember.

Venus, with masses of dense clouds reflecting the light of
the sun, bright to the eyes of the beholder upon the earth
—but a planet surrounded by a dense cloud. There were
Jupiter's cloud belts, too—clouds from which pieces could
fall, pieces which could drop through space.

Could they?

The scientists didn't know exactly what happened. It
was surprising both how much and how little they knew—of
meteors, for instance, of what happened to the molten metals
which fell from unknown places, what happened to the gases
when they were freed from the pull of their mother-planet.

How much they didn't know; how much he didn't know!

One thing was certain: it was impossible to say that any
specific thing could not happen. One could believe that life
could not exist on the moon; one could not be sure.

What *was* life?

What was the mist which had seized Brett Hall, where did
it come from and where did it go?

Did Botticelli know?

10

"THERE's the house," Bruton said. "The House of the Angels. It's the name *he* gave it!"

They were in a big blue Buick, driving along Lakeside Drive. There were imposing houses on either side, and the one which Bruton pointed out was on the right, backing on the lake. It had its own private beach; it looked as if it had everything.

It was large and modern, built in the shape of an E without the middle section, and of white stone. In front was a sweeping lawn, beautiful as a lawn could be, and flowering shrubs were already in blossom in the beds which were planted out with spring flowers. Two gardeners were working on the lawns, one mowing, one with a weeding-tool. An arch-shaped sign held the name: The House of the Angels.

Traffic flowed by.

Bruton drove past the house, took a right turn, then another. He drove into the back entrance of one of the houses on the other side of the road.

"Sometimes we have luck," he said. "This belongs to McCall. I hear that McCall came back and gave a *very* good report on you, Sap." Bruton tried to make that something to grin about.

"Nice of him," Palfrey said absently. "But he was helping before, wasn't he? It hurt, but he helped."

"Oh, sure," agreed Bruton. "He's that kind of guy."

He pulled up outside a painted doorway in a frame house which looked old and almost antiquated compared with the house which belonged to Botticelli. A tall, thin negro with a very long neck smiled a nervous greeting and stood aside to let them enter. Another, dressed in chocolate brown, stood by a small lift; and they were taken up almost at once. Palfrey smiled at the negroes and looked almost vaguely about him. As the lift stopped, Bruton said impatiently:

"I sometimes wonder if you did get over the shock."

"You couldn't wonder more than I," Palfrey said, and suddenly chuckled.

Bruton pushed a hand through his wiry grey hair.

They stepped into a small landing. This was an attic apartment at the top of McCall's home. Palfrey knew that there were four rooms, one used as a living room, one as a dormitory, two as "offices". In fact, at one of the windows a man was always stationed, with a movie-camera by day, and a camera which could take pictures by night, using different rays, not a flash-light.

Every movement Botticelli had made, every person who had called on him, had been observed for some time past. Now and again special reports had been made to London, and each film had been developed and sent to London for him to study. That had first enabled Palfrey to prove that the Lennards were connected with Botticelli, had also told him that some people, known to have vanished, had been to visit him.

An elderly man, almost bald, with a round face, a button of a nose and rimless *pince nez*, opened the attic door to them. At sight of Palfrey he drew in a long, exulting breath, then shot out both hands and gripped Palfrey's right, and shook it as if he couldn't let go. His round face, traced with lines of sorrows which would never be wholly forgotten, creased into a hundred wrinkles as he beamed his welcome.

The door closed.

"Come, quick, Kramer!" he called. "Come, see who hass come to visit us." He had a mid-European accent, with a hint of guttural; and there was a suspicious moisture at his pale-blue eyes. "Quick, quick, you leg of a lame donkey!"

Another man appeared, tall, very thin, with a beak of a nose, a long, narrow jaw which finished in a point. His big eyes were hooded by heavy, sleepy lids; he looked as tired as the shorter man looked alert. But the pose faded when he saw Palfrey.

"The miracles themselves," he said, very gently. "Come in, come in, my friend." He made the "d" sound almost like a "t". "Vot brings you?"

Bruton said: "I don't get it. Two grown men break down and look as if they could burst into tears because a guy looks in to see them. It wouldn't be so surprising if he was a good guy, but Sap Palfrey——"

"Oh, be quiet with you," the round-faced man said. "Kramer, get something to drink for a celebration."

"That's what I like about you, Masak," Bruton said, "you can always think of something for someone else to do."

Masak the Czech got the drinks; Kramer the German poured them.

Half an hour later, all four were in the bedroom, with the blinds drawn and a small screen up. The sixteen-millimetre projector was plugged in, already to work. Masak was working it, Kramer went out to maintain the ceaseless watch on Botticelli's house.

"You are ready?" Masak demanded.

"Yes," said Palfrey.

They had not seen any processed film for the past ten days; and the first five minutes showed different people going into the house across the road, but no one familiar, no one who looked like any person known to work with or for Botticelli. Among the callers were several girls, all very easy on the eye.

None of these came out.

The weather was wet or blowy or fine, one day the mist was so thick that it was difficult to see across the road—but this had been a normal lake mist, Masak and Kramer had assured them.

Masak changed a reel.

Bruton lit cigarettes for himself and Palfrey.

"There vos two people we do not see before in dis feelm," Masak declared, as the bright light shot out and the picture was thrown on to the glass-beaded screen. "Also Kramer take very good pictures, but zen—ze lady is so photogenic, isn't it?"

Two or three ordinary-looking people arrived at The House of the Angels. The camera had been so placed that its long-distance lens almost looked into the hall, and everyone on the porch could be seen clearly.

A green Cadillac swept off the road into the drive of Botticelli's house. Palfrey and Bruton remembered Forrester's report about a green Cadillac at Estafillo.

A man got out.

Palfrey opened his eyes wide in astonishment. Bruton drew in a sharp breath. The camera whirred, and Masak murmured something about the lady being very lovely, isn't she? Then the woman appeared, in close up, and she had a beauty which seemed unreal. It was like looking at the face of a woman who had been made to reveal to all women what beauty was.

Her movements, her complexion, her dress—all these things added to that beauty. She wore a red dress and a small hat, with white shoes, white cuffs, white handbag. The man handed her out of the car and then turned towards the door, which was already opening.

"Forrester," Bruton breathed.

"That's who it is," Palfrey agreed softly.

"And who's the girl?" Bruton was staring as the door closed on the couple. "Seen them before?"

"No," Palfrey said.

"For a woman with a face like that a man might do anything," Bruton growled. "Have they been again?"

"Oh, yes, two times, three," said Masak, his face glowing in the light of the lamp as it shone upwards from the projector. "They are inside der house now. The man, his name is Forrester. The woman is Isabella Melado, a Spanish name, no? The best beauty that Botticelli has. Vot a pity, vot a pity," Masak went on, "such a lovely von and such a bad man. You seen enough?"

Palfrey was thinking: "That's the name of the girl Forrester wrote about. Isabella Melado." He dared to hope. "Can Jim be fooling Botticelli?"

If Forrester were spying, why hadn't he sent a report? Was he afraid it would be intercepted? Was he biding his time?

"We'll see it all through, please," he said.

Masak nodded, as if pleased by this thoroughness. They sat and watched different callers, including some men and women who were highly-placed and some who seemed unlikely ever to play any part in Botticelli's plans.

Isabella Melado did not appear again.

Nor did Jim Forrester.

.   .   .   .   .   .

Palfrey said: "Don't be an ass, Corny, of course I'm going. Nothing will happen to me in there. Botticelli won't come right into the open. If anything's going to happen, it will be when I've left the place. You take it easy. Keep everything covered in the ciné, and be around in case I'm in a hurry to get away."

"You need company," Bruton said. "You need me."

Palfrey said, almost musingly: "Soon, but I don't think you and Botticelli would get on."

Bruton scowled.

It was the evening of the day that they had seen the pictures of Forrester and the Spanish girl. Darkness had spread over the lake, but there were bright lights on Lakeside Drive, and the sky behind them glowed with the reflected light of a hundred thousand neon signs, many flashing and changing colour, giving the night, and the glow which spread over the water, a different hue each passing second.

Traffic noises came more clearly from the city.

Palfrey stepped into a chocolate-brown Chrysler which had seen better days, and drove from the hotel where he and Bruton were staying. Bruton followed in another car.

They had been back to the top apartment at McCall's house once, and left by the back stairs. Unless the house was being closely watched by Botticelli's men, and there was no evidence that it was, they had not been seen.

Palfrey, who knew the city fairly well from past visits, drove slowly towards East Wacker Drive, then towards the lake. He wasn't thinking of Chicago itself, the traffic, the blaring horns or the shrill whistles or the police. He wasn't even thinking much about Forrester and the Spanish girl, Isabella, or his hopes that Forrester might be fooling Botticelli, a spy at last in The House of the Angels. He had not lived for a minute free from the eerie fears which the touch of the mist had made for him.

He drove smoothly, and without effort.

He knew the exact moment when Bruton's car turned away, leaving him on his own.

The roads leading to Botticelli's house were always watched. If a man drove up to the house and was followed by another who drove past and waited near by, Botticelli would know.

So Palfrey went on alone.

Although the fear lurked in the background, like part of the air he breathed, he was less conscious of fear than he had been for a long time. He pulled up near the front door and sat for a moment, with a feeling that was almost of relief. He had not decided what to say to Botticelli, but knew the kind of thing; he had planned certain tactics, but had no idea whether he would have a chance to put them into operation.

It had been extremely difficult to obtain any reliable account of the temperament and the normal behaviour of Botticelli. He was a man whom all people knew yet none knew well; and outwardly, he kept a poker face—a handsome poker face.

Palfrey opened the car door.

A man appeared, as if out of the air, but Palfrey had seen him lurking near a tree.

"Going some place?" the man asked.

"Oh, yes," said Palfrey. "I'm going to see Mr. Botticelli."

"He know you're coming?"

"He's probably expecting me," Palfrey said, "although he doesn't quite know just when."

He was aware of someone else near; he felt almost as he had felt at Brett Hall, when he had gone to look for the mist; for the intangible thing which could strangle the life out of powerful men.

A beam of light shot into his face, and stayed for several seconds. He kept his eyes averted, but took out his wallet, extracted a card, and handed it to the first man, who glanced down and said:

"Palfrey, would he know Palfrey?" Then the light was switched out.

"This way," another man said.

Palfrey followed him into the house. If he hadn't known before, he would have known now that only people who were known or expected were admitted into Botticelli's home without the strictest inquiries.

The door closed behind Palfrey.

The hall was square, with a white-painted wooden staircase leading off on one side to a half-landing. The narrow floor boards were of some reddish wood; redwood itself, possibly. There was a faint, invigorating smell of polish. The first impression was pleasing; there were skin rugs and good-quality furniture, although nothing ostentatious. On the panelled walls were a few paintings, all of the heads of girls or women; of Botticelli angels.

Palfrey was left alone, yet he knew that he was watched. He could have sat, smoking, fighting against the fears which the house brought crowding; instead, he moved from picture to picture. They were all styled on the original Botticelli's work. Some of the artists were named, all of the paintings were good. It was made clear that these were copies taken from famous paintings, and the paintings were usually named.

The house was very quiet.

No sounds came in from the outside; the place might be a thousand miles from anywhere. Yet Bruton was watching from the attic room across the Riverside Drive; others were watching; and there were the men in the grounds of The House of the Angels.

The minutes began to drag.

Suddenly Palfrey heard a sound outside, startling in the quiet; a rushing sound. Then windows rattled, a door shook, and the wind howled.

In a moment, it was gone.

"Odd," Palfrey said, and waited for another gust. It didn't come.

Palfrey finished looking at the portraits, and spent longer than he wanted to over the last few. Still nothing happened; it was almost as if he were alone.

Yet he had that sensation of being watched.

Then he heard footsteps, of a woman approaching. The steps were sharp and clear on wooden flooring, but now and again muffled as she trod on a rug. Palfrey looked towards a passage through which the man had gone. The woman drew nearer. Palfrey moved to a chair nearly opposite the passage, and saw a woman turn into it.

She was the woman who had been with Forrester when the film had been taken.

Palfrey stood up.

Around him were the copies of paintings of lovely women; and towards him came a woman who compared favourably with them all; surpassed them all. The way she walked was like a kind of music. She did not smile, but looked pleased to see him, and Palfrey had an impression that he had not dreamed of getting at this house.

The woman looked *good*.

Beauty could have many guises, and in the hanging pictures goodness was the one that mattered—and here a woman came to surpass the pictures. She would have been a perfect model for the Botticelli who had left the world such priceless treasures.

As the woman Isabella Melado drew nearer, she smiled; but her eyes had a questioning look, as if she were seeking in Palfrey's face the reason for his coming.

"Dr. Palfrey?" Her English was slightly accented.

"Yes," said Palfrey, and his eyes crinkled at the corners. "Señorita Melado?"

Unexpectedly, she laughed; as if that were so surprising that it forced the laugh out of her. Laughing, her beauty had a quality that almost hurt; it wasn't true, nothing could be so beautiful as this—and *bad*.

"That is right," she said, but did not trouble to ask him how he knew. "Mr. Botticelli cannot see you at once, but if you can wait for a little while, he will be happy to see you."

"And how long is a little while?"

"Perhaps half an hour." Her eyes, honey-brown, were questioning again, and Palfrey felt strongly that she was trying to convince herself that he was here for a straightforward purpose.

"Then I'll wait," he said.

"That is good. Will you come with me, please?" She stood to one side, then led the way up the stairs. At the half-landing, beautifully lighted by concealed lighting round the sides, was a painting of such exquisite form that Palfrey stopped and actually exclaimed.

In a flash, he saw the difference between the real and the false; the work of the master and the work of the disciples. The face of the woman in front of him seemed to be alive, the honey-brown eyes glowed, the blemishless skin, almost the colour of the eyes, had a bloom on it. Feature by feature, the artist's model must have been superbly beautiful; Palfrey had not a moment's doubt that this was a real Botticelli.

And a woman who was remarkably like the picture stood by Palfrey's side.

"You admire the painting?" Isabella Melado asked.

"It's—beautiful beyond words," Palfrey said, and stared, then made himself look at her; he managed to smile, too. "For the first time, I think, I believe in re-incarnation."

She understood at once, her English was as thorough as it was good. She flushed slightly, and the compliment pleased her. Together, they moved away, to a main landing.

There were other paintings here, but all like those downstairs, none like the original in the landing.

Isobella Melado led the way into a pleasant, nicely furnished room. There was nothing ostentatious. It looked a woman's room; there were chintzes at the windows and the loose coverings of the chairs and couches were of the same flowered chintz. Several bowls of roses and one of carnations made almost the only touch of ostentation; for in March they cost a fabulous price. Television, radio, books and magazines gave a homely touch. There were no pictures here, only wall-plaques; when he drew closer, Palfrey saw that they were modelled in the same fashion—models of Botticelli heads.

"Please sit down," said Isabella, and leaned forward and touched a bell-push. He didn't hear it ring, but the door opened almost on the instant, and a girl came in wearing a wine-coloured dress, simply but beautifully cut. She also wore a tiny apron of beautifully worked lace, and walked with almost as much ease and grace as Isabella.

"Paula, will you please bring in the cocktail cabinet?"

"At once, señorita." The girl's gaze flickered towards Palfrey as she turned and went out. Palfrey made himself keep a poker face. It wasn't easy. If that girl were sent out into the streets of Chicago she would cause a sensation. She had the same kind of loveliness as Isabella. Hers wasn't so perfect, but few could have told the difference.

"You will smoke," asked Isabella, and held out a gold cigarette-box.

Palfrey took one.

"Won't you join me?"

"No, I never smoke," she told him. "I do not like it when women do." She lit his cigarette. That brought her closer to him, and he was very conscious of her.

He leaned back.

"You are, of course, an Englishman," she said. "Have you been to America so often?"

"Several times."

"Why is it you wish to see Mr. Botticelli?"

Palfrey said: "I've heard a lot about him, and would like to find out if he lives up to his reputation."

"In other words, you do not wish to tell me," said Isabella, and shrugged her shoulders. She was amiable enough, though, not at all put out.

Paula came back wheeling a small cabinet which she placed before them. Then she pressed a small lever at one side, and the top unfolded, showing bottles, glasses, everything they would need.

"Is there anything else?" asked Paula.

"No, not now."

The touch of formality about the way they spoke was intriguing. It was the preciseness of English spoken by people who did not own it as a mother tongue. There was a kind of gravity, too, which Isabella Melado had broken only once, with that spontaneous laugh.

He had an Old-fashioned . . .

He finished his first cigarette, and lit another. They talked idly; afterwards he could never say exactly what they talked about. He made no attempt to pump her; he wanted to hold everything in reserve for Botticelli. The one thing certain was that the beginning of the visit hadn't panned out as he had expected. Isabella did most of the talking—and he felt a curious contentment in sitting next to her, listening to her soft voice, watching her honey-coloured beauty.

Then he saw her expression change. One moment she was leaning back in a corner of the couch, speaking almost dreamily, and the next she was standing up, looking towards the door through which they had entered. Somewhere outside there was a sound of a bell ringing; and suddenly, a bell in this room rang sharply. Like an alarm.

She cried: "Stay here!" and rushed across the room, but when she opened the door she stopped dead still.

Palfrey moved swiftly after her.

Before he reached the door he heard a man scream.

11

PALFREY reached the door as the scream came again.

Isabella went swiftly, as if sensing his presence, and tried to shut the door, but he grabbed the handle and pushed her to one side.

Forrester was in the passage.

Forrester stood with his back to the wall, hands spread out, palms pressed tightly against the wall, mouth wide open, eyes staring at something just in front of him.

At swirling *mist*.

"Come back, come back!" Isabella cried, and pulled at Palfrey's arm. "You cannot help, you——"

Palfrey heard a crackling noise, strange and unfamiliar; it seemed a long way off one moment, and very close by the next. The mist swirled wildly—almost as if it had heard the noise and was turning to face some threat. That was a strange impression, but another, much stronger, lasted for several seconds before the blinding flash came.

This mist had *shape*; it swirled and moved ceaselessly, as if a man were moving arms and legs about, stirring the cloud which emanated from him.

Then came the flash!

Palfrey felt sharp pain at his eyes. He staggered, and felt hands touching him, drawing him away from the spot. He was conscious of more than one pair of hands but of one voice—Isabella's. He heard a door close. The explosion rang in his ears and the flash still blinded him, but suddenly he remembered, pulled himself free and strode towards the door—or where he thought the door was. A chair was in his path; he kicked against it, and nearly fell.

"Please stay here," Isabella said, "you will be all right in a few minutes, and he is not hurt."

Palfrey stared towards the sound of her voice. He could just make out her figure and the shape of her head; but her face was blurred, all its beauty hidden. He waited for a few seconds, and his sight gradually returned.

He swung towards the door.

Isabella was alone in the room with him. She made no

attempt to stop him, but when he reached the door and turned the handle it would not open.

"He is not hurt," she said quietly, "and you need not worry now, everything is all right."

Palfrey said roughly: "I want to see him."

"But I tell you he is not hurt."

"I don't believe you."

He could see her much more clearly now, and saw that the beauty of her face was in fact unspoiled by any expression of fear or of distress. Her eyes were very calm. She raised one hand, almost as if she were giving him her blessing, and she said quite clearly:

"I shall not lie to you, Dr. Palfrey. We do not lie in this house."

"All right," he growled. "Prove it, let me see that man." It was on the tip of his tongue to say "Forrester"; but he kept the name back. He wanted all the tricks up his sleeve for Botticelli. But he did not think that tricks would avail him much; the sight of the mist, the flash and the explosion had shaken his nerve. He was all right now, but under pressure he might not be so good.

Isabella stood looking at him.

"Very well," she said at last. "Come and see."

She did not take him through the door which was locked, but through another, then along a passage, up a short flight of stairs, past several closed doors. At last they turned into a bedroom. It was small, with a single bed, a pine wardrobe and dressing-table, and a carpet which fitted wall to wall.

Forrester, still fully-clad, lay on the bed.

A girl was loosening his shoe laces, another had unfastened his collar and tie, and was undoing the buttons at his waist; the proper things to do with anyone unconscious, or suffering from shock or collapse. Forrester's eyes were closed, and he was breathing heavily through his mouth.

Palfrey went to him.

The girls stood aside.

Palfrey realised afterwards that they were like Paula; not "like" in the sense that they could be mistaken for her, but they had the same kind of face, the same "Botticelli" loveliness.

Now, he was concerned only with Forrester.

He felt his pulse; it was fast and uneven. Isabella was right; apart from shock there was nothing the matter with him.

His eyes flickered.

Palfrey leaned over him, ostensibly to feel his forehead. The girls were behind him, and could not see Forrester's face.

Forrester opened his eyes, and his lips moved.

"*Get out of here,*" he breathed.

Palfrey didn't hear the words, just lip-read them; there was no possibility of mistake, but there was desperation in the way Forrester breathed, in his haunted eyes.

"*Sending message,*" he added, "*you get out. Deadly.*"

One of the girls moved, as if she were suspicious. Forrester closed his eyes, and his mouth went slack.

The girl had a hypodermic syringe in her hand.

"He must have rest," she said, "and you must leave now." She actually pushed Palfrey to one side. "I'll look after Jim."

She turned the bedspread and the sheets down, and bared Forrester's arm. She stood between Palfrey and the bed, making it difficult for him to stay where he was. The other girl spoke from behind him.

"Please, Dr. Palfrey——"

Tight-lipped, Palfrey stared at Forrester's face. Of course Forrester wanted him to go, but that didn't mean that it was right to do so. If they could have two minutes together without the risk of being overheard: if they could have one minute, even half a minute——

Forrester screamed!

Palfrey saw the girl dart back, the hypo waving wildly. Forrester struck at her, clutching at her wrist. He was trying to get off the bed, to force her away and to strike her, all at the same time. She struggled, but he had the strength of a man demented, and she dropped the syringe.

Forrester let the girl go, and snatched the syringe; a new expression appeared in his eyes. Palfrey couldn't be sure whether it was real or feigned, whether this was an act or whether Forrester felt such terror.

"*I'll give you a dose!*" he shouted, and plunged the hypo towards the girl. "I'll make you——"

She darted back.

"Get help!" she cried, and Palfrey saw the door already open, saw the other girl disappearing. "Palfrey, get out, he'll kill——"

Forrester leapt at her. She couldn't get away, because
Palfrey was between her and the door. Forrester had dropped
the syringe, but he grabbed her by the neck. His fingers
tightened, as if he were going to choke the life out of her.

Palfrey made himself go forward, to pluck at the strangling
fingers.

"Now, you don't want——"

Above the girl's head, Forrester shot him a look which
told the truth: this was an act, Palfrey wasn't to interfere;
he was to stand by and watch the girl's life choked out of her.

Forrester seemed to mean to kill.

Suddenly, he let her go.

She had lost consciousness, and crumpled up. She didn't
even gasp. There was no sound in the room except Forrester's harsh breathing; and Palfrey's too.

Forrester croaked: "Laboratory down here, under ground,
where they make the creatures of the mist. Called *elementa*.
Trying to find out what—what's in them. Not funny. Some
basic raw materials found various places, including Sierra
Nevada, Spain. Professor Rebonne in charge here, devil on
two legs. They think I'm being converted to hideous new
religion." He paused, still gasping for breath; he knew
exactly what he was saying, was trying to cram as much as he
could into the precious seconds they were alone together.

"Go on," Palfrey begged.

"If you stay too long, they'll—kill you. Listen—dig
deep, approach from below. Hundred feet, possibly more.
Don't let them know you're doing it, or——"

He broke off.

Terror showed in his eyes as he listened; and, not far off,
there was the sound of men or women, running.

"Don't worry about me, fooling 'em, got to," he gasped.
"Remember Rebonne—dig deep—new religion—fantastic
power of *elementa*, and Bott's a megalo——"

He stopped.

He thrust Palfrey to one side and leapt towards the door,
reached it and put his head down, then raced along the
passage. Palfrey heard him screaming like a wild man, heard
the screaming reach a new high pitch, heard a scuffling sound
—and then silence.

A moment later, Isabella came into the room, flushed,

anxious until she saw him. It was hard to believe that she wasn't as concerned as she sounded.

"Are you all right?" she asked.

Palfrey didn't answer.

"Dr. Palfrey, are you——?"

He said savagely: "No, I'm not all right. That man is nearly demented. What the hell do you think you're doing to him? He's being——"

"He has been very ill," she said, "the treatment is necessary ——and his terror is mostly imaginary, he has nightmares."

"I don't believe it."

"It is true," she said, very quietly. "Some respond as he does, others hardly notice the effect on them."

"The effect of what?" Palfrey growled.

Isabella said: "I can only tell you that we are making experiments which we believe will be of great value to mankind, Dr. Palfrey. If Mr. Botticelli wishes to tell you more, no doubt he will. I cannot. Perhaps I may tell you that Mr. Forrester is not the only person on whom the experiments are being tried. All of us here have been experimented on, few of us have suffered any ill effects."

"That doesn't make it any less diabolic."

"Dr. Palfrey," she said abruptly, "I am not able to argue with you. Please come with me." She led the way back to the pleasant room, and said abruptly: "If you would like a drink, please help yourself."

She went out.

Palfrey watched the door close behind her, and seemed to see Forrester rushing out of the other room. He could imagine Forrester's scream. He could hear Forrester speaking those white-hot words, uttering each one as if he meant to burn them into Palfrey's mind.

He had won a chance to talk, but what had it cost him?

Never mind what it cost him, provided it wasn't his life!

Palfrey forced himself to accept that. He had *news*. Forrester was alive, a spy in Botticelli's camp; he might make the difference between complete success and utter failure.

Botticelli was a megalomaniac; there was talk of a "hideous" new religion—with Botticelli the Messiah? There was the knowledge that Rebonne, of Paris, was the chief research worker, that the laboratory was underground, that Forrester himself lived in terror of the *elementa*, had actually allowed himself to talk of "another planet".

Here was plenty to work on, and—he must get out.

Now, Palfrey began to feel the coldness of fear.

Forrester had been terrified, and not least because he had believed that they might kill him, Palfrey. He mustn't let them. *He must get out*, taking his news, giving the outside world the clue that it had been waiting for.

He lit another cigarette, and said, to himself: "Take it easy." If he showed the slightest sign of panic now, they might associate it with Forrester. If he gave them any reason to believe that Forrester had passed on secrets, he wouldn't have a ghost of a chance of getting away.

Had he one, now?

How could anyone fight against that mist; the *elementa*?

It was hideous; and all he knew of Botticelli was as bad.

Yet there was such beauty here.

Could one believe that Isabella Melado lied to him, and was touched with evil?

She had talked as if it were unthinkable that anyone in this house could lie, but here was beauty living side by side with horror.

He had to get away.

He did not hear the door open, but suddenly a man came into the room. The silence with which he moved was uncanny; when Palfrey saw him he felt an unnerving flood of emotion.

He stood very still.

Botticelli came towards him.

12

SANDRO BOTTICELLI did not smile, even with his eyes. He stopped a few feet in front of Palfrey and studied Palfrey's face as if he were looking for something which he could not expect to see anywhere else. It was a tense moment of mutual appraisal.

Palfrey did not speak.

Here was the man whom he had said confidently was the worst man in the world. He had seen many photographs of him; and they had all been good. Each showed the same iron-grey hair, brushed straight back from his forehead, the clear grey eyes, the aquiline nose; oh, here was a man almost as handsome as Isabella Melado was beautiful. Botticelli's features were so regular that they hardly seemed real.

That was Palfrey's most vivid thought: the man wasn't real.

He was dressed in a suit of medium grey, beautifully cut, and wore a wine-red tie with a strange pattern on it; a pattern, as it were, of little wisps of cloud. His eyes were very clear, but if man had been able to create a robot truly in his own image, then the robot's eyes, empty of all expression, might have been like Sandro Botticelli's.

Quickly, suddenly, that changed. Life seemed to pour itself into Botticelli.

"It was good of you to wait for so long," he said. He did not offer to shake hands. "And I am sorry that you encountered such an unfortunate incident. However, no great harm was done." He spoke very precisely; like Isabella and the girls, and his accent was only slightly American. "I have, of course, heard a great deal about you."

Palfrey said mildly: "A thing I never like hearing."

"You must blame yourself, the newspapers and the public's avidity for news," said Botticelli. He still did not smile. "But even without all that I would doubtless have heard a great deal about you, and I suppose it was inevitable that we should meet before long."

"I think perhaps we didn't meet early enough," Palfrey murmured.

"Perhaps. How can I help you?"

Menace and danger seemed a long way off. In this mood, Botticelli wasn't a man to fear. A megalomaniac? Founder of a hideous cult?

Could Forrester be wrong?

"Perhaps you have not found everything here as you expected it," said Botticelli, "but does that really surprise a man of your wide experience, Dr. Palfrey? Things are so often not what they seem. But I am being inhospitable!

Shall we go to another room, Isabella and the—ah—lesser angels like to come and relax here?"

Palfrey felt the irony of that ". . . and the—ah—lesser angels . . ." and frowned as he stared into Botticelli's face. Was there a suspicion of a gleam in them, a hint that he had really been joking?

If there were, Palfrey didn't see it.

Botticelli led the way out. They went across the landing into another, smaller room; as much a man's as this other had been a woman's. On the walls were just two pictures, and the hand of the master could be seen so clearly in them that the effect was something like that of the picture on the landing. The same concealed lighting showed every line of the faces.

Botticelli said, as if dryly: "Beauty is its own inspiration, isn't it, Dr. Palfrey? Shall I take you into my confidence a little? I have searched the world for an artist with one-half of the genius of the great Botticelli. You have seen the result downstairs. They are as photographs to the living person. Has it ever struck you that the same can be said of all artists? Except possibly Epstein, whose work I do not admire for I worship beauty, the world is empty of genius and full of dull competence. Would you agree?"

Palfrey said flatly: "Possibly. I haven't given it much thought."

"One of the shortcomings of men with good minds is that they are apt to forget how many people have bad ones," Botticelli said prosily. "Why don't you sit down?"

Palfrey sat down.

"I'm sure you'd like a drink," Botticelli said, and pressed a bell, just as Isabella had; and the same thing happened, except that a different girl came in. "Will you smoke a cigar?" asked Botticelli, and offered a carved cigar-box.

Palfrey said: "Thanks." He pierced the end of the cigar with a needle-point blade in his knife, lit it and then had another Old-fashioned. He didn't drink, after the first almost casual "good luck". Botticelli sat beneath one of the paintings, with his hands loosely clasped in front of him. His magnificent head was turned slightly towards the fireplace, where a log fire burned sluggishly, pale-blue smoke rising slowly up the chimney. "Now, how can I help you, Dr. Palfrey?"

Was he playing cat-and-mouse?

Palfrey said slowly: "I'm not sure. Unless you can tell me what happened with Forrester, where the mist comes from and what it is."

"When you ask such a question, I realise how little you know," said Botticelli sadly. "Yes, I can tell you." He did not pause for a moment. "That was a manifestation in the physical form of a substance or a creature we call *elementa*." Could he *mean* this? Could any man in his right mind talk about a "manifestation in the physical form"? "It is a new form of life—an elemental form—which we are creating. Sometimes, it gets out of control." Botticelli shrugged. "We shall find the way of stopping it," he said quite solemnly. "It terrified Forrester, who——"

"The hypodermic syringe terrified him more."

Botticelli said: "Yes, perhaps it did. Forrester is having a difficult time, but he is over the worst. He is learning what the rest of us here have learned—that the mind can dominate the body—and can control itself, its fears and hopes, and the body's aches and pains."

Palfrey said: "That's all been said before. It——"

"It has never been believed," said Botticelli, quietly. "It is necessary to undergo intensive physical and mental training before understanding becomes possible. Perhaps a little demonstration——"

He broke off.

"I don't want any demonstration," Palfrey made himself say. He still did not know if Botticelli were deliberately playing with him.

"Don't you, Dr. Palfrey?" Botticelli's forefinger was on a bell-push set in the desk. The nail, a perfect filbert shape, glistened with natural-shade nail varnish. His gaze held Palfrey's, in a kind of defiance. "I think you'd better have one, all the same."

The door opened, and a girl came in.

"Yes, Sandro?"

"Who is in Devotional today, Mary?"

"Rebecca is," said the girl promptly, "and Telisa, Mitzi, Hiliare, Elenora——"

"Ah, yes. Ask Elenora to come, will you?"

"Yes," the girl said. She smiled and went out. She was in the early twenties, and lovely in her dark-eyed, olive-skinned way.

"While we are waiting, I will explain one or two things which doubtless puzzle you, Dr. Palfrey," said Botticelli. "Isabella is anxious that you should not be unduly mystified, and while I doubt your ability to grasp the essentials, it will do no harm now. In the first place, your man Forrester is a convert—or he wishes to be."

Palfrey didn't speak, and showed no disappointment.

"He was remarkably courageous, although he did not know what he was fighting," Botticelli went on. "While in Estafillo, he was visited by one of the *elementa*, who was under our control, and seeking information about your organisation, because of your known interest in us. While they have an intelligence, the *elementa* do not behave logically, as we do. One went into Forrester's room while he was there, instead of waiting until he had gone out. Forrester attacked the one which raided his room and, by a freak accident, struck its one vulnerable spot, causing a cut and smearing its 'blood' or blood plasma on the corner of an ash-tray. This 'blood'—there is really no other word to describe it—contains the substance which generates the mist. The *elementa* can disappear behind this mist at will. Anything which is touched by the 'blood' is enshrouded for a while. But of course you know that."

Palfrey didn't comment. But how much ignorance dare he admit; and how far should he try to bluff?

Botticelli's smile lingered, as if he suspected how little Palfrey knew.

"With your big Russian agent's help," he continued, "Forrester was able to get the ash-tray out of Spain and into England, Dr. Palfrey. As you know. The *elementa* followed both the Russian and Forrester. They got an ash-tray from the Russian, but it wasn't the right one. So they looked for and followed Forrester, and——"

"Why were they so anxious to get it?" demanded Palfrey abruptly.

Botticelli began to smile more widely.

It was as if he could read Palfrey's thoughts, and knew exactly how to cope.

He was all-powerful here, and—a megalomaniac? One who would gloat over another man's fears?

"The *elementa* are not strictly speaking human beings," Botticelli said. "They are creatures born out of our attempts to make the perfect man. They have a kind of flesh and a kind of blood——"

"Why are you telling me all this?" Palfrey demanded abruptly. His heart beat faster now. If this man intended to let him go, would he talk so freely?

Botticelli went on: "I am telling you this so that you may understand that what you are trying to do is to fight against a phenomena as powerful and implacable as a force from another planet. They are under control here, within reason, but even I am not sure how complete the control is. That is why we take great care. Sometimes the *elementa* get out of control. Some did when they visited you in England. Their instructions were to capture McCall, and prevent a discussion with you. We then believed, wrongly, that he had certain essential information which he could pass on to you. The *elementa* became frightened and ran amok. The result of panic is always the same—and is, as you will understand, similar to the consequences of any attack they make at our orders.

"There is always an explosion which generates great heat, and turns many solid substances into boiling mud. Obviously this self-destruction causes a great deal of local damage."

Palfrey broke in flatly: "Are you telling me that you actually create these creatures and let them loose, although they can ignore your control?"

"We make them, and some get beyond our control," agreed Botticelli. His smile remained, a Mona Lisa smile on a man's face. "In such vast experiments, Palfrey, we must take some risks, and I have little patience with the theory of the absolute sanctity of human life. But to return to this ash-tray." He went on without a pause. "It was smeared with the 'blood' of *elementa*, and we did not want you to get a specimen and conceivably learn how to make the mist. They have a very different existence from ours, but they do breathe, and they have shape, even though they can exist in a gaseous state. The gas, as you know, can be as solid as a brick wall. It becomes very thin at will, enabling *elementa* to get through spaces impossible to human beings. The whole life flow of the creatures is in the blood plasma, and we are learning to give human beings certain of the *elementa* qualities. True, we can't yet fly at their height, experiments have proved that they can exist far above the stratosphere. But we can enshroud ourselves with mist, as I have told you. Ourselves, as well as other things. Oh, they are quite remarkable, Palfrey. Now, let me repeat: Forrester struck one of the *elementa* through the protective gas, and the ash-tray, broken in contact with a wall, cut the *elementa* in the neck—nicking the vein comparable to our carotid artery. We knew that if the specimen reached you there was a chance that British research physicists would discover the secret of *elementa*'s bodily condition. They were then controlled by my agent in Spain, who ordered them to attack Forrester while he was in the air. Forrester baled out of the aircraft. Isabella and Elenora, who you will soon meet, were there to—ah—help him. They rescued him, with the ash-tray—which we have here, and which we have been able to use to great advantage. The plasma—pink and oily, not at all like human blood and plasma—is seldom encountered, and appears to be present in the *elementa* only during the process of transition from one life stratum to another. Do you understand?"

"What is a life strata?" asked Palfrey.

Botticelli said softly: "It is like trying to explain great literature to a man who does not know his ABC. You will have to try to grasp the essentials, quickly. Forrester came here with us. He became greatly attached to Isabella Melado. He has begun to see our great conception, and Isabella would like to help him. So he is at the first stage of conversion. He knew that you were here, expressed a wish to see you and was on the way when the *elementa* attacked him. One of the worst features of early days of conversion is the terror of *elementa*. Very few converts ever lose the fear absolutely. I do not myself, and with the initiate, fear is very vivid. You see, they are just beginning to understand what the creatures are. The initiate gets a feeling that he is going mad, and when that is coupled with physical terror, the result is like D.T.s, or like the early stages of a cure for drug addiction. However, Forrester will be nursed through this stage, although I don't know whether he has the necessary qualities to continue with the conversion."

"Conversion to——" began Palfrey stiffly.

"Excuse me," Botticelli broke in, when a buzzer sounded. "Yes, Mary . . . very well." He flicked off the buzzer. "Elenora will be a few minutes longer," he said. "What were you saying?"

"I was asking what Forrester is being converted into," Palfrey said. His mouth was dry; some quality in the manner of this man, perhaps his absolute certainty, was more frightening than any threat.

"Don't you know even *that*?" Botticelli glanced down at his nails. "You do, of course, you just don't believe. Very well, Palfrey. There is a stage in human existence when it is possible to make the mind, the spirit or the soul—call it what you like, all three are inextricably intermingled—control the body absolutely. I use the word deliberately. One aspect of it is well known in India, of course, and *yogi* in its most advanced state has been practised with some success by Europeans. And there are other authenticated incidents of mind over body control, usually among what we impudently call the primitive peoples.

"I have been given a strange gift, Palfrey. I can control matter. I can also teach others to do so. I shall not, of course, tell you how it is done, but it needs great application and absolute—I use that word again deliberately, *absolute* devotion. All other loyalties, all other likes and dislikes, the emotions, the habits, the customs—all of these must go. You would be surprised how many find it possible to make those sacrifices—and at first they are very great sacrifices indeed. Elenora had the greatest difficulty in leaving her father, whom she greatly loves. Saturnino, in Spain, left his wife and children. But"—Botticelli paused, as if he were about to add something unpleasant—"Saturnino was unreliable, after all. He was not fully satisfied with *my* integrity. He came from the same village as Isabella, and she went there to reason with him. Instead, they clashed. Each was accompanied by *elementa*, over whom each had control. As a result, Saturnino's *elementa* attacked Isabella's home— with what results you know."

Botticelli paused again, but Palfrey didn't speak.

"I had sent two agents, a man named Lennard and Elenora, to help Isabella. They got her away, using the mist to hide her, and also to hide their car when they left the town. In that way, of course, they planned to confuse Saturnino. However, that was unnecessary; he had died as a result of a storm at sea created by the two conflicting groups of *elementa*. Since then, I am glad to say, Professor Rebonne has found a way of making sure that the final control is in my hands, not in those of the agents. We cannot afford to have such fratricidal quarrels, can we?"

Palfrey said stiffly: "So that's the cause of the horror in Estafillo."

"The full explanation, Palfrey."

"Not quite. What happened to Andromovitch?"

Botticelli began to smile.

"Your friend is quite well," he said smoothly, "and undergoing a period of indoctrination. I am hopeful that he will become a valuable convert. He already has a gift of controlling matter, which is, after all, a question of will-power. Don't worry about him, Palfrey."

"Where is he?"

"Never mind," evaded Botticelli, "you will hear soon enough." His voice was very soft. "Now—you yourself have seen the *elementa*, you know exactly what can happen when the *elementa* get out of control. At Brett Hall my agent —one of your servants—tried to regain control and was killed. Their strength is terrifying, but they exhaust themselves quickly—if they did not, you would never have survived the attack. But once they are completely under my orders, and they are very nearly now, imagine what a remarkable army I shall have!"

Palfrey said roughly: "You must be crazy! With forces like this beyond your control——"

"Oh, if they should turn on us, we get good warning, and put ourselves out of range," said Botticelli off-handedly. "They are incidental, too, if extremely useful. The most important factor for you to understand is that we shall use them if you—your Governments, your Secret Services, anyone with power or influence—harass us in what we are doing."

"What *are* you doing?"

"We are setting out to dominate the mind and the body of man everywhere," announced Botticelli, "and I will show you what I mean."

As he spoke, the door opened and Elenora, the daughter of Senator Samuel McCall, came into the room.

.   .   .   .

Her corn-coloured hair was braided and wound tightly about her head. She wore no make-up. She was dressed in a single garment, a diaphanous slip caught up at the waist and falling in tiny pleats half-way down her beautiful slim legs. She had the face and the figure of an angel.

She smiled gravely at Botticelli; as gravely at Palfrey.

"Elenora," Botticelli said, "I want you to show Dr. Palfrey how oblivious you are of physical conditions."

"Of course," she said, and her manner was easy and natural, with no sense of strain. She held out her right arm, lightly tanned by the Spanish sun. Botticelli opened a drawer in his desk and drew out a knife; a small, curved knife with a blade which looked razor sharp.

He raised it.

"No!" exclaimed Palfrey.

Botticelli slashed at Elenora's arm. The blade went in. She did not flinch. Sweat stood out on Palfrey's forehead; he felt as if he were choking, horror clutched him so.

Botticelli withdrew the blade, and Palfrey looked upon the bright steel and upon Elenora's arm, which was without blemish.

.   .   .   .   .

"Elenora," Botticelli said, quietly, "will you go into the Inferno?"

"Of course," she said again, and turned and went out.

Palfrey felt his lips working, felt the sweat running down his forehead, could not sit still. He leaned against the big desk.

"What—what is she going to do?"

"Just watch," said Botticelli, "and afterwards perhaps you will begin to understand." His voice had that soft, persuasive quality which it had held when he had spoken to McCall's daughter. "While faith is strong no harm can come, and hers is very strong. Watch——"

He pressed another button.

A window appeared in the wall behind him, long, narrow; glowing red, as if a huge fire were raging beyond it.

Palfrey clenched his hands, gritted his teeth and made himself go forward.

Fire was burning with white-hot fury. The floor beneath it was white-hot, too. As he stood close to the window, Botticelli moved his hand, and a blast of heat-laden air struck Palfrey, who backed away wildly. Botticelli had opened a tiny window within a window; now he picked up a brass paperweight and tossed it into the room of fire, the room he had called the Inferno.

The solid brass was molten within a moment of reaching the floor.

Then McCall's daughter appeared.

She was quite naked.

Her hair was loose, falling in a shimmering cloak to her shoulders.

"*No!*" cried Palfrey, and could not keep the scream back. He swung wildly round on Botticelli. "Get her out, get her out!"

"Watch," breathed Botticelli.

Elenora, McCall's daughter, stepped on to the white-hot floor, where a tiny glistening blob showed what was left of a solid brass ball. She walked across it, turned, walked back again, then looked up at the window, stood amid the burning, and *smiled.**

.   .   .   .   .

Palfrey saw the door of Botticelli's room open. He was still fighting to regain his composure, still dreadfully affected by what he had seen.

Elenora came in.

There was no mark upon her flesh, no sign of burning.

---

* "In a parking lot in Radio City, surrounded by skyscrapers, a ditch was dug, twenty feet long, four feet wide and three feet deep. It was filled with tons of oak logs, twenty-six bags of charcoal and set on fire. At the end of twenty-four hours the pit was a red-hot inferno. No creature of flesh and blood could come within ten feet without being burned. The temperature was 1,400 degrees Fahrenheit.

"At the stroke of eight, a little man dressed in the oriental manner approached the trench. He removed his shoes, rolled up his trousers and stepped into the fiery furnace. His feet sank into

13

"You see, Palfrey," said Botticelli, in that quiet, confident voice, "these are matters which are beyond your understanding. So many other things are beyond the mind of ordinary man. I am—different." He was in deadly earnest, now. "I am a man apart, Palfrey, and I believe it possible to control man's mind so completely that one becomes, as it were, the supreme being."

He stopped, but did not seem to be affected by the enormity of his blasphemy.

Palfrey couldn't find words.

"It will take some time for you to grasp this," went on Botticelli. "That doesn't matter. I am making tens of thousands of converts, in all parts of the world; and the *elementa* give me the one thing I need—an impregnable defence against attack by ordinary forces. Go and tell McCall this; tell your Government; tell the world's leaders. This has started, and nothing can stop it."

Half-blinded by the vision of that inferno-like room and the woman walking across the white-hot fire, Palfrey found it difficult to speak.

"For your own ends, you'll risk killing——"

"Oh, sentimentality hasn't a place in any affair of major issue," Botticelli said. "There is a war, your friends get killed —do you take it upon yourself to avenge their death? Of course not. Think of the number of deaths through road accidents in the course of a year. If a friend of yours is killed, do you take it upon yourself to exact a form of punishment? Of course not—there are authorities to which you

---

embers over his ankles. A large crowd, including skin specialists, leading medical authorities, cameramen and reporters watched breathlessly. Ambulances and fire engines were on hand.

"The man, Kuda Bux, walked through the centre of the pit. . . .

"As he completed his second run, doctors rushed towards him.

"Kuda Bux's feet were not even warm."

Ripley's *Believe It Or Not*, August 2nd, 1938, published in England by John Long.

rightly defer. And death—come, Palfrey, *death* as death doesn't distress you, does it? Surely your philosophy allows that death is simply a stage in life. Men have been dying for so long that it is normal enough, and in no way shocking—in fact, some people actually look forward to it, to find out what is going to happen next. Death is *exciting*, Palfrey."

"What would happen if someone tried to make life exciting for you?" Palfrey made himself ask.

Botticelli actually waved his right hand.

"Oh, the time to think about that is when it comes. I have much more to do in this world before I pass on! Take me seriously, Dr. Palfrey. You are unlikely to have trouble from the—ah—elemental visitors, unless of course you interfere with them again. That is up to you. I'm sorry that your friends suffered, but I don't advise you to take up the sword on their behalf. Leave that to me. Report to your Government, say truly that here are things beyond your understanding. What could be simpler?"

Palfrey didn't speak.

"If you are not satisfied that I have told you the truth, wait for a few weeks," Botticelli suggested. "You will find out."

Palfrey felt like choking.

The Supreme Being——

There Botticelli sat, in the absolute certainty, that he could command worship. Here, he was all-powerful, except against the creatures he had created. He boasted of thousands of converts all over the world. He could order the *elementa* so that they could strike at all the known defences of man.

He believed that he could become all-powerful by dominating the mind of man; and in trying to prove it, might cause the death of millions, and the death of nations.

That was the greatest danger; not that he could succeed in any kind of world domination, but that he might bring suffering to many multitudes.

If Palfrey could get out of here . . .

At least he had reason to hope; and no reason to think that Botticelli had been playing cat and mouse. Botticelli wanted him to go and take the fantastic message to London, to Washington, everywhere.

If he knew what Forrester had told him . . .

The door opened, and Isabella Melado came in. For the first time there was a marked change in her manner; a kind of tension which made her move briskly, made Botticelli look at her sharply, stifling a rebuke in his lips.

"What is it?" He was abrupt.

"I think you should come and see for yourself," she said. "Our agent is here, from the State Department."

From—Washington.

There was only a moment's pause before Botticelli moved towards the door. Isabella looked at Palfrey, without speaking, and from the door Botticelli said:

"You will excuse me, Palfrey."

They went out.

The door closed.

It was as if an end were threatened to the world. Botticelli had changed on the instant, and if he learned how much Forrester had said . . .

Palfrey went to the door, and tried to open it; but it would not open.

There was no other door.

There was no window that he could see.

He lit a cigarette and stood there, waiting, with choking fears of Botticelli and of the evil thing he had released frightening him.

He did not know whether he was being watched.

He seemed to be here for an age.

Then he heard the door open, and greater fear welled up when he saw the expression on Botticelli's face.

The man was alone. He looked—murderous. He stared at Palfrey as if he would kill him with his bare hands. Palfrey actually found himself backing away; tried to think of a means of fighting that would give him a chance, but could see none.

Botticelli said: "Stay where you are, and listen to me. A group of my converts have been arrested in Chicago, another group in Washington, another in Los Angeles. They have been accused"—he almost choked—"of treason, of plotting against the state because they worship *me*. They must be released. Tell McCall to tell the President that if my people are not free within twenty-four hours, this country will experience the greatest disaster in its history. Do you understand? They must release my people."

Palfrey felt the deadliness in the man, knew that he meant exactly what he said. The relief at his own reprieve was almost forgotten in understanding of what Botticelli believed himself to be.

Mathilde came in.

Botticelli said: "He may go, Mathilde, send him away."

Send him away.

Mathilde came to him, quite gravely, and he did not know what she was going to do, until she had done it. The prick of a needle in his arm was sharp and painful, and he flinched. She smiled. Botticelli sat at his desk, glaring at the wall.

A thwarted deity . . .

Palfrey felt his head reeling, felt his knees bending and felt mist swirling about his eyes, but he felt no pain now, only absolute helplessness—and a stranger feeling than that, a kind of peace. It was as if tension which had been in him from the time that he had seen Forrester was being drawn out of him.

He knew that he wasn't struggling; he hadn't the will to struggle.

He was being carried.

He felt himself being lowered, and realised that he was sitting in a comfortable chair. Hands which had touched him, dropped away. The mist swirled, but it was not so frightening. A man whom he could not see said quietly:

"We have the strength of *elementa*, Dr. Palfrey, and it cannot be opposed or overcome. Tell McCall, tell your friends, that Botticelli's people must be released. They *must* be."

The voice faded.

Palfrey felt drowsy.

He did not think of Botticelli or Forrester, of Bruton or Masak and Kramer and what they would think if he were not soon back. He did not think of the pictures. He kept seeing images on his mind's eye; of Isabella Melado, of Paula and Mathilde. Lovely, lovely creatures . . .

He could not understand this change; it was as if someone had taken control of his mind—*of his fears.*

Even that thought did not alarm him, then.

What could make him feel like this?

Vaguely, he thought of hashish; or marihuana; any of the

dream narcotics. It was as if he had taken some of the drugs and had drifted off into this misty world peopled by lovely women whom he knew, who smiled at him; or who laughed, as Isabella had laughed, or smiled like Elenora. The laughter was soft, muted, friendly—not mocking.

Isabella—Paula—Mathilde—McCall's beautiful daughter.

Next, he felt a sense of movement, as if he were being carried along a smooth road in a car which had perfect springing. Or in an aircraft. That was the kind of movement —a sensation of comfort and speed. It was as if he were flying through the clouds, that white cloud rested against the windows; one could not see out, but one felt safe and free from fear.

That was the marvel of it—freedom from fear.

The movement stopped.

He heard little sounds, oddly familiar; muted voices; and then he was lifted. He was still sitting down. This time it was a hard seat; that was all he knew.

Hands which had held him dropped away.

He heard doors slam, but the sounds were muffled; as if the mist not only blinded but also deafened him, so that noises close to his ear sounded as if they were a long way off.

A faint purring sound followed; a car engine, of course. They had taken him out of The House of the Angels, and now he was sitting in some unknown place, surrounded by dark mist. He was aware of it, as he was of the hard seat, yet he was not distressed or fearful; just—at rest.

But fear lurked near.

"Tell McCall . . . Greatest disaster . . . my people . . . must be released at once . . . my people, *my* people, *my* people!*"

14

A MAN said: "The guy's on fire, that's smoke."

Another man said: "I don't smell any smoke, maybe it's steam."

"How would it be steam?" the first man asked. "Where's the boiling water?"

"It's just fog, that's what it is," a third said. "It's a patch of fog."

"You look around," said the man who had spoken first, "and see if you can see fog any place else."

For the next few moments there was silence.

Palfrey was vaguely aware of the voices. He sensed that several other people were present. He didn't want to wake up from the pleasant drowsiness.

A man touched his shoulder.

"Hi, you," he said, "wake up."

Palfrey screwed up his eyes. He shivered, suddenly and uncontrollably, and someone exclaimed:

"He's waking, see that?"

The hand on his shoulder was firm; not like the hand of the girl when she had touched him. The voices were American. That wasn't surprising, as he was in Chicago. So his mind was working freely. He wished the man would stop shaking him, he needed longer to wake, but he supposed they would have to have their own way.

He opened his eyes.

There were just a few traces of mist, that was all: traces about his legs and his shoulders, little wisps which passed him floating with great unconcern towards—where?

He saw lights reflecting on the water.

"You can't sleep here," the man who had woken him said, and Palfrey looked round to see a tall, heavily-built man in uniform; a policeman. Half a dozen people were near by, others were coming up. Somewhere in the distance cars were humming. Palfrey realised that he was on a public seat on Lakeside Drive.

"You okay?" the man asked, and shone a torch into his face. "You . . ."

His voice trailed off.

Palfrey closed his eyes against the light, which didn't go out. He sensed a change in the policeman's manner, and it brought the first flutter of alarm that he had felt since he had left Botticelli, but it didn't go very deep.

"Say, look at him," the man breathed, and gripped his shoulder with his free hand and kept the light fully into his face. "Mister, is your name Palfrey? *Doctor* Palfrey?" He pronounced the first syllable as "Paw". There was an edge of fierce excitement in his voice, and his grip on Palfrey's shoulder was hard, hurtful.

"That's right," Palfrey said. "I'm Palfrey." He made it sound more like "Polfrey".

"Listen, Ully," said the policeman to a companion, "get back to the car, have a radio call sent back—we got Palfrey. That's the guy they broadcast for tonight, he's wanted real bad. You okay?" he asked Palfrey again. "Sure you're okay?"

"Oh, yes," Palfrey said, and stifled a yawn. "I'm a bit tired, that's all." He smiled as he heard the policeman mutter something under his breath.

"You'll get plenty of rest," the policeman said. "You come with me, doc. Move away, there, move away."

A police patrol car was drawn up on the side of the road. One man was at the wheel, talking into a microphone. The other, holding Palfrey's arm as if he held something precious, helped him towards the car. Palfrey didn't want any help. He yawned. He felt tired. He knew vaguely that it had been a remarkable night, but the prospect of having plenty of rest was attractive.

He dozed in the police car.

. . . .

Cornelius Bruton looked into Samuel McCall's eyes, dark blue into light blue, storm into calm.

They were in a suite at the Stevens. It was nearly dawn, but the curtains were still drawn. Cars were hooting and engines racing out in the streets, for this was truly a city which never slept.

McCall said: "He's on his way, and we'll know all about it when he gets here."

"Oh, sure," said Bruton. "Sure, we'll know all about it. He gets picked up sitting on a seat near the lake, like any bum. That's after we've turned Botticelli's House of the Angels inside out, to look for him. I know, I know, I insisted on doing that, and——"

"Botticelli co-operated," McCall said mildly.

"I'd like to know what that guy has for blood," Bruton said. He was angry, glowering. "That place gave me the creeps, and those women——"

McCall was still mild.

"Botticelli said that Palfrey had been there and left just

after nine o'clock. We know that they can use this mist, and hide their comings and goings. We know that Palfrey materialised out of a mist. Now Palfrey's been found."

"What happened in between?" Bruton demanded harshly. He swung away from McCall, and began to pace the room. "I wish I could tell you how bad I feel. If I hadn't been inside The House of the Angels I'd have felt better, but——" He broke off, took out cigarettes, lit one savagely and tossed the match at an ash-tray. It missed, and flamed on the floor. He went and picked it up, blew it out, and flicked it away again. "I can't believe what I saw even now. Those——"

"Angels," murmured McCall.

Bruton said: "Sure, that's right, those angels." His voice went flat on him. "You weren't there, you don't know what it felt like. There was Botticelli looking as if he'd been made out of wax, and in every corner you saw you found a girl who ought to have been hanging on a wall in a frame. All right, all right, so they were beautiful. You ever eaten too much ice-cream?"

McCall chuckled.

"Palfrey has been found, he's on his way here, and as soon as he can talk you'll know what it's all about."

"I wonder," said Bruton. "Here's another thing. Masak knew that Forrester went into that house, but we didn't find Forrester. He knows that Isabella Melado went there, too, but she was about the only member of the specie *angelicus* who wasn't there. I know, I know, they surround them with mist and spirit them out of the house, but we didn't see them go. And Palfrey's found on a park seat, *steaming*. That's what the report says—steaming. And he's sleepy and disinclined to talk. You know what?" He swung round on McCall. "He ought not to have gone in that house alone."

"I wish I knew why you're still so worried," McCall said. "If we were still looking for him, it would be different."

Bruton stopped just in front of him. His deep-set eyes were filled with shadows. His face was small and sharp-featured, the kind of face that might have been chiselled out of granite, although the lips were full and unexpectedly soft.

"Sure," he said. "It could be different. I know. I'll tell you what's got into me, Mr. McCall. I'm scared."

McCall said: "We're all scared."

Bruton rubbed the end of his nose.

He went to the door, opened it and looked into the passage. He slammed the door and crossed to the window, opened it and looked out. A few clouds floating sluggishly across the stars was all that he could see above. He leaned out, peering down into the street. This was a side street, and there were few lights; but not far along the glitter and glow of neons was competing with the first grey light of the dawn.

A few wisps of steam were coming out of manholes in the side street, and the steam caught the colour of a neon sign; blood red. Red-tinged mist seemed to be floating upwards, dispersing before it reached the windows.

Bruton drew back.

"Clouds, mist, vanishing tricks and Botticelli," he growled. "What *does* that guy use for blood? You want to know something? Botticelli hasn't got a smile in him. He's as solemn as they come, and that was the first thing you noticed about Hitler. And something else. I've known Palfrey for twelve years. Twelve *years*. That's one hundred and forty-four months. I've been on a hundred inquiries with him. I've known every kind of torment and torture on a job. I've known a time when it looked as if everything we call civilisation would be smashed to pieces, and let me tell you something: I've never known Palfrey scared the way he is now. He's scared of a few puffs of mist! And so am I. So are you. So is everyone who's had any experience of it. Those men at Brett Hall—do you know what happened? Three of them went mad after the attack by mist. *Mad*. Understand? *Mad*."

"You know, you'll soon need a rest," McCall said quietly.

"Aw, forget it! I'm just worried about Sap." Bruton gave a sudden, swift grin. "When he gets back, if he's not too bad——"

He stopped.

He went to the door as if there were dynamite at his heels, opened it and then reared up and came tottering backwards, uttering a gibberish sound. It reached McCall, and the Senator seemed to feel his blood curdling, his own mouth opened.

Mist swirled about.

Bruton got inside, kicked at the door, then slammed it.

The mist was shut out, but Bruton didn't move, just stood and gaped, as if he feared that it would find a way through the keyhole or down the sides. His breath came in deep, convulsive gasps, and he had lost every vestige of colour.

McCall, looking and feeling almost as bad, stared at the door.

Bruton muttered: "That's what it does to me. That's what it does to anyone." He stood with his teeth clenched and his arms stiff by his side, then slowly moved towards the door. "The hell," he said, and stretched out to touch the handle.

"Bruton!" exclaimed McCall, in a cracked voice.

"The hell," Bruton repeated clearly. "If I'm going crazy, let me go quick."

"Bruton!" yelled McCall.

Bruton pulled open the door. There was no mist at all in the passage, but there was a girl; one of Botticelli's "angels". She was smiling, and the way she looked at Bruton seemed to suggest that she knew just how he had felt; and that it amused her.

"Dr. Palfrey left this behind," she said, and held out a golden cigarette-case. Bruton had often held it, knew that there was a tiny dent on one corner, and that the monogram was of Palfrey's initials and his wife's, intermingled.

He moistened his dry lips.

"Thanks," he said. "Good of you. Will you—come in?"

"No, thank you." She smiled and turned away.

Bruton turned back into the room. He rubbed the cigarette-case, his thumb going round and round, round and round. Then he said:

"So they're polite *and* honest. That's what they'd like us to think! Listen, McCall, if a thing can make me feel so scared, I don't know any way to fight against it. And it's got Sap Palfrey. If it can get him, it can get anyone."

He broke off again, and looked towards the door.

There were the footsteps of several men in the passage.

Bruton hesitated, then moved towards the door again. He kept his hand on the handle for several seconds, as the footsteps drew nearer. The bell rang. Bruton still hesitated. It was as if he were frightened of what he knew he was going to see—as if the thought of Palfrey's condition affected him almost as badly as the mist had.

Then he opened the door.

Two well-dressed men from Police Headquarters were with Palfrey. They were big, powerful looking and puzzled. One stared at Palfrey, who stood in the doorway with his head on one side, an absurd little smile on his lips. He had a nice colour. His eyes were rather sleepy, but they were smiling. He had one hand in his pocket, and the other raised in front of his chest.

"Why, Corny." He grinned broadly. "Waiting up?" He moved forward, holding out a hand. "Kindly thought. These two gentlemen have been good enough to escort me here. I told them I was quite capable of getting here on my own, but they were very kind. I—why, Mr. McCall!" He drew back a little when he recognised McCall, then went forward with both hands outstretched. "Very happy to see you again, sir! Good of you to come."

He came into the room, swaying.

One of the plain-clothes men said: "He's been this way since we found him. If you ask me——" He touched his forehead with his forefinger, and nodded his meaning. "As you're here, Mr. McCall, we don't need a receipt for the body."

He backed away.

Palfrey was yawning, stretching his arms above his head and looking about the room as if he had never seen it before. Bruton had moved away from him and was watching with a wild look in his eyes.

"Bed, that's me," said Palfrey hazily. "Bed and sweet dreams, dear Morpheus, oh for the dizzy mists of sleep. Mists. Mists of sleep. That's good." He spoke and behaved for all the world as if he were drunk, and he approached Bruton and stood in front of him, pointing with an unsteady forefinger. "Do you good, too. You look tired and harassed, old friend, as if the demons of hell have been chasing you with a torch of treacle and brimstone. No, not treacle. Never mind, hell's bells and fire will do." He yawned and tapped his lips. "Sorry."

The door closed on the man from Police Headquarters.

McCall stood looking at Palfrey. Bruton went up to Palfrey, gripped his forearm, and said:

"You can snap out of it. They've gone."

Palfrey looked down at him, grey eyes puzzled, pink cheeks slightly flushed. He looked almost babyish.

"Snap out of what, old pal? Sleep, that's what I want." He smiled, patted Bruton's shoulder, freed his arm and went towards the bedroom door. He stopped and turned round slowly, looked into McCall's eyes and beamed. "Got a message for you—oh, yes. Botticelli says that some worshipper friends of his have been arrested. Must be released." Beneath the almost drunken stupor he was in, there was the lurking fear. "Important. Botticelli says that if they're not released, he'll cause the—ah!—greatest disaster this country's ever known. He probably will, too."

Bruton said roughly: "Do you know what you're saying?"

"Oh, every word."

"Palfrey," began McCall. Only to pause before he went on: "You sound as if you think Botticelli can do it."

"Of course he can," said Palfrey. "All powerful, isn't he? Supreme. If you'd seen what I've seen——"

Just for a moment, the buried fear leapt up like a tongue of flame.

"He'll do it, release those people. Here in Chicago, Washington, Los Angeles——" He stopped and gulped, then grinned foolishly. "Forgive me, won't you? Very tired. Exhausting day. Don't forget to tell Washington. Good night."

He went into the bedroom, but did not close the door. After a few seconds they heard a bed creak. Then a shoe dropped to the floor, another followed it.

Palfrey began to hum a tune from a new musical.

McCall said: "It's unbelievable."

"Know who these people are?"

"Some groups of a religious sect, suspected of treason. They're being held——"

He broke off.

"Well?" Bruton barked.

"But no one knew, it was all done secretly. If Botticelli told Palfrey——"

"Let me see if I can knock any sense into him," Bruton said, and went into the bedroom.

Palfrey stood in his underpants and nothing else, stifling another yawn. It was possible to see the packed muscles of his shoulders, the strength of his chest, the ripple of his muscles under skin which had been slightly tanned. He was going unsteadily towards the bathroom, still humming, and did not appear to notice Bruton. Two minutes later he returned to the bedroom, got into bed, pulled the clothes over him and turned his back on the window. He didn't turn out the light.

"Sap, let's hear more of what happened. Did you talk to Botticelli?"

"Eh? Oh, yes. Was granted an audience with Great White Chief. Impressive chap. Wants his people released, and—means what he says. He—Corny!"

"What?"

"I tell you he means what he says!"

The fear was in the open, now, the effect of whatever dope he had been given was gone.

"Fetch McCall!" he cried. "McCall! Senator!" He actually got out of bed, but Bruton pushed him back, and McCall came hurrying. "Senator—he meant it. Every word. He can control the mist, *elementa*, he—he *meant* it. Never more sure of anything."

McCall said: "But I can't——" and broke off.

"Try!" cried Palfrey, "try! Telephone Washington, do all you can——"

He sank back in bed.

"Head's going round," he said clearly. "Damned drug. Be careful. Botticelli's—a great man." He broke off. Then: "Man?" he queried. "Man?"

Abruptly he lost consciousness.

.   .   .   .   .

He was unconscious most of the night, and sick and in a strange mood all the next day. He could not understand himself. He was frightened, yet memory of Botticelli wasn't a memory of evil.

Nor was memory of Isabella, Elenora, Mathilde.

Late that evening, McCall came in.

"Glad to see you up," he said to Palfrey gruffly. "Feeling yourself again?"

"Nearly."

"Good."

"Had any luck?" Bruton demanded.

McCall said: "No, and I didn't expect any. The Secretary was polite, but——" He shrugged. "No doubt these men under arrest were plotting the overthrow of the State. They had pictures of Botticelli, too—seemed to venerate him, I'm told."

"Worship," declared Palfrey. "Yes. I know." He moved about the room slowly, feeling as if he had the weight of the world on his shoulders. "I almost felt the same way. They've developed a drug, which——" He paused, then twisted a few strands of hair round his forefinger. "Well, they know how to make converts. Forrester's fighting them. Forrester says . . ."

He told them.

Then he said: "Has anyone been to the House of the Angels today?"

"Yes," McCall said. "F.B.I. men went to see Botticelli. He's gone. The house seems empty."

As he spoke, wind struck the window of the room, but none of them noticed it.

Throughout the night, the storm went on.

Throughout the night, officials in Washington and London studied Palfrey's report of his conversation with Botticelli, and Forrester's warning. Inquiries were put in hand about Professor Rebonne, the physicist whose atomic research had won world renown; he was known to be in America, but had not been seen for some weeks.

Palfrey's report of his own mental condition on returning from The House of the Angels made many eyebrows raise. If there were a common reaction, it was that Palfrey was working too hard, and might be the victim of hallucinations.

With the storm still blowing up, Palfrey slept.

15

BRUTON pushed back the bedclothes on the second morning and licked his lips. Palfrey was facing the window, and seemed to be sleeping. Bruton yawned, scratched his head, stretched, and got out of bed. He went unsteadily round to

Palfrey, whose lips were set, who breathed through his nose and who looked more himself. No one knew how defeated he had felt, but Bruton had a good idea.

Bruton also knew that he feared a disaster: Botticelli had affected him like that.

Palfrey didn't stir.

The window shook under a gust of wind.

Bruton lit a cigarette, went into the bathroom and took a can of orange juice out of a small ice-box, pierced it and drank. Then he plugged in his razor, shaved, put on an electric kettle when he had finished and sauntered back into the bedroom.

Another gust of wind struck the window.

It was just ten o'clock.

Palfrey started, and turned round. Bruton pushed his hand through his stiff hair, and smiled faintly; ironically. He thought it was going to be all right. He went in and had a shower, and when he had finished, the kettle was singing. It was a fetish of Palfrey's to make his own tea whenever it was possible. A sign, he often said, of encroaching age.

Wind howled along the street, smacking at the windows, and Bruton went to have a look outside. As he pulled aside the net curtains, his heart began to pound, and he felt like choking.

Thick mist hung about the street.

Bruton didn't open the window; something almost physical stopped him from letting the mist in. He felt his teeth clenching. He pressed as close to the window as he could, and looked down. A few people were hurrying along the street, coat collars turned up—dark-clad, huddled, damp and miserable-looking. And yesterday had been a glorious day, the forecast had promised sunshine. Bruton could just see Clarke Street. Traffic there was thick and crawling, and occasionally he could hear the hooters blaring impatiently, but the almost continual howl of the wind drowned most sound.

He heard a movement, and spun round, his heart making a wild leap.

Palfrey was standing by the side of the bed; a sleepy-eyed Palfrey.

Bruton snapped: "You stay in bed! You need——"

"I'm all right," Palfrey said, in his ordinary speaking voice. "What's the matter with the morning?"

"Windy City's being windy. And misty."

Palfrey said: "Oh."

He moved towards the window. Whatever had taken possession of him at Botticelli's house had left him now. His face was set and stern, and his eyes were almost closed. The blustering wind shook the windows. Across the road, a hanging sign was turning over and over its bar, like a child's monkey-on-a-stick. A hat appeared for a moment in front of the window, whisked up from the street, like the hat of an invisible man.

"How long's the wind been blowing?" Palfrey asked.

"Not long." Bruton scowled. "Come to think of it, I didn't notice it until ten minutes ago. When I woke, it wasn't blowing. But what difference does the weather make?"

Palfrey turned to look at him. He didn't smile; and the shadows lurking in his eyes startled Bruton.

"I'm getting nervous about the weather," he said. "Storms in particular. I didn't tell you about Saturnino, and the storm off the Spanish coast. Botticelli told me." He hesitated before he explained, and then he said very slowly: "I'm back to normal, and afraid to breathe. Botticelli scared the wits out of me; the whole set-up did. They pumped something into me that made me think Botticelli might be——"

He broke off.

"Good?" Bruton asked gruffly.

"More than good." Palfrey caught his breath. "Holy? Not that, not quite——"

Wind smacked at the window.

"He threatened a disaster," Palfrey added harshly. "If he could make a storm——" He stopped again. Then: "Corny, it was a nightmare. I saw McCall's daughter walk through fire. Understand? And Botticelli slashed at her arm with a knife, and didn't draw blood. I saw Forrester in terror, but that's the one good thing, he's there. And there's little doubt they're trying to convert him in the way they started on me. Injections, to help control your mind. It's— diabolic."

"The kettle's on," Bruton said gruffly. "Get back into bed."

He went into the bathroom, to make the tea. When he came back, carrying it on a tray with two cups and saucers, Palfrey was standing by the window, his face pressed close against it. The sound of the wind was now almost continuous, the traffic noises were drowned except for the occasional screech of a horn. A sheet of newspaper floated past the window, danced skittishly and dropped out of sight.

It was very dark; the sky was overcast.

"Tea, sir," Bruton said, forcing himself to sound flippant.

Palfrey turned. "Thanks." He was back in the grip of fear again, Bruton believed; the fear which had been with them since the beginning of this affair. "How often do you get wind like this in Chicago?"

"You never heard of our freak weather?"

"I've heard of it." Palfrey kept sipping his tea. "It's getting darker and the mist is getting thicker," he said. "It'll soon be fog." He moved to the window and looked out again. Almost against his will, Bruton joined him. Banks of mist floated sluggishly past the window, and it was almost impossible to see the traffic in Clarke Street.

It was like looking at grey cloud from the top of a mountain.

The room was a place of shadow.

Bruton said testily: "Okay, we'll have some light." He turned to go for the light switch.

Then light came, from outside.

It was as lightning, a swift and dazzling flash which blinded them and filled every corner of the room. It was so bright that it showed every tiny thing in the room. And it filled the sky and the street and the whole city.

It died.

And as it died, a thunderous roar filled the vacuum quiet of the morning, a shattering, deafening, horrifying roar; as if the heavens had opened, split by the lightning, and this were the cry of agony which followed.

.   .   .   .   .

Bruton gasped: "Sap, I can't see."

"You'll be all right."

"I tell you I can't see."

"I can't see, either, but we're only dazzled."

"I can't *see*!"

"Just stand where you are," said Palfrey, patiently. "You'll be able to see in a few minutes."

"How the hell do you know?"

"It happened before," Palfrey said. "Something very like it. Remember—at Brett Hall."

He was seeing that misty shape, the tentacles stretching out for him—and then the flash which had blinded him, and the explosion which had crumpled part of the staircase. There had been just such a flash last night, when Forrester had stood pressed against the wall, striving to get away from the writhing creature enshrouded by mist.

The two friends were silent for several minutes.

The wind howled and whined, and windows and signs rattled, and the mist raced past the window, although they could not see it.

Gradually, their sight came back. The things in the room were vague at first, and each man saw treble—the bed, the cups, the lamps, everything here seemed to be going round and round in circles.

Bruton said squeakily: "You're right again."

"Am I?" Palfrey turned away from him, bent by the side of the bed, and drew out a suit-case. He opened it, rummaged through the contents and said: "I thought so, they're in the car."

"What are in the car?"

"Dark glasses," Palfrey said. "I've a nasty feeling that we're going to have some more of this. Know of a shop near by where they sell goggles? Anything with really thick dark lenses."

"Any drug store——"

"We don't want toys! Try Marshall Fields—no, wait, we'll go together." Palfrey was at the window, pulling the thick curtains across savagely. "See if we can get any service, I feel as if I haven't eaten for a week." Every word he uttered, every movement he made, carried a hint of savagery. He flung on his clothes, while Bruton tried Room Service, and didn't get an answer until Palfrey was almost ready.

Outside, the fog made the sky and the streets dark, but there had been no more thunder and lightning.

"Forget Room Service," Palfrey said jerkily, "see if you can get Masak on the telephone." He was knotting his tie.

Bruton put in the call.

Wind smashed against the window and set up a howling that was like the wail of a thousand terrified cats. Then it stopped, and with awful suddenness the blinding light came again. But for the thick curtains, it would have been as dreadful as before. Bruton cried out and slapped his hands to his eyes, Palfrey swung round towards the door. The telephone dropped and dangled at the end of its cord. Palfrey moved and picked it up, gave Masak's number and waited.

Thunder smote the air, like the roar of a thousand guns. The room shook, a brush fell off the dressing-table.

The hotel exchange operator said: "We don't get any reply, sir, a lot of lines are busy or out of order."

"All right, thanks," Palfrey said. He put the receiver down. "Come on, Corny." He tapped his pocket, checking that he had his gun, and went on: "Not that bullets will help much today."

They went out.

The wide, carpeted passage was quiet, no one was about. A floor clerk sat at her desk near the elevators, and looked up with a vague smile.

"They say there's a bad storm," she said, and went on totting up pencilled figures.

An elevator slid to a hissing standstill, the doors opened, the attendant stood aside for them. He looked pale, and his eyes were scared. Two other people were in the elevator car; a man and a woman. There was tension in their faces, in the way they stood.

"You hear that thunder?" the man asked.

"Bad, wasn't it?" Palfrey smiled.

"I've never heard anything so terrible," the woman said. "And that flash of lightning." Now that she had started talking, she began to tremble. "I was blind for a long time, I didn't think I would ever be able to see again." She choked back a sob.

"Don't you worry, honey," the man said, "we'll be safe enough down in the coffee-shop, that's way down below the street." He patted her arm, and glanced at Palfrey and Bruton as if to say: "You know how it is with a nervous woman."

Three people came in at the next stop, two youths and a

teen-age girl with long, silky hair and a golden skin and glistening, excited eyes.

"You hear that thunder?" a boy asked. "Gee, could an atom bomb be any louder?"

"*Please!*" gasped the woman.

"Don't you worry, honey," the man soothed.

"I'm sorry, ma'am," the boy said awkwardly.

"It's kind of exciting," said the girl, and her eyes shone as if she really meant that; she and the boys almost certainly did. There was something reassuring about a capacity for excitement which could make them forget that fear existed.

"We're right here," the attendant announced.

They stepped out into the big entrance hall. It was crowded; not just full, as it would usually be, but crammed with people. There was a muted whisper of voices. When a man sneezed the sound was like an explosion; and a woman gasped in fright. As Palfrey and Bruton forced their way through towards the doors they saw the strained expressions on the faces of the people.

Near the doors, three policemen, caps on, were in a little group.

"Sure it's a bad storm, don't we have the biggest storms in the United States of America?" one of these demanded. "It'll pass by, don't you worry!"

Palfrey reached him.

"You going out?" the policeman asked, almost truculently.

"Yes."

"Don't advise it," the policeman said. "I just don't advise it, not while the storm lasts."

"Very urgent business," Palfrey said. "I'm a doctor."

He felt that he was being watched by the hundreds of people in the hall and the wide passages leading off. Old men and young, old women, teen-agers and children were jammed tightly into every inch of space.

Palfrey stepped into the street. Bruton followed, and the girl and her two companions came hurrying after them, still exhilarated. The sky was like a great pall of sulphurous smoke. A few people were in sight, but Palfrey had never seen the streets of an American city so empty. Cars and taxis crawled past, some bright colours dimmed by the fog. Few horns blared. Two newspapermen stood by their stall calling out in muted, defiant voices. People watched the sky and the street from doorways; most of the shops were crowded with those taking cover.

There was a sense of waiting; waiting for disaster.

"I just don't recall a shop where——" Bruton began.

"Marshall Fields, remember," Palfrey said. He knew where the store was, and led the way, sometimes breaking into a run. Traffic slid by. The wind smote the streets and walls and windows, and at some corners they had to battle against it; at others there was hardly any at all. But whether close by or far away, it whined and howled; and all the time signs were clattering, hats were being blown along the street, newspapers flew about.

They reached the huge store.

Each entrance was crowded. People were staring at the sky, and its darkness was now so great that it was like night lit only by some sulphurous yellow glow.

The huge store was crowded, especially near the doors, but few people were buying. Store clerks were standing about in little groups, most of them looking towards the doors.

Palfrey and Bruton found the right department. . . .

"Yes, sir," the assistant crowed, "we have the very thing you want. Special goggles, as used by close observers of the atomic explosions way down in Nevada. . . ."

They'd bought the goggles and left the store all in ten minutes.

A long line of taxis was drawn up near by when they got out, and they stopped at the first one.

The driver said: "Where you want to go?"

"Lakeside Drive, by Cross Street."

"Don't know how close we can get," the driver said. He was chewing and looking at the sky as he spoke, as if he were asking whether it were wise to go. "There's been some damage over there. Okay, you get in, I'll take you some place."

They got in, and the cab moved off.

There was a thick wedge of slow-moving traffic at the next intersection, but the lights were in their favour. It took them ten minutes to reach the lakeside, then they travelled more quickly. Other traffic was moving quicker, too—fully ten miles an hour.

The driver leaned back.

"Some bad crashes when that lightning struck," he said, and paused to chew. "So we don't hurry, see."

"Just get us there."

"I'll get you some place."

Headlights were needed in order to see the kerb; fog showed in the beams, yellow and glistening. The driver switched the lights off. A hundred yards along the wide street he grabbed the wheel as a gust of wind struck the car and sent it slewing round. Another taxi, coming towards them, swerved wildly in the same direction.

As if warned by instinct, the driver jammed on his brakes and covered his eyes with his hands.

The flash came with blinding horror. People on the sidewalk screamed, cars in the roadway went out of control and crashed, some ran along locked together as if in a drunken dance. Palfrey's taxi jolted to a standstill. The driver sat huddled over the wheel, his eyes still covered, head bowed. No other traffic moved.

Palfrey said stonily: "I'll drive."

Bruton didn't try to restrain him.

Palfrey pushed the driver to one side, and the man went without any protest, quite mutely as a passenger in his own cab. Palfrey took the wheel. He could just see the glow of parking-lights, but it was difficult to drive. He pushed his goggles up, taking a chance; there had been long intervals between the earlier flashes.

Only here and there did a car move. From the crowded doorways, people stared blankly, blindly. Some were weeping, a few were running about wildly, as if the thunder and the lightning had driven them into hysteria.

The dark pall still hung over the city.

Palfrey turned into the Lakeside Drive. A hundred yards along, a policeman stepped out into the roadway, one hand raised. His face was the colour of pastry before it was put in the oven.

"Where do you think you're going?"

"A house along here. Botticelli's house."

"Well, you can walk. There's been some trouble farther

along there." He spoke gaspingly, as if the shock were still on him. "You can't take the car."

"All right."

Palfrey and Bruton got out. Palfrey stuck a twenty-dollar bill into the jacket pocket of the driver, who was beginning to look about him dazedly.

They walked on.

Trees were down, windows of the houses near the road had been broken, a channel of water ran along each side of the street; the water had obviously rushed up from the lake and spilled into the roadway.

They could hear the seething water smashing against the beaches and the sea-wall. Suddenly the wind howled with fury, and that awful wailing sound came again, herald of horror. Palfrey snatched at his goggles, Bruton pulled his down, and they waited, holding their breath.

The flash came——

They were not blinded, but the thunder rocked the earth and deafened them. They crouched against a thick brick wall, with a dozen other people, and waited fearfully until the awful sound had died away. They could not hear ordinary noises, and Palfrey now understood the silence which followed each outburst.

He was the first to move.

"Let's go," he mouthed to Bruton.

Bruton made himself stand upright, braced his shoulders and walked into the wind. It caught them in furious gusts, now throwing them against each other, now forcing them apart. Once Palfrey was blown back at least a yard; once Bruton was lifted off his feet and hurled into the road. But there was no moving traffic.

A lull came.

In spite of it, they could still see mountainous waves racing inland from the lake, washing over the gardens of the once-beautiful houses on the lakeside, coming up towards the road and falling back just before it reached it. The lake was a seething tumult, as fiercely hostile as the Atlantic in the fury of a mid-winter gale.

The wind whined and howled across it.

Palfrey and Bruton could hear again now, but there was a ringing sound in their ears all the time; no sounds were clear or natural, and they did not try to speak. They passed a few dazed people struggling with furniture, pictures, clothes and luggage near houses which had been flooded. Children were helping, too, and police were everywhere.

More police were arriving, some in cars, some on motor-cycles. They passed Palfrey and Bruton, who reached a corner. On the other side of the road was a big house, a beautiful place of pale-cream-coloured brick which had looked superb in the light of the previous evening.

A great jagged hole gaped in the roof; one of the walls was down. Inside, they saw two beds, one hanging over the edge of the hole; what was worse, a woman lay in it. There was blood on her face and blood on her neck. Beneath her, police were working and others were trying to shore up the wall before the rest of it collapsed.

Palfrey forced his way past the crowd.

He mouthed at Bruton: "How far?"

"Two hundred yards," Bruton's voice just reached Palfrey's straining ears.

They passed another house, which looked undamaged except for flooding. But the one next door again had been demolished, only rubble stood where a mansion had been. Trees had been uprooted and were now lying across the road and on the ground. A huge pond of muddy water, ruffled by the wind, filled the hole where the lawn had been.

Police stood and looked about as if the destruction had robbed them of the ability to move; all were muttering, and Palfrey caught some of the words, guessed at many others.

"Could of been a meteor," a big, florid-faced Irishman was saying. "What else would ye call it?"

"If you ask me——"

"Carney, we aren't asking you," a chunky lieutenant said brusquely. "Get on with the job."

The job was keeping people away and on the move; helping others who came, shocked and dazed, from the great houses. The fog was upon them all the time, a dark pall with that sulphurous, yellowish glow behind it; as if even the sun had to admit defeat.

"Getting on with the job" didn't keep anyone silent. The

voice of terror sounded, even on the tongues of men who showed most courage. Meteor, some said, or atom bomb. And the thoughts crowded Palfrey's mind as he went on—until they came within sight of Botticelli's gates.

The house was not there.

16

PALFREY took off the goggles and stared at the huge crater where Botticelli's house had been. Rubble had been thrown for miles by the explosion, but most of it was crammed in the grounds. Nothing stood where it had been; no brick, no tree, no flower or shrub. The green lawns had been scorched, and were black and dead-looking. The branches of trees had been stripped of all their budding promise.

Nothing was left but destruction—and a great hole filled with mud. A big car could be put into that hole.

Bruton said just above his breath: "Well, what do you know?"

Some way off, the wind was howling and blustering, but here it was calmer, and the fog seemed to be lifting a little. Palfrey didn't put his goggles back on. A police lieutenant came striding up, a man smaller than most in uniform, white to the lips, eyes glassy with loss of sleep or with shock. His lips were set in a thin line as he drew up and glowered at them.

"What the hell do you think you're doing? Get going."

"Your job," Palfrey said. "Our job." He slid a card out of his pocket, signed by McCall; sight of the signature brought a moment's relaxation to the lieutenant, whose shoulders sagged and who looked fit to drop.

"You want to know something," he said. "At half-past ten this was a big house with garage for six cars, a greenhouse and a hot-house. Sure, and stables. There was Botticelli and his dames, and maybe a lot of other people. And now there isn't any house. There isn't anything. Just a big hole in the ground filled with mud. Thick, slimy, yellow, stinking mud," he went on, grinding the words out. "Thick, slimy——"

"Take it easy," Bruton said stonily. "One of the guys

here was a friend of mine." He took a brandy flask from his hip pocket. "No one left at all?"

"No one and nothing."

"Sure?"

The lieutenant said in a voice which was almost a scream: "Didn't God Almighty give you any eyes?"

Palfrey said: "And we're looking. Take it easy." He stared into the police officer's face, and there seemed to be some strange confidence in his; something which helped.

"Aw, I'm okay."

Palfrey and Bruton moved nearer the hole. The lieutenant was as right as a man could be; it was a huge crater, filled with thick slimy, yellow mud. And it was moving; writhing. A faint wisp of smoke or steam rose from it. Palfrey felt himself go cold, and sensed the horror which sprang to Bruton's mind. They stood staring, until Palfrey said explosively:

"It's boiling! We've seen mud like that at Rotorua. Boiling volcanic mud."

"I think you're right," Bruton said. "Only there it comes out of the earth, and here——" He broke off. He lit a cigarette, slowly, and tossed the spent match into the crater; it floated on the mud for a few seconds, and was gradually sucked under. "Sap," he said, "you went into that house. You see Botticelli?"

"Yes."

"Isabella?"

"Yes."

"I guess you saw Elenora and Mathilde, too," Bruton went on, in his strange, high-pitched voice. "And Paula and half a dozen others. And Jim Forrester. I've seen some of those girls coming out of the house. You ever seen girls who're easier on the eye? You ever seen girls so beautiful? Now look at them. That's where they are, stewed up in that boiling hell-hole. Botticelli doesn't count, but those girls——"

Palfrey said: "There isn't anything more we can do here. Let's see if Masak's all right."

They went across the Riverside Drive, which just here was unrecognisable as a roadway. A crowd of police and firemen were working on McCall's house, the front of which had been blown away. The roof was gone, too, the attic apartment was bared to the sky and the fog.

The fog *was* lifting.

Masak was still at his place of duty, sprawled on the floor; Palfrey saw that in some pathetic way he had managed to hug the camera to his body, saving it, although he must have known that he was going to die.

There was no sign of Kramer.

.   .   .   .   .

The fog over Chicago lifted gradually during the next two hours. The dread which nearly everyone felt eased slowly, too. There had been only the four flashes of "lightning" and four explosions. Two of these had centred on Riverside Drive, near Botticelli's house. It was now known that one had been half a mile out in the Lake, where a small steamer had been sailing. That had been sunk without trace. The fourth had been in the downtown district, and the destruction and loss of life had been far greater there than anywhere else.

Everywhere, the people were dazed.

Police and firemen, military and volunteer helpers from a hundred clubs and organisations went into action with emergency dressing-stations, field-kitchens, all that was needed to help the injured, the sick and the shocked. The shocked were worse, perhaps, than any others. Hundreds walked about aimlessly, a few still sightless, mouths partly open, bodies sagging. There was not so much fear as blankness in their faces. Messages went to all parts of the city and suburbs, to have the shock victims picked up and not allowed to roam about at will.

Scientists were at the scene of the explosions within an house.

By midday, long before the fog had lifted completely, every radio broadcasting station and every television transmitter had sent out the same message: rumours that an atomic bomb had been exploded above Chicago were untrue. There was no evidence whatsoever of radio-activity in the ruins or in the boiling mud. The theory that a meteor of unusual size had struck the earth was being explored. America's greatest physicists were on the spot. There was also the more likely possibility that Chicago had been struck by a freak storm, the worst in the world's history.

Palfrey sat listening to a broadcast in his room.

". . . and who's surprised at that?" asked the announcer. "Chi always has the biggest in the world, hasn't it?"

His chuckle when he finished was masterly, and made even Palfrey smile. It must have cheered up a million listeners. The television announcers were as cheerful, the newspapers took the same line. One man, a television news announcer named Cardell, was brilliantly reassuring.

Reports of what had happened in the city came in steadily, by telephone and by messengers. There had been little or no panic, even when the first wild rumour of atomic warfare had spread around. As if by habit, the people had carried out the air-raid drill which had been practised for several years. Very few had been on the streets after the first explosion. There had been a great number of small accidents, few of them fatal. In all but the worst-hit areas, telephone, gas and electricity mains and water services had been restored to normal.

At half-past two, when the first pale glim of sunshine was finding its way through the mist which had followed the fog, McCall walked into Palfrey's room at the Stevens. Bruton was already there, with two other Z 5 agents who operated in Chicago. These two and Bruton were sifting reports from Police Headquarters; they had already been sifted there.

Palfrey said: "Hi." He stood up from a table which he was using as a desk. "At least you weren't hurt."

"I'm all right," said McCall. He looked twenty years older; otherwise he was probably telling the truth. He knew that his daughter had been in that house, which partly explained his shattered appearance. He knew that Chicago had suffered a threatened disaster.

"I think we have confirmation of what we've feared for some time." Palfrey spoke very slowly, saying "we" when he could have said "I". "The reports of those people who are dispassionate enough to be believed are all about the same. The first indication of anything unusual was of a big wind blowing up in the lake. That wasn't altogether abnormal, storms do blow up from nowhere; but this one was of much greater velocity than most. Before it had been officially recorded, it had churned the lake into a whirlpool. We know that most of the shipping near by was either sunk or smashed to pieces on the beaches."

McCall nodded, into a pause.

"But it was comparatively local," Palfrey went on. "There was something reported as a tidal wave, but it didn't extend more than five miles from its central point of impact. Ten miles along there were exceptionally heavy waves, but not tidal. Twenty-five miles away comparatively little was felt of the wind, just a few big waves. The explosions were heard, but the only phenomenon was the fog—or the overcast sky."

McCall nodded.

Palfrey said: "Senator, I don't know exactly what's happening. I've always made it clear that I don't know, and that it scares me. But I'm sure of one thing. We're likely to have more of this kind of phenomenon. I think that all Governments should be warned that they might happen, that the people in the big cities should be warned to be ready to take to the air-raid shelters as soon as a warning is given. It's much safer to be under cover than out in the open. Most countries have an atomic-raid-protection drill. I think they should put the drill into operation right away."

McCall said: "I agree, fully."

"And I think we ought to go very warily with Botticelli's agents and groups," Palfrey said. "He told me he was always prepared for trouble. He may have been for this—I'm not taking it for granted that he's dead."

"And—you feel certain he caused this?"

Palfrey said: "It's a hell of a thing to be sure of, but we know the *elementa* exist, we know what a fear of them can do. Think you can persuade Washington to hold off his groups?"

"When they see the evidence, they'll listen. Can you persuade London?"

"I've been speaking to my Chief, by radio telephone," Palfrey told him. "He's co-operative."

McCall said abruptly: "I can't believe any *man* can cause——"

"Let's face it," Palfrey said. "Botticelli's had physicists working for years, and they stumbled across this; half-mist, half-man, call it *elementa*, call it what you like. He's got them under his thumb. Sometimes they rebel, sometimes they run into trouble of some kind, which he says he doesn't understand—although that could have been to fool me. We've a lot of supporting evidence that he really can control it—and that it can be deadly. Look at it all ways. These disappearances, in a mist. Occasional small explosions, without any evidence of what was causing them, reported from many parts of the world. Then, not long ago, the big disturbance in Spain. I've been studying Andromovitch's report from there, before he vanished. On the night that Forrester was attacked there was a fierce storm, with lightning out at sea. It was phenomenal, both in its violence and its timing. There had been one a little more than a week earlier. Those storms never happen within two months of each other—or they never have in the past. And there were characteristics about that particular storm which didn't square with the usual electric disturbances in the area. Botticelli says that *elementa* rebelled and attacked Saturnino. I can't say I think he's a liar."

He stopped, to draw very deeply on his cigarette.

McCall and the others waited.

"And two or three phenomena were discovered afterwards just inland from the point of the storm. In a small valley three miles north-west of Estafillo some peasants found that the earth had caved in, and that a small pool of boiling mud had appeared. It caused a lot of alarm. Nothing of the kind has ever been seen there before. Two or three other mud pools were discovered, as well as several craters in the rocky mountain-side which the locals said hadn't been there before. But that's all. Nature cutting up rough!"

McCall said: "Anywhere else?"

"Only the mild dose at Brett Hall, and compared with this it was very mild." Palfrey stood up. "We've got our back-room boys on it, we've got every agent working on it, and we haven't a hope—unless Forrester's still alive. That's what it amounts to. There's one thing that makes me hope. He said we had to dig deep, to get into The House of the Angels from beneath. As soon as we can, we'll try. If they had some super air-raid shelter——"

He didn't finish, but went towards the window, and looked out. It was wide open, now. All the mist had gone, and in the past ten minutes the sun had burst through the slight haze which was all that was left of the fog. It was pleasantly warm. Out in the street, everything seemed normal, people were hurrying or dawdling, traffic was going at its usual hell-for-leather pace, horns were blasting their way, whistles were shrilling. "Back to normal," he went on, without looking round. "For a while, anyhow."

McCall said slowly, heavily: "We'll take all the precautions we can, and try to get beneath the house. If—if any of Botticelli's followers get into trouble and he does this——"

He caught his breath.

"Hell to think that he can," Palfrey said, with a bitter smile.

The telephone bell rang.

Bruton got up.

"I'll get it," he said.

Palfrey went on, as if there had been no interruption.

"If Botticelli sees himself as a supreme being, if this is an effort to establish a world religion, if——"

He broke off.

McCall said: "How strong are they? How many? Can they let loose these storms anywhere else?"

Bruton, standing at the telephone as if he were made of wood, suddenly moved. Palfrey saw a glint in his eyes, as he said quietly:

"Okay, we'll be right down." He put the receiver back. "The police want us over at The House of the Angels, Sap," he said. "More questioning."

McCall seemed not to notice Bruton's air of subdued excitement. He was alert again, depression gone. Palfrey made no comment, murmured excuses to McCall and left him standing by the window.

In the passage Bruton burst out: "They've found one of the girls alive, Sap. Could be McCall's daughter. If she's alive, then Forrester might be."

17

RIVERSIDE DRIVE was transformed.

Several bull-dozers were busy, clearing up the wreckage of some houses and gardens. An army of troops and civilians was at the sea-wall, moving with regulated frenzy to get it restored. Men were working like ants about all of the damaged buildings. Parts of the road surface had been repaired, and one-way traffic was allowed along the whole of the Drive, even outside The House of the Angels. Here, and at several other places, police were keeping the traffic moving. The rest of the drive, the gardens and the adjoining thoroughfares was a dense mass of people, all come to stare.

Bruton slowed down in his car, a green Pontiac, about two hundred yards from The House of the Angels.

"I can park here," he said. "You ever realise what a lot of rubbernecks we have in the States?" His voice was still jubilant; Bruton was the most mercurial man Palfrey knew, and perhaps the toughest.

"Knowing you, how could I miss it?" Palfrey asked dryly.

He got out. They spoke to a sergeant of police, who immediately started to bellow at the crowd, and so cleared a way. Other police helped. Palfrey didn't look right or left into the excited faces of the people. But he sensed the excitement; much more than simple curiosity had brought the thousands here.

There was little fear; few people even looked nervous. Those who had suffered were no longer here, but being cared for, helped, comforted; and now these others, who had been fear-stricken during the morning's fury, were agog to see the damage, to talk, to guess and add to rumour.

"Pop," a boy called, almost under Palfrey's nose, "you think it was an atomic bomb?"

"Now you heard the radio say it wasn't, son."

"Aw, who'd believe *that* crap?" the boy asked disgustedly. "Pop, whaddaya think it was?"

"I don't know, son."

"Well, someone ought to know."

A fencing had been erected round the grounds of The House of the Angels, and police stood on guard outside the three entrances, and others patrolled the fence. In the grounds two bull-dozers were pushing and hoisting nosily. No steam was rising from the mud-filled crater, and the mud itself appeared to have congealed. A big hut had been erected in a corner, and Palfrey saw two men going into it, pale-faced, earnest; and one of them was Robare, probably the world's greatest nuclear-fission expert.

An ambulance stood near the hut.

A fireman, wearing a steel helmet, was climbing out of a small hole in the ground.

Two or three officials checked Palfrey and Bruton, then called across to the man in the steel helmet.

"Hi, Cap, here's Dr. Palfrey."

"That so." The Captain moved towards Palfrey, taking off his helmet and wiping his forehead. His face was beaded with sweat, his face was lined, his eyes were glassy and red-rimmed. "Glad to know you, Dr. Palfrey." They shook hands; his was sticky hot. "And Mr. Bruton, I guess," the Captain said. "I'm Captain Hartmann."

"That right, one of the girls is alive?" Bruton demanded abruptly.

"Oh, sure. She's alive. We'll have her up before long. We found a hard spot and tunnelled a hundred feet under the ground. It's so hot down there, it's like working next door to hell!" Hartmann forced a smile. "But it was hotter when we first started. Temperature of that mud's dropped by five hundred degrees in three hours, the experts tell me."

"This girl," said Palfrey, "is she hurt?"

"She's hurt all right. A doctor got into the tunnel and gave her morphia," Hartmann reported. "I guess she'll soon need more." He wiped his forehead again. "It's so hot where she is, no one can work for more than a little while without coming up. I recommended asbestos suits, but I guess that was panic measure."

"Can you be sure you'll get the girl up alive?"

Hartmann said: "No, sir, we can't guarantee that at all. She's alive now. Her legs are crushed, and so is the lower part of her body. She's oaky from the waist up. They don't come as beautiful as that very often. That Botticelli——"

"I'd like to go down and see her," Palfrey said, in a manner that was almost apologetic.

"Now, listen, doctor, it's dangerous down there. I've found a big tunnel, kind of underground passage, but it was badly damaged. The roof might fall down on us any minute. It's shored up, but there's no telling——"

Bruton said: "You're wasting your time, Captain, you may as well let us go down now as later."

Hartmann stared into Palfrey's eyes.

"Okay," he said. He looked too tired to fight it out.

. . . . .

The tunnel led down into a shaft which was wide enough for two men to walk along side by side, and deep enough for an average man to walk upright. Palfrey had to bend his head; Bruton did not need to. Hartmann had sent a lieutenant with them, and he was leading the way.

They wore goggles of fire-department issue, and asbestos gloves and steel helmets. Palfrey and Bruton carried a powerful torch; so did the lieutenant. At intervals, the walls had been shored up with heavy timbers. Here and there the roof had fallen in already, they had to climb over piles of rubble.

It was hotter than on the hottest summer day; as if the earth itself were burning.

Neither of them spoke.

Palfrey saw the obvious; that this tunnel had led from The House of the Angels. It was much deeper than ordinary cellars, and where the walls were broken, slabs of reinforced concrete showed. It might be an atomic air-raid shelter; many wealthy people had built them when the first war scare had swept across half the world.

Had Botticelli?

The tunnel sloped downwards, and then opened into a big hall. This was higher than the tunnel itself. It was almost bare, except for a few boxes and some big crates. These were all empty. Palfrey knew at once that pictures had been packed in some of them; perhaps some of the pictures which had hung on the walls of the house which no longer existed.

He could think, even now, of the beauty of those Botticelli paintings, precious beyond the world's wealth—and now part of the seething mud.

A group of men worked in one corner. An electric drill was snarling, a nerve-racking din. Two men used picks, two more had shovels, and the rubble from a part of the wall was being cleared into wheelbarrows, and taken away. Each man was dripping sweat. Most were stripped to the waist, but each wore asbestos gloves and steel helmets. Two men were carrying the body of a third, crushed and broken. As he drew nearer, Palfrey recognised the man Lennard, who had travelled so widely with McCall's daughter. Lennard, even in death, was exactly like his photograph.

The lieutenant said: "The next shift will be coming soon, doctor."

Palfrey went nearer.

The girl was lying on her back, and she was McCall's daughter. Her eyes were closed, but she looked calm, and not in pain. Only a few heavy pieces of rock were on her legs, now. There was a big bandage at her waist, and Palfrey knew that whatever else, she was not likely to walk again.

He didn't make himself go nearer.

Soon, the doctor in charge said: "Let me get closer." He edged his way towards the girl. A man grunted as he lifted a piece of stone from the girl's legs, and let it fall to one side. The doctor hid the girl's body from Palfrey's sight, but her face still showed—that lovely, angelic face, possessing a beauty which would have made men turn to stare wherever they were, whoever they were. The doctor said: "Give me more of that wool, please."

A man handed him a roll of cotton-wool and some big rolls of bandages. The doctor strapped part of Elenora's right leg; then splints were fixed and a board was slid under her, so that she could be lifted. Men brought her out, carrying her very gently.

"She's still alive," the doctor said, as if speaking to himself, "but I wouldn't like to say how long she'll stay that way."

"Doc," a man said, "you want some air."

"Sure, I know."

The doctor turned away, but as he did so an orderly exclaimed:

"Look at her!"

The doctor and Palfrey swung round. Elenora's eyes were opening.

"It's fantastic," breathed the doctor. "She ought to be——"

He stopped. Elenora's eyes opened wide; and mirrored terror. No one, seeing her, could have been untouched by it. Terror was in her eyes, her face, in the way she kept so stiff and still.

"Millions," she muttered. "Millions will die, millions. He's not—he's not——"

She broke off. The doctor was kneeling by her side, speechless. Her gaze was on Palfrey.

"Find him, stop him!" she cried. "He's the Devil come back, he'll kill millions to get his own way, he'll——"

"Where is he?" Palfrey asked desperately. "Where is he? And Forrester—*Forrester*. Where——?"

He broke off as the girl's eyes opened very wide, and she said in a strong, clear voice:

"You must kill Botticelli, that will end it all."

She stopped.

Another rescue squad took over from the party which had found Elenora, while Palfrey was still there. A lieutenant in charge went close to the rubble, listening intently with special instruments fastened to his head, earphones tight against his ears. The heat was so great that Palfrey felt the sweat running down him. It was in his eyes, too, making the pupils look very bright, and the lids greasy.

Bruton muttered: "There was another tunnel. It looks as if she was caught trying to get away."

"The rescue squad didn't find anyone else," Palfrey said.

Bruton sniffed and rubbed his nose. Palfrey went to the lieutenant, who was taking off his earphones. "Can you hear anything else, lieutenant?"

"No, sir."

"What's beyond the rubble where the girl was trapped?"

"There's three or four feet of broken concrete," the man told him, "and beyond that, I wouldn't know. The roof might fall in at any moment, I'm sure of that. No one is to go farther until we can get it shored up."

"Someone else might be alive."

"Don't you kid yourself."

Palfrey said: "You don't mind if I try, do you?" His voice was very mild.

There was a moment's pause, and then the lieutenant said: "Sure, you go and commit suicide, doctor."

Bruton said slowly: "Do you think it's necessary, Sap?" He spoke as if he knew that the question was really a waste of time. "Think it will help?"

"If Botticelli's alive, we want him in a hurry," Palfrey said.

"He might not live long if he's trapped down there." He gave the lieutenant a quick, brittle smile. "I'll take an oxygen lead and mask with me. You keep your fingers crossed."

Bruton said roughly: "I'm going first. That's the place for a small man."

"There's room for two," Palfrey answered mildly.

.   .   .   .

Was Forrester alive?
What had made McCall's daughter change?
Was Botticelli down here?
Was Forrester alive?

.   .   .   .   .

They crept over the heaps of rubble, inch by inch. Their breathing was soft but laboured; now and again, Palfrey heard Bruton give a stifled sneeze—a scared sneeze, as if he were fearful that even that slight noise might bring the roof in. The "roof" was actually the earth above them, and when they glanced up they could see great cracks in it, knew that the lieutenant was quite right; and if there were another fall their chances of getting out alive wouldn't be worth anyone's money.

Now and again, a small stone fell from the roof or from the walls at the side.

There were indications that there had been concrete along here, too, but not so thick and not reinforced, like that farther along. The beams of their torches shone on the odd shapes of the broken concrete and the fallen rock; created shadows; fell glistening on water which was dripping slowly from the roof; or on great bricks which hung down, as if inviting them to come faster, recklessly, and so to rip their heads open against it.

The worst fear was of what might happen behind them. They could only see ahead. Their movements might have started a tremor in the earth which would cause a fall which would close up the tunnel, and kill all hope of their escape.

Palfrey was slightly in front now.

Sometimes, if he crouched low, he could walk. Sometimes he was forced to move on his knees. As often, he was full length on his stomach, crawling.

Bruton stifled another sneeze, then swore under his breath.

There was one relief; it was not so hot. They were sweating as much with the effort as with the heat itself. The worst of the heat had been at the mouth of this tunnel, fifty feet behind them now and, Palfrey was sure, àt least ten feet higher. Twice they had clambered over rubble which had been at a lower level than where they had started; as if once there had been steps here.

They heard only the sound of their own movements.

Each moment had its own tension, its own alarm. Palfrey tried not to think of what might happen behind him but the thoughts forced their way in. So did thoughts of Drusilla, his wife, staying quietly on the Riviera with their daughter Marion; and of Alexander the Second, at his school in the south of England. Palfrey knew that he was very conscious of the nearness of death.

Drusilla's picture was very vivid.

So was the picture of Elenora, lying there, her lovely young body crushed, lovely face not even bruised.

He felt a tug at his left hand.

"Stop, Corny," he whispered.

Bruton was only a foot away from him, a little to his left. He stopped. Palfrey turned the beam of his torch behind him.

"What is it?" Bruton whispered.

"Oxygen line," Palfrey said. "I'll have to let it go."

Bruton didn't speak.

Palfrey had been holding the line; and the mask was fastened to his waist. The mask by itself would be no help at all. He unfastened this, let it and the line fall, and then he said quietly:

"Okay."

Their main hope of rescue had gone now; before, they could have got some oxygen through; now there was no hope of being rescued if the roof caved in.

Neither spoke as they went on. The beam shone on those strange shapes again, casting weird shadows. Water dropped, *plop-plop-plop*, making the only sound.

"It's still a tunnel," Bruton said, keeping his voice so low that Palfrey could hardly hear him.

"Eh?"

"It's a tunnel. It *was* a tunnel."

"Oh, yes. Someone has been along here before. They didn't expect to have an earthquake."

Bruton grunted.

This had just been a tunnel dug in the earth, which had been shored up in places—but only with the purpose of stopping it from collapsing, not to give it strength. The inescapable fact that it was man made was the magnetic hope which drew Palfrey on. Others had made this tunnel; so others had used it.

Suddenly, they came upon a narrow stretch where there was no rubble. The walls and roof seemed to be of solid rock, not fallen earth. Just ahead were half a dozen steps, hewn out of the rock—and the tunnel itself stretched a long way on. They shone their torches along it, and the light was swallowed up in the darkness.

Bruton said: "Well, we ought to be way under Lake Michigan!"

Palfrey said: "Yes, probably. I wish I knew how far on this goes." He pushed back his steel helmet, and scratched his forehead. He was filmed with sweat, but felt almost chilly; and the explanation of that came to him suddenly.

"Feel that?" he exclaimed.

"What's that I'm supposed to feel?"

"A wind," Palfrey said. "Keep still!"

They stood tensely, Palfrey with his head bowed beneath the low roof, Bruton with his head erect. They heard that dull *plop-plop-plop* of the water, but nothing else. That didn't matter. They could feel the breeze, no more than a current of air stealing its way towards them, caressing their hot faces and chilling them.

"If you ask me," Bruton said, trying to repress his excitement, "that's air-conditioning. Come on!"

He moved forward.

Before he had taken two steps, the ground shook beneath their feet. They stared at each other, touched with a horror which had been forgotten in hope but came back now with redoubled force.

Next came a rumbling roar behind them; a gust of wind whined out of the rubble-filled tunnel, rushed past them and went howling into the unknown.

There was no way back.

18

"THAT'S it," Bruton said. "That's everything."

The rumbling and the trembling had stopped, and the wind had fallen, except for that soft, caressing stream of air. For some seconds they had kept quite still, thinking not only of the tunnel but of the life that they had left behind them.

Palfrey could hear a cry——

It was an imagined cry; the cry that Drusilla his wife would utter if she knew where he was. It was as if she had some premonition, had seen that tumbling earth, and screamed, then buried her face in her hands to try to shut out the horror.

And Palfrey could imagine that scream now.

Bruton said roughly: "Do you want to stay here all day?"

Palfrey made himself relax, thrust the torch in front of him and walked on. There was room for them to walk side by side. He still had to keep his head bent. The sounds of their footsteps were clearly audible, and the echo of the sound seemed to follow them and whisper about their ears. So did the echo of the rumbling, which seemed as if it would never stop.

Then they came to a blank wall of rock which blocked the tunnel.

They could not go on; they could not go back.

. . . . .

The light from their torches converged on the wall of earth in front of them. It filled the tunnel from wall to wall and from floor to ceiling, and there was nothing to suggest that it had ever been dug out, or that the tunnel had ever gone farther than this. The rocky earth was roughly hewn, as it would have been by men carrying hand-drills or pick-axes. Here and there quartz glittered beneath the powerful light, and in two places water seemed to trickle, shimmering black, out of the rock to the earth below; but the earth swallowed it up, and there was no pool.

Bruton said: "So it's the finish," in a voice so dry that it seemed to come from a painful throat.

"Yes," Palfrey said, distantly. "Dead-end. Full stop.

Period." A strangled laugh forced its way from his lips. "Not what we prayed for. I wonder how long——?"

He stopped.

"We just made a foolish mistake," Bruton said, his voice now well controlled but filled with bitterness. "We know everything, don't we? We've spent a lifetime dealing with emergencies, and what little mistake did we make this time?"

"Well, what?"

"No iron rations," Bruton said, and waved his left arm about. "With rations we could have died in comfort. Now we'll have it the hard way."

Palfrey was pulling at a few strands of hair.

"Yes," he agreed. "Bad. But let's start thinking. Did you feel that air current coming along?"

"Forget it."

"But it was there. I felt it."

"Sure, I felt it, too," Bruton said viciously. "I can tell you what it was. The roof was going to fall in, wasn't it? When a thing like that happens, the whole of the earth around starts to fall away from its bed. That creates pressures which draw the air along the tunnel. When we thought we were finding something, we were really being warned that we hadn't a chance. I don't know that I approve of it," Bruton went on, and he gave a giggle of sound.

"Of what?"

"The end coming this way for you and for me. We deserve something much more heroic. Even I can say so, this being no time for false modesty. On the other hand——"

He stopped.

He was trying desperately to put a good face on it; trying to pretend that it didn't matter. Yet he was feeling the same hopeless dread as Palfrey; the same emptiness; the same realisation that the past was the present and the future had been snatched from them. "On the other hand——" he said, and then suddenly his face twisted, and he closed his eyes as if he did not want Palfrey to see his expression.

"On the other hand," Palfrey echoed very gently, "it might be as well if we don't live to see what's going to happen up there."

Bruton said huskily: "We've worked together so often we

even think alike." He stopped, and there was complete silence except for that *plop-plop-plop-plop* which seemed to come from farther away. "Well, are we going to try to get back?"

Palfrey said: "They'll try to reach us."

He turned slowly, and shone the torchlight about the walls, as if in desperate hope that there would be a doorway which they had not seen. There was nothing. The water dripped, the quartz glittered, the tiny waterfall oozing out of the rock looked very like oil.

Was it water from the lake?

"We may as well start back," Bruton said gruffly, and actually moved forward. Then he screeched wildly, and dropped his torch. He sprang back as it struck the rocky ground. The light went out. Palfrey's torch was in his hand, but Bruton's sudden movement and Bruton's sudden gasping breath shook his nerve. He fumbled for the switch.

"*What was it?*" he demanded harshly.

"The floor—moved," Bruton said chokily. "Put that light on, for God's sake!" He was panting like an exhausted dog. "I tell you it moved!"

Palfrey's fingers were clammy as he groped for the switch. He touched but did not press on it. Light came. First there was a soft glow rising from the floor, touching the sides of the tunnel. Then it spread, and grew brighter, rising as high as the roof, spreading towards them and bathing them in its glow.

Bruton gasped: "What is it? *What is it?*"

It grew brighter still, pure white and dazzling; it shone upon their faces and then into their eyes, and out of the light came a vision of such beauty that Palfrey was held in emotion as tightly as in any vice, could hardly draw breath, was empty of thought and of feeling except a strange and compelling sense of wonder.

He heard Bruton groan.

He saw Bruton pitch forward in a dead faint, but did nothing to save him. He could only stare into the radiance of the woman who was bathed in light. He knew her; it was like looking upon the face of one once beloved but gone to distant places, not forgotten but seldom thought of.

This was Isabella Melado.

She seemed to float out of the light, but that was a trick of the imagination. She was moving, yes; walking up steps into the tunnel, which was now filled with that glowing light.

Palfrey felt a strange contentment creep upon him.

"Help your friend up," commanded Isabella, "and then please follow me."

.   .   .   .   .

Cornelius Bruton was not a big man, but most of him was bone and muscle, and he weighed over eleven stone. Palfrey helped him to his feet, then hoisted him to his shoulders; and instead of feeling the weight too much, Bruton seemed easy to carry, and feather light.

Isabella, having commanded, turned away. The light shone against her dark hair, and Palfrey saw through it, wispily. Her silhouette was superb. Following her, he saw that a part of the floor had risen and was behind her; a trapdoor, rising upwards. That was what Bruton had seen. Now Isabella went downwards, gradually disappearing, and Palfrey stepped through the hole in the floor and followed without thinking of anything else.

These steps were hewn in the rock.

Soon, he was in a passage, lighted well, but not with the glowing radiance of the light in the tunnel. Palfrey thought he knew the simple explanation; then light had spread through darkness; now he was used to it.

Isabella walked with floating ease, reached a doorway, opened it and stood aside for him to pass.

The first thing he saw was the portrait of a woman who had lived five centuries ago, yet might have been painted from Isabella Melado herself.

It had been moved to safety; there was no mark or blemish on it. On the wall by its side were other pictures, two of them from Botticelli's study, others which Palfrey had not seen before. He did not speak of these, but stared at them; then Isobella led the way into another room, a lovely, comfortable room, where several women were sitting in easy-chairs—women whose photographs he seemed to have seen, all with faces which made them qualify as Botticelli angels.

One was Paula.

He thought of Elenora . . .

Isabella led him into another, smaller room, where there

were two couches, a divan and several easy-chairs. Almost with a sense of surprise he realised that he was still carrying Bruton. He put the American down in one of the easy-chairs and, mechanically, raised his legs and rested them on a pouf. Bruton's thick-soled brown shoes were covered with clayey mud from the tunnel, there were mud-stains on his trousers and one on the back of his hand. A scratch on the tip of his nose bled slightly.

Palfrey took out a handkerchief and dabbed the scratch.

He felt that he did not want to look at Isabella, yet at last he was compelled to turn and peer into her eyes. Her expression was grave, but those honey-coloured eyes held a smile which reassured him. Could *she* be evil?

Had Botticelli fooled her?

Did she know that Elenora had died calling him the Devil?

"You are very tired," she said. "I think you should rest. Your friend will be well, very soon. Sit down and rest, please. I will have some sandwiches sent to you."

Palfrey said: "You're very kind." Crazy. It was all he could say, yet. He had to be careful, to watch all he said and did, had to find if Forrester were alive, had to find Botticelli.

He had to *kill* Botticelli, if Elenora had been right.

Isabella turned and disappeared.

Palfrey stood looking at the door through which she had gone, standing there for a long time. Then he turned to Bruton. The American was leaning back, grey head on a dark-brown cushion, and his eyes with their short, black eyelashes were twitching. He turned his head from side to side, and grunted. His face was lined and streaked with the yellow mud, but apart from the scratch on his nose there was nothing to show for his fall.

"All right, Corny," Palfrey said. "We're quite safe."

Bruton stopped moving his head, and for a moment he lay absolutely still. Then he opened his eyes sharply, and their piercing glance fell upon Palfrey; their dark blue seemed almost black.

"What's this?"

"Sanctuary," Palfrey said.

"Where are we?"

"There was another tunnel beneath ours," Palfrey explained. "It's all right."

Bruton sat up and blinked, then looked about him. Several pictures of Botticelli angels were on the walls, and he stared at each, then got up and walked to one of them, stood two feet away and examined it with his head on one side. He looked a wiry, truculent figure as he stood there; a Captain Kettle without a beard.

He turned swiftly.

"Did I see Isabella, or was it a vision?"

"You saw her."

"And I remember," Bruton said, smiling with a sudden fierce gaiety. "The light came up, and I was so scared I couldn't keep my knees from shaking. Then I caught a glimpse of her face, and I thought I'd crossed the line and seen the angels in heaven." He broke off and began to smile. "Crazy, wasn't I?"

"Why more than usual?"

"To be scared."

"Aren't we always?" Palfrey asked. "And can we help it?"

"I don't know," Bruton answered, hesitantly, wonderingly. "I don't feel so scared now. I feel *good*. I feel——" He laughed again and rubbed his hands together. "I feel *fine*. In fact, I don't remember feeling like this since Robina said she would marry me!" Robina, Bruton's wife, was Drusilla Palfrey's sister. "You know," Bruton went on in a voice which echoed a wondering bewilderment, "when I was down in that tunnel and heard the roof falling in, all I could think about was Robina. I felt as if she could hear everything, and knew what was happening. That's what made me feel so bad, I suppose. Now"—he put his head on one side, and tried to scowl, but could achieve no more than a mock frown—"do you feel as if nothing could go wrong in the whole, wide world?"

"I know what you mean."

"Why, sure you do," cried Bruton. "When you came back to the Stevens the other night, you were so skittish that I thought you were drunk! That's just the way I feel. Life is good, life is wonderful. And yet——"

He didn't finish.

Palfrey said: "We know that a thousand people were dreadfully injured this morning, and half of them will probably die. Thousands more are wandering about as if they'll never forget the horror of it. There was Elenora too. She talked of millions dying, and yet——"

"We can think about now without losing a moment's sleep," Bruton said gruffly. "I ought to feel like hell. Instead"—he took out a cigarette, put one to his lips, lit it and drew slowly—"I feel—peaceful." He was puzzled, trying to understand why this was happening, what had happened to cause the transformation.

The door opened.

Paula wheeled in a trolley. There was a slice of melon, with sifters of ginger and sugar by it; sandwiches; coffee in a percolator, which bubbled gently beneath a tiny spirit stove.

"I hope this will be all you need," she said.

"Fine," said Bruton abruptly. "Wonderful!" He looked at Paula with his head on one side, smiling that unbelievably contented smile. "How are you, honey?"

She laughed.

"Well, I'm fine," she said. "Aren't you?"

"I'm trying to guess why I feel that way."

"I shouldn't worry about it," Paula said. "We all feel fine here. Why shouldn't we?"

She didn't give them a chance to ask more questions, but turned and went out. The door closed softly behind her. Bruton drew on his cigarette, then stubbed it out, while letting the smoke curl from a corner of his lips. He shook his head, slowly, and then was caught out by a sudden yawn.

Palfrey said sharply: "Don't go to sleep!"

Bruton stared. "But Sap . . ."

"We've got to keep awake," Palfrey said. "The last time I went to sleep with these women about, I——"

"You're not yourself." Bruton grinned again. "Tired out —exertion, I suppose. Feel good. Nice girl, Isabella."

"Damn you, keep awake! Elenora——"

"Elenora," echoed Bruton. "Know what you mean, but— who knows she was right? She may have said he was the Devil, but take it from me, Isabella's a little angel. Isn't she?"

He grinned.

Palfrey turned away abruptly.

He had a feeling that he was watched, but couldn't see a window or any place where man or woman could be standing; yet the room seemed full of eyes. Staring, watching, appraising, accusing.

He yawned.

He began to move about the room so as to keep himself awake, but they'd drugged him; somehow they'd drugged him. Bruton was already dozing.

"Corny, wake up!"

Bruton's eyes were closed.

Palfrey went unsteadily towards a chair, dropped into it and yawned. He felt a bewildering mixture of fear and of contentment; it was as if all his fears had been proved groundless, and he need not worry; yet beneath it all was an awful fear—the kind of dread a man might feel if he were damned to the knowledge that a million people would die unless he could think of the right thing to do.

Elenora——

Isabella——

He went to sleep.

. . . . .

Isabella Melado stepped in the room, and Forrester followed her. They stood looking down on the sleeping men. The woman was smiling, faintly, and when she glanced at Forrester her eyes were very calm.

"I like your friend Palfrey," she said.

"He's all right," Forrester muttered.

"In some ways, quite handsome," she said. "Such fine, silky hair. I think he will be a very good worker, when he is with us. So clever, as you say, and with a genius for organising, that is what we need so badly here. There is too much for one man to do."

Forrester said abruptly: "I don't think you'll ever get Palfrey on Botticelli's side."

She looked surprised.

"But, Jim, why not?" When he didn't answer, she went on: "*You* became converted, didn't you?"

"I see it your way and Botticelli's way now," Forrester admitted. "I had some help, though. I'm in love with you, and you're so sure."

"Of course I am sure," said Isabella. "I have known him

for so long now, and everything has happened as he said it would. There will be trouble in the beginning, but when everything is over, a greater peace than the world has known, with only one man——"

She broke off.

Forrester said: "I don't think Palfrey will work for Botticelli. I'm positive Bruton won't."

Isabella went to him, took his hands, raised them until they were on a level with her breast, and then said very quietly:

"Jim, you must help to make them. We can do much, as you know, the drug conditions them, but in their periods of full consciousness, when the doubts rise up, you must be there to convince them that Botticelli is a Supreme Being, is——" She paused, and the room was deathly quiet. Then: "They will serve him soon, or they will die," Isabella said. "There is no room here for prisoners. Make them serve him, Jim."

Forrester didn't speak.

Neither Palfrey nor Bruton stirred.

"If Palfrey can be made to serve, he can save so much trouble," Isabella said. "Make him understand that Botticelli is not bad, but good."

Forrester said almost wearily: "I keep forgetting."

He turned away, and she watched him go.

He wondered what she was thinking.

He wondered if there were now any chance at all of getting out of here.

He went to a small room, which was empty then, and lit a cigarette. He was conscious, like Palfrey, of being watched. He was aware, as Palfrey had been, of a curious contradiction, a conflict of emotions: fear and contentment. At moments when Isabella was with him he felt sure that she was right, that Botticelli was a man to venerate.

At others——

He shivered, suddenly. He remembered the warning to get beneath The House of the Angels. He remembered Elenora coming up to him and saying in a frightened whisper:

"He is going to destroy the city. The only way to stop him is to kill him."

"You're crazy!" Forrester had said.

"I tell you he is going to destroy Chicago," Elenora had insisted. "I've heard his plans, he's concentrating the *elementa* here, *all* of them. He's the only man who can, the only man, without him they're just part of the elements, with him they're evil. We must kill Botticelli."

She had stopped, because one of the angels had come near.

Now, Forrester knew that she had been condemned to death, and not brought here with the rest of them. He was not sure why.

He did not know whether he was here because Isabella had interceded for him or because Botticelli believed he could be useful.

Forrester kept thinking of Elenora.

Kill Botticelli, she'd said, and the rest would resolve itself. *Kill Botticelli.*

Perhaps that was the one thing left to do.

19

SAMUEL McCALL, who had taken over a suite at the Stevens now that he knew that his own house would be unusable for some weeks, looked up from the notes he was writing when the telephone bell rang. A Z 5 man named Cinzane, small, dark-haired, an Italian who had been a naturalised American for the past thirty years, moved with almost cat-like speed and lifted the receiver.

"Yes," he said.

"Yes, that's right, Mr. McCall's right here." He put the receiver down. "That's London," he said.

McCall picked up his telephone.

He looked very tired, and his eyes, usually so bright and fine, were sunken and bloodshot. His forehead was lined with deep grooves. His jaw was set, and new lines ran from the corners of his mouth down to his chin. By his looks, he had aged twenty years in the course of that day, but his voice was firm.

There was muttering on the line, followed by a clear English voice.

"Mr. McCall?"

"Speaking. Is that Kennedy, of Z 5?"

"Yes, sir," Kennedy said briskly. Apart from a few squeaky noises, atmospherics of some kind, he might have been speaking from the next room. "Is there any news?"

"No," said McCall.

"None at all?" Kennedy's brisk voice took on another tone; the depth of anxiety sounded in it.

"Palfrey and Bruton started to crawl through that tunnel, and the roof fell in," said McCall. "The tunnel is known to be at least a hundred yards long. Palfrey took a measure along with him, and it's been drawn back. It showed one hundred and three yards. Allowing for it going up and down over rubble, say one hundred. Fifty yards are blocked. There is little space to work in, and the danger is that if mechanical tools are used, the rest of the roof will cave in. If we were looking for anyone else, I would have had the rescue work stopped by now—and I think higher authorities will stop it soon, whatever I say."

Kennedy said very slowly: "I know you'll do everything you can. Do you think——?"

He broke off.

"If you were going to ask me if I think there is any chance at all, the answer is no," said McCall quietly. "I shouldn't think anyone will stay alive in that tunnel for very long. They've no extra supply of oxygen, and no one made sure that they took food and water along. I'm afraid we have to give up all hope."

Kennedy said stonily: "Very well, sir. Is there anything else?"

"Nothing that's good," said McCall. "You know that your man Forrester is probably dead. The one girl who was rescued alive is also dead. They had no time to operate." There was a long pause, while McCall's lips worked; but he steeled himself to go on: "Botticelli is missing or dead, with Isabella Melado and all the other girls at the house. You've had the latest details about the explosions, I suppose."

"Oh, yes, sir. And the early physicist's reports. Very slight traces of radio-activity, but it's almost certain that this explosion wasn't atomic. And the similarity between this storm and others which have been reported in various places is most marked. I'm sending the fullest report by air courier tonight, with copies for UNO—everyone who should have one, in fact. But I don't know what we shall do without Palfrey. I think he's the exception."

"To what?"

"The rule that no one is indispensable," Kennedy said. "I knew only one man who might be able to take up where Palfrey left off."

"Who was that?"

"The Russian, Andromovitch," Kennedy told him. "He disappeared in Spain, just after one of the storms, but we had a message yesterday, saying he is free. If he shows up . . ." Kennedy paused; when he spoke his voice was sharper and more official. "I'll do everything I can, sir, whether he does or not, and no doubt an appointment will be made soon to replace Palfrey. Have you any special instructions?"

"You mean requests," McCall corrected quietly. "No, I don't think so. We've nothing at all to work on. Nothing at all. There's just one thing——"

"Yes, sir?"

"I want to write to Mrs. Palfrey and to Mrs. Bruton," McCall said, very heavily. "I don't know whether it will help, but I would like to try."

Kennedy burst out: "I wish to God you could tell them! I don't think I can face it, I——"

He broke off.

Something in the way he caught his breath made McCall wait with increasing tension. He heard the atmospherics, like muttering voices a long way off.

The Italian came closer, as if he wanted to know what had changed the expression on McCall's face. The room was very quiet. The blaring of horns and the chug-chug of engines outside came clearly into the room. People walked along the streets, heels tapping sharply. To those who had not suffered, the morning's "storm" had been a sensation, that was all. A newsboy's voice could just be heard; he would be calling out a later sensation still—about Palfrey and Bruton. Already the destruction of Botticelli's house, the lightning which had blinded, the explosion which had wrecked so many buildings and killed so many people were

"old" news items. The radio, the television and the newspapers were no longer preoccupied with what had happened
—but with what had caused it. And now the headlines, some
two inches high, told of the disappearance of Palfrey and
Bruton, giving a garbled story of Z 5 which prepared the
readers for new sensations.

All this, and more.

Then McCall heard Kennedy's voice again—an excited
Kennedy, who had lost the emptiness which had sounded in
his voice before he had stopped.

"Are you there, sir?"

"Yes, Kennedy, what is it?"

"You remember that I was talking about the Russian
Andromovitch," Kennedy said, and he could not keep the
excitement out of his voice. "He has just telephoned. He's
safe, he thinks he can help to find out what this is all about,
and he's fit and ready to take over."

McCall said slowly: "I guess I understand, Kennedy."

"I'd like him to see you as soon as possible," Kennedy
went on. "You'll stay in Chicago for a few days, won't
you?"

"I think so, yes," McCall said. "And I'd like to meet this
Russian." He didn't smile. "Good-bye for now, then."

"Good-bye, sir, and thank you for the call."

McCall rang off.

"Thank you for the call." That ingrained courtesy was
something you would never eradicate from Englishmen like
Kennedy. It was hard to explain, but it was there—a kind
of formal courtesy which could be misleading. Palfrey had it.
Palfrey *had* had it.

And Kennedy could be excited, so soon, about a man who
had the credentials and the qualifications to take Palfrey's
place.

A Russian, too.

There was work to do.

PART THREE

STEFAN ANDROMOVITCH

20

STEFAN ANDROMOVITCH was so tall, broad and massive that people stared at him wherever he went. It had once been said that Palfrey could not have selected a less suitable man for much of the hush-hush work of Z 5, because whatever else he could do, Andromovitch could never conceal himself. An average man might have a chance of escaping notice; not the Russian.

"But remember," Palfrey had always replied to this criticism, "in every other way he's worth two of you. Or possibly ten!" And Palfrey had given that almost whimsical smile which annoyed so many people who did not know him well, and confirmed that Stefan Andromovitch was Number 2 of the group.

The Russian landed at O'Hara Field three days after McCall had talked to Kennedy on the telephone, and the stewardess on the aircraft, pretty as air stewardesses nearly always were, looked at him with the kind of affectionate smile which was reserved for very few passengers.

"I hope you have a wonderful visit, sir."

"Thank you," Andromovitch said, in his deep, precise voice. "You have given it a wonderful start."

She would remember that for a long time . . .

She would remember the Russian's fine features, too, and the expression in his eyes which reminded her, vaguely, of the eyes of some of the best pilots in B.O.A.C. She remembered several other men who had had the same kind of effect on her. A passenger named Palfrey, who had crossed the Atlantic several times; Sam McCall, the envoy-extraordinary who was always flying to and from Washington; just a few others, including the ageing Bishop of Llansed . . .

No one met Andromovitch at the airport.

Two Z 5 agents, in separate cars, followed him from the airport. He was in a big Ford taxi, and the driver was still leaning back—yet looking ahead, expertly making jokes about his biggest passenger and roaring with laughter.

"You want to know something?" he said, "I once had a grizzly bear as a passenger. Yes, sir, a real grizzly from Oregon. And I'll tell you something else, he wasn't so big as you. No, sir! You got plenty of room for your head?"

"Nearly enough room," Andromovitch answered mildly.

They reached the centre of the city, and soon he was entering the Stevens Hotel. At least thirty people stood and watched him, and a woman said:

"He sure is the tallest man I've ever seen."

Porters, bell-boys, reception clerks, guests, all looked startled when they first saw Andromovitch; but when he gave that grave smile, all found themselves smiling back. He had that effect more than anyone in Cinzane's experience.

Cinzane was standing by the elevators, watching as every head turned and diminutive bell-boys gaped. One little Negro shoe-black stared open mouthed, and was still staring when the elevator doors closed on the Russian.

The attendant and five other passengers, the tallest over six feet and almost a head shorter, did not utter a word. Andromovitch smiled at them as he went out, and the attendant said unsteadily:

"Good—good day, sir."

Andromovitch went along to the room which had been reserved for him. It was on the same floor as Bruton's and Palfrey's, but in a different corridor; Room 791. He went in, and closed the door. He waited for a moment, then looked into the two rooms and the bathroom; they were empty. He put his hand-case down at the foot of the bed; he had brought little luggage. He waited by the telephone, and it rang suddenly.

"Hallo."

"Hi, Stefan," Cinzane said. "You have a good journey?"

"Very good, thank you."

"That's fine. No one followed you from the airport. It wouldn't be true to say that no one took any interest in you," Cinzane added, with laughter in his voice. "Mr. McCall's here right now. He'll come along and see you."

"I'm looking forward to meeting him," Andromovitch said, as if he meant it.

He sat down on a chair which would have been too large for most men; it was just big enough for him. He waited fully five minutes, quite impassively. He heard nothing, and McCall didn't arrive.

He stood up.

He didn't frown, but he looked more alert than most of the people who had seen him remembered. He went towards the door, reaching it in three long strides. He hesitated for a moment, and then slowly opened the door.

Just along the passage was a little writhing patch of mist. Ahead of it, was Samuel McCall.

.   .   .   .   .

A few minutes earlier, McCall had said: "No, I don't want escorting round the corner, thank you." But he had waited for Cinzane to put some papers away. He was used to being followed, for Palfrey had not allowed him to go anywhere without an escort.

Cinzane went out, and McCall followed. The passage was empty. Their footsteps made no sound on the carpeted floor. They reached the corner, Cinzane a foot or two ahead of McCall.

The Z 5 agent turned the corner——

McCall heard a sudden, startled cry, then a groaning sound. And he saw writhing mist. All his instinct was to turn and run, but he could not. He forced himself to go on. He saw Cinzane lying on the floor, with a swollen neck—and his head lay at a strange angle.

He didn't move.

The mist was swirling just in front of McCall, as if it had come out of the floor. It seemed to have shape. His blood seemed to freeze. It was not only the sight of the mist, and of the writhing shape which seemed to be in its midst; there was his own sense of utter helplessness, the fact that he could not move right or left, backward or forward.

The creature might be winding itself up to launch an attack. Tentacles of mist seemed to be shooting out, writhing, drawing nearer.

Then a door opened.

McCall knew that, but he did not look up. There was just

the mist and the threat, and the sight of Cinzane's broken neck. He made a muttering sound, deep in his throat, and pressed back tightly against the wall, feeling as if his last moment had come.

Then he saw the giant moving forward, powerful hands outstretched, as if to carry the fight.

He met the *elementa*.

There was a moment of frightening violence, a screaming and groaning and writhing, the Russian was almost covered in mist——

A vivid flash came. McCall was thrust savagely against the wall, banged his head, felt consciousness slipping away from him; he slid down slowly.

He did not see Andromovitch standing there, taking in great gulps of air, with sweat pouring down his face.

It was an age before the Russian moved. Then, slowly, deliberately, he picked McCall up and carried him into the room.

.   .   .   .   .

The Russian watched McCall stirring in his chair. He saw the distress on the old man's pale, lined face. He knew something of the ordeal which McCall had undergone already, knew also the effect it had had on him. Now, the American looked a very old man, like one who had not much longer to live.

Outside, men were roping off a part of the passage which had been damaged, hotel residents were not allowed to go along here. Men from the Research Laboratories were already on the way to inspect the damage. There was no sign of the mist, but there was a pale-red stain on the wall and the floor and mixed with the rubble of the wall and floor.

McCall opened his eyes.

Andromovitch was sitting in the easy-chair, with a pen in his hand and some papers in front of him. He glanced up and smiled.

McCall said unbelievingly: "You—you're *alive?*" He looked terror-stricken.

"I am alive," agreed Andromovitch dryly. He looked much better, although still bruised. "I have been studying the way they fight, Senator—they always go for the throat. I have very great strength, and——"

He shrugged.

McCall gulped: "I—didn't believe I'd ever live to see a thing like it. Did you kill——?"

"Yes, it's dead."

McCall blurted out: "Can you do it again?" There was tension in every curve of his body; tension very close to fear.

"I think so," Andromovitch said slowly. "I cannot guarantee to do that very often, but I have a measure of protection. If there were an attack in numbers I'd be as helpless as you. But for individual attacks—yes, I can protect myself and perhaps my friends."

"How did you learn how to do it?"

"I studied the way they worked in Spain. They captured me, and tried to convert me." The Russian's smile was a delight. "I don't think I was a very good subject, but one thing I did learn."

"What?" McCall asked jerkily.

"They are controlled by Botticelli," the Russian told him. "He has trained hundreds, perhaps thousands of men and women to control the *elementa*, and these converts, as well as the *elementa*, worship him. To the *elementa* he is simply their creator; their God."

The giant paused, and McCall looked frightened; as frightened as he had been by the creature in the passage.

"The one way to break the power of the *elementa* is to kill Botticelli," the Russian went on. "The only way."

"Do you know where he is?"

"No."

McCall said roughly: "Palfrey's gone, Bruton, others——"

"I know they've gone," Andromovitch said. "I know Forrester's gone, too. If he's alive, the others have a chance."

"What makes you sure?"

Andromovitch said: "Anyone who's been attacked once is less susceptible to another attack. That's why I can defend myself. Why Forrester can, too. I've touched *elementa* and wounded them. I've been smeared with their blood, and been enveloped by mist. Anyone smeared with the blood is enveloped, that's how Botticelli stages the disappearing tricks. That's why it's going to be almost impossible to find. We're looking for *cloud*."

.   .   .   .

The Russian turned away, reached the window, opened it
and looked down into Clarke Street. The roar of the traffic
came in, lights outside flashed on and off, even in the street
there was light enough to read by. Since he had said "we're
looking for cloud" the Russian hadn't spoken.

"Listen to me," McCall said hoarsely. "Out there, three
days ago, hundreds of people were killed, thousands were
blinded, more thousands shocked. The hospitals are full of
victims. The doctors' surgeries are full. Some people will
never recover from what happened. This can happen over
and over again if we don't find Botticelli, and we can't stop
it."

"We're looking for him wherever he's been and wherever
he has known agents," Andromovitch said. "He has
hundreds of agents we don't even suspect, in high places as
well as among the masses. He has almost deified himself.
His followers will make any sacrifice for him, hundreds of
them have been killed in experiments with *elementa*. The
simple truth is, Mr. McCall, no one has any idea where he is,
and no one is likely to betray him."

McCall said abruptly: "So the only hope is Palfrey,
Bruton and—this man Forrester."

"That's right," said the Russian. "The only hope."

.   .   .   .   .

Palfrey watched Forrester.

He had been awake for half an hour. Isabella had been
in to speak to him, followed by Mathilde; now Forrester was
here. He hadn't said much. Bruton was still asleep, but
stirring. Palfrey was conscious of his own conflict between
fear and contentment again, and fought against the lethargy
which contentment would bring.

He didn't know whether Forrester knew what he was
doing, how he was fighting. Forrester seemed aloof, indifferent, impersonal. Palfrey kept thinking of the drugs
which had been pumped into him, and how he had screamed
out. He knew the effect of the drug on himself, how he was
half-persuaded to accept these things as good.

How was Forrester affected, now?

Had it changed him?

Forrester was either different or afraid that he was being
watched. Certainly he had shown no eagerness to talk to

Palfrey, hadn't tried to pass on any message either by look or word. He was sitting in a large armchair, one leg draped over the other, cigarette drooping from his lips. Everything he said seemed forced.

"It will not be long before Botticelli will want to talk to you," he said. "I don't know how much you've learned about him."

"Precious little," Palfrey said.

"That isn't surprising, I suppose. Know how many converts he has?"

"Tens of thousands?"

"Millions," Forrester said.

Palfrey said sharply: "I don't believe it."

Forrester's grin was cynical and resigned.

"You'll come to believe it, one day. The one thing this old world's been waiting for is a new religion, didn't you know? Now we have it—Botticelli's Beauty Worship." That was almost sardonic, the first time anything like feeling had crept into his voice. "You don't know why he had these beauties here, trained to do what they can—to walk through fire, to have their arms and bodies slashed, to go into a cataleptic trance and wake up as if nothing had happened."

Palfrey said thinly: "No, I don't know."

"You ought to," Forrester said, and grinned again. "It follows on logically. Nothing if not logical, this new religion! Botticelli has always worshipped beauty. That's how he started on this. First of all he just bought beautiful things from pictures to women, and gradually it grew on him. People began to kow-tow before him, for he's quite a looker himself. Strong will-power, too. A few girls lost their heads over him. He read a lot about the old religions, then studied hypnotism and yogi. Yogi fascinated him most. He practised it. He found that there were methods of getting results more quickly—drugs could quicken the pace of the mental conditioning the Indians acquire with their monumental patience. He developed drugs which could mould the mind and make individuals susceptible to another's will. Call it a monstrous form of hypnotism, call it what you like, but it works. He can make these people do what he wants, can make them regard him as supreme being."

Forrester stopped.

Bruton was awake, now, and listening intently, his gaze fixed on Forrester.

Forrester's voice was low-pitched, his manner still cynical; it was impossible to be sure what he was feeling and thinking.

"So he's trained girls like Mathilde and Elenora and thousands of others. When they leave here they go as missionaries for Botticelli. They can walk through fire, and if seeing a girl walk through fire isn't reasonable proof that she's more than an ordinary human being, I'd like to know what is. Mostly, these girls work among people like the Spanish peasants, among the illiterate and the superstitious—they work where the results are certain to be good. You get a good following for any new religious movement, even among the upper social classes, and among the lower ones it goes so far that you can't stop it. Remember these women can put on what looks like a miracle to you and me any time they like."

He stopped again.

The door opened, and Isabella came in, with that faint smile that always seemed about to break. Palfrey felt quite sure that she had heard everything that Forrester had said and that Forrester knew she had.

"Hallo, Isabella," Forrester greeted, but he didn't get up. "I've been telling Palfrey how things stand. As instructed! He knows where we have the converts, and how absolute is Botticelli's power."

Isabella was looking at Palfrey, completely ignoring Bruton. There was a long silence before she said:

"It is only a matter of time before Botticelli's mastery is acknowledged everywhere, Dr. Palfrey. If it can be done without bloodshed, he would be much happier. But if it can't, then a word from him, and——"

She didn't finish.

"Chicago was just a fleabite," Forrester said dryly.

"The important thing to remember is his absolute control, not only of people who serve him but also of the *elementa*," Isabella went on. "They know what the rest of the world will find out."

Palfrey said chokily: "What?"

"That Botticelli is immortal," she said solemnly, "that he cannot be killed."

·　　　·　　　·　　　·　　　·

Isabella believed that.

Palfrey could not be sure whether Forrester did or not. Forrester's manner hadn't changed at all, and he had left with Isabella. The two prisoners were alone. After the first few seconds Bruton hadn't said a word; he still seemed dazed. It was very quiet, here.

Then the door opened and Forrester came in, moving swiftly, his expresson one of acute alarm, one hand raised and a finger at his lips. Palfrey felt his heart racing; this gave the answer to his silent question; *Forrester was still loyal.*

Bruton jumped up.

Forrester whispered: "You're to see Botticelli put up a show. Don't try to do anything, or you won't stand a chance. Just sit tight." He stopped speaking, and ran his hand over his damp forehead, then he spoke in a more normal voice: "I have to take you to Botticelli. You saw the fire test, Sap, didn't you?"

"Yes."

"You wait until you've seen this," Forrester said. "It'll convert you."

21

FORRESTER led the way, and girls followed the three men, none of them very close behind. Bruton stared straight ahead, as if more deeply affected than Palfrey by what had happened and by fear of what would happen next.

There was sweat on his forehead.

They went along a narrow passage, and then into a round room, like a small Roman amphitheatre. There was a raised rostrum at one spot with doors behind it, leading from some room or passages beyond. The wooden seats were placed in circular fashion round it, a dozen tiers in all. There was only a sprinkling of people; there was room for several hundred, but Palfrey doubted if fifty were present.

He sensed their tension.

He followed Forrester to the bottom of the gangway immediately opposite the rostrum. He sat down. Two girls slid along the seat and came near him; two more sat by Bruton's side.

Forrester was between the two men.

The room was shaped like the planetarium which Palfrey had seen when he had first come to Chicago. The ceiling was bowl shaped, perfectly plain but for a few painted stars; none of them seemed to represent stars in the firmament. It was a pale blue; so were the walls, so were the draperies at the rostrum.

The tension grew.

Everyone stared towards the doors behind the rostrum, with an expectancy that was almost painful. Palfrey couldn't steel himself to break the silence. He glanced at Bruton, whose lips were working, and whose forehead streamed with sweat.

Then, a girl came from a doorway. There was a long-drawn-out sigh from practically every man and woman present. Every eye was turned towards the girl, whom Palfrey had never seen before.

She spread her arms towards the people, as if bidding them to kneel. They knelt. They stared towards her, too, until she moved to one side, and waited—as if she knew that the supreme moment was near. Palfrey had a weird notion; that he could hear the thumping of fifty hearts, the beating of fifty human pulses.

Then Isabella appeared, in a white robe.

Next, Botticelli.

He was dressed in a simple gown, of powder blue, more like a Roman toga than any other form of dress. He wore a crown of some tiny blue flower. He stood quite still, as everyone except Palfrey and Bruton bowed their heads and cried as if in agony, in supplication and in prayer. Palfrey watched while human beings, most of them superbly lovely girls, prostrated themselves before Botticelli.

Even Forrester did that.

Next, the people rose, stood for a moment and sat down. Palfrey forced himself to look away from Botticelli towards Bruton. Forrester had a hand on Bruton's arm, as if he were forcing him to sit still. Bruton's expression was unbelievably savage, he looked as if he longed to kill.

Then they brought on to the rostrum a cauldron of some

boiling, seething, white-hot metal. The heat of it rose to the ceiling, scorched their faces and dried their breath. The great cauldron stood in the centre of the rostrum, while Botticelli and Isabella watched.

The girl who had first come here moved towards the molten mass.

It must be searing her hair, her eyes.

She drew nearer.

Bruton screamed: "*No, no!*" He jumped to his feet, tore himself free from Forrester's grasp and tried to jump on to the rostrum. The girls near him moved swiftly. He fought savagely, but their young strength was too great for him. They pulled him back to his seat, and then one sat on either side of him, so that he could not leap up again.

The girl on the rostrum placed her hands on that white-hot cauldron, and then climbed into it.

Bruton's scream seemed to tear Palfrey's head in two.

.   .   .   .   .

The girl rose out of the molten mass, like a fabulous image of *She*, turned, prostrated herself before Botticelli and turned away.

.   .   .   .   .

Another girl took her place.

She was as young and as lovely, clad in a diaphanous blouse and pleated skirt. She did not utter a word when she reached the rostrum, but stood quite still, looking adoringly at Botticelli. He beckoned her. She moved towards him. He touched her hand, and she bowed low and then fell upon her knees. As she knelt there, with the tension growing until Palfrey felt at screaming point, pale-grey mist began to envelope her.

She disappeared.

And into the silence, Forrester said quietly: "All of us can do that, we can vanish in mist at will."

There was only a patch of mist on the rostrum; opaque, because it hid Isabella and Botticelli.

The mist lingered for seconds which ticked slowly by. Then gradually the girl materialised, prostrated herself again and backed away. She stood some distance from Botticelli, staring fixedly at the ceiling. She stood there like a living sacrifice, like a lamb preparing for the slaughter.

Mist appeared, near Botticelli.

Mist, writhing like the shimmering heat waves off a desert, moved towards the girl. She did not look at it, but towards Botticelli. The writhing shape drew closer and still closer.

The silence was like the silence of death.

Then, into it:

"*No!*" screamed Bruton.

His cry seemed the signal for the mist to move with awful speed, to hurl itself against the girl. At last she moved. For a moment, terror showed on her face—the terror of death. Then, the *elementa* clutched at her throat, and as she fell there was a sharp, explosive sound.

. . . . .

There she lay, with her broken neck.

Bruton was shrieking, but the girls would not let him go, and nothing he could do would make them. Palfrey tried not to hear, but he could not fail; tried not to see, yet kept seeing his friend out of the corner of his eye.

There were other *elementa* on the rostrum.

They neared Botticelli.

He stood up, and walked to the spot where the girl had been, and where her body lay. The *elementa* crept towards him in that deathly silence; for this new scene had quietened even Bruton.

The *elementa* pounced!

Botticelli just stood immobile; and as the writhing creatures flung themselves at and about him, a great noise filled the auditorium, a great wind blew, there was a vivid, blinding flash. . . .

When Palfrey could see again, Botticelli stood there, unhurt. The rostrum was damaged, much as the staircase at Brett Hall had been. There were faint pink stains near Botticelli, the kind of stains that he had seen before.

The people there were all prostrated before Botticelli.

"You see," Forrester said chokily, "they can't kill him. He is indestructible. The only way to defeat him is to kill him, and you can't do that."

Palfrey didn't speak.

The two girls beyond Forrester stood up, carrying Bruton

out between them; and Bruton was still and limp—unconscious, perhaps—dead.

Dead?

Palfrey had known him all the years of Z 5's existence, had no closer and no greater friend—yet did not think of him. The girl had stepped into molten metal. Another had submitted herself to the choking death, a sacrifice to "prove" the immortality of Botticelli.

And Botticelli had overcome the *elementa* simply by standing there.

Forrester's voice echoed in his ears.

". . . *he's indestructible. The only way to defeat him is to kill him, and you can't do that.*"

.   .   .   .   .

They gave Palfrey a tablet and some water, and soon he went to sleep in the room where Bruton lay.

.   .   .   .   .

Palfrey and Bruton woke almost at the same moment, an hour or for all Palfrey knew, a day after he had fallen asleep. They opened their eyes warily at first; then Bruton grinned sheepishly and Palfrey smiled.

Bruton sat up at once, Palfrey stretched himself and looked round. The room was the one where Isabella had first brought them, and no one else was there. It was pleasantly warm. The lighting was a good simulation of daylight.

Bruton stood up, waited until Palfrey shifted his position and then walked slowly about the room, taking each step with great care. When he had completed his circuit he stood in front of Palfrey with a marvelling expression in his eyes.

"Did I make a fool of myself at the show?"

"You'd probably say so," Palfrey temporised.

"I can just remember," Bruton said, and then added in the same marvelling way: "This is the first morning for months that I've woken up free from fear."

"My second," said Palfrey, "and the other didn't last very long."

"I thought you were the optimist!" Bruton paused. "Fear's been like a weight pressing down on me. I couldn't shift it, but—it's gone."

"That leaves one worry."

"Which particular one?" Bruton asked.

"The people who don't feel as if all their troubles are over," Palfrey said. "I'd like to get word to Drusilla."

Bruton nodded slowly: "And Robina." He rubbed his nose, winced, then squinted down at his finger. "Must have scratched it," he said. "We aren't free from the troubles of the flesh!" He dabbed his bleeding nose with a handkerchief. "I need a shave, too."

"In a few minutes you'll start complaining," Palfrey said. "Then we'll both feel at home."

Bruton chuckled.

The most remarkable thing about the next two hours was that they took what happened almost for granted. They could remember what had happened without the horror. There was little sense of surprise, and none at all of anxiety. The worry about their wives did not go very deep; it was as if they were sure that the women knew they were not dead.

Forrester came in and led them to a bathroom. He said little, and that little was casual. There was an electric razor, a shower, everything they needed. And after that, breakfast. Paula, one of Botticelli's "angels" brought it in; bacon and eggs nicely cooked, toast, wheat cakes, maple syrup, coffee. The girl laid the table for them, and took little notice of the way Bruton watched her. But she was aware of it, and the smile she gave him when she went out was wholly delightful.

Bruton chuckled.

"They're man proof," he remarked. "And I'm hungry!"

He could talk like that——

In the hour which followed they became more quiet. Recollection began to hurt. Palfrey could see the haunted look in Bruton's eyes. Whatever drug they were given dulled their awareness for a while, but didn't kill it.

Then the door opened and Isabella Melado came in, bringing with her all the beauty of Spain.

"He would like to see you," she said simply.

She led the way out of the room and across a passage, into another smaller room, where Sandro Botticelli sat.

Behind him was one of the great paintings.

In his eyes there was something of the clearness of the eyes of the painted faces.

He did not smile.

He was dressed immaculately; was a little too handsome to be true.

He stood up, looking from Bruton to Palfrey.

"I can see that you feel better," he said. "Good. The drug can help but cannot convince you. That you have to do for yourself." He paused, looking at Palfrey, forgetful of Bruton. "I am seeing you myself because I want you to go back and tell your Governments what you have seen. I hope that you will believe what I am going to say to you, because otherwise the great cities of the world may be subjected to severe attacks. You see, Palfrey, I was prepared to wait, to work by stealth. You prevented that with your agents, you made difficulties, forced me to retaliate. Now there is no drawing back. I must be accepted, everywhere—or I shall compel obedience. Remember, I ask for nothing except freedom to convert the world.

"If you cannot secure that, I shall have to use the *elementa*," Botticelli went on. "They are all that is bad, vicious and treacherous. I can control them, through my people. No one else can."

All the sense of horror was coming back.

Bruton's face had gone ashen grey, he was trembling, he couldn't keep his lips steady. Sweat, first in little beads, then in tiny streams, gathered on his face and dropped to his lips, trickled under his jowl. His eyes were glittering.

Botticelli said very softly: "The choice is not mine, Palfrey—I give you and the Governments complete freedom of choice. My people must be freed, none must be threatened again. I must be free to preach, to make converts, to accept worship. We have converts in every city, town and village, every nation, every Government, even in the homes of the people. You have been watching my activities for a long time; you know where my leaders are."

Palfrey said gruffly: "Yes, I know."

"You'll never succeed——" began Bruton, and choked on the words.

"But are there enough?" asked Botticelli, in a soft tone.

Isabella asked: "Will you look at this, Dr. Palfrey?"

She was sideways towards the one long, blank wall, and when she pressed a button a relief map of the world showed up, each hemisphere in bold relief. There were shining spots on this, all tiny and some no larger than pin-heads. Clusters of these were in London and New York and other large cities; there were more in India and in China than in the United States or Great Britain. As he looked, Palfrey felt as if the brightness of the dots had some special message.

"These are the places where Sandro has his followers," Isabella said. "These must be free to do as they wish."

Palfrey looked at the glowing dots, like stars upon the face of the earth.

He did not see the mist at the door.

22

THE mist was there, thin and tenuous, now at one end of the tiny gap between the door and the floor, now at the other. Little tentacles stretched out, as if hands of a many-armed creature were trying to get farther in, to reach the closed door and to open it.

Isabella did not see it.

Botticelli, watching her and Palfrey, did not see it.

Bruton lay back in his chair, eyes closed, hands lying along the arms, face grey. If he heard or saw anything, he did not speak or show any sign.

The mist writhed. . . .

Palfrey watched the shining dots, and remembered all that he had learned about Botticelli's activities. Men and women had been bought or persuaded, somehow won over, and they came from all branches of life, all Governments, all places of authority. Members of Parliament and Congressmen, senators, soldiers in high authority, naval leaders and air-force commanders. In the fighting services, then, and in the great financial houses of Wall Street and of London's City, in Paris and Vienna, Berlin and Moscow, Pekin and Bombay —throughout the world, often in unexpected places, Botticelli had made "converts".

In the villages and the great cities, among the workmen building houses, making automobiles, manufacturing the goods and producing the food for the people, making the weapons of a war which would annihilate man—among all these groups, Botticelli had his "converts". Many of these were in surprising places, and were men and women whom he had believed likely to be loyal.

They served this self-styled Supreme Being.

Palfrey did not see the writhing mist; the tentacle stretching up, like a shapeless hand with ephemeral fingers twitching and grasping for the handle of the door.

"It can be a great power for good," Isabella said. "The one great power."

She was watching Palfrey, and he sensed that she was trying to convince him, exerting all her own faith in Botticelli. Botticelli watched with equal intensity; they did not give a thought to Bruton or the door; only to him. He studied the maps, reminding himself of the reports which had come from so many different places; Paris, where a lovely girl, Octavie, had disappeared in front of her father's eyes.

And Spain—the visiting Americans, the lovely Isabella. Spain, where one of the worst storms had taken place, and pools of boiling mud had appeared in the place of solid rock.

Boiling *mud*.

That changed the tempo and the direction of his thoughts. He turned away from the wall, to face Isabella; and the way she looked at him, pleading now, held a kind of desperation. He did not really understand why it mattered to her and to Botticelli that he should believe them; but undoubtedly it did. In a different way from Bruton, he began to fight.

There was boiling mud and physical destruction; there were the flashes of lightning, the thunder and the fog, all material manifestations. These were physical, weren't they? Things to feel, touch, which could hurt and be hurt, kill and be killed. A house disappeared, a lake became a tidal wave, fog blacked out a city. Quite suddenly, he could understand the sudden fury which had possessed Bruton; he felt much as Bruton did, but without the emotion, without the anger.

He wished that he did not.

"What still worries you?" asked Isabella.

"He doubts everything," Botticelli said coldly. "Let him go. If he cannot convince his leaders——"

Botticelli shrugged.

"Be patient a little longer," Isabella pleaded. "Dr. Palfrey, do you realise what you can do, how much suffering you can save? You have seen what can happen in a small area, and——"

Bruton screamed: "*Look at that door!*"

. . . . .

The door was opening, and at the side were the tentacles of mist.

At Bruton's scream the door stopped moving for a moment, and then it crashed back against the wall.

Bruton drew in a shuddering breath.

Botticelli shouted: "*No!*"

All that followed was in a split second of time, yet later Palfrey could recall every trivial incident, almost every whirling shape. First, it thrust the door open and rushed forward. Botticelli's cry stopped it for a moment, as if it did not know which way to turn. It was spitting, writhing, twisting, and Palfrey stood with horror and fear, knowing that he was looking upon the face of evil, unable to move or speak or to evade the danger.

"Keep back!" cried Bruton, "*keep back!*"

He was shouting at Isabella.

She did not keep back, but went forward with her hand outstretched. The mist, like flames which had been robbed of colour, spat and licked towards her, and she drew nearer. Bruton drew his legs up, Botticelli neither moved nor spoke. Palfrey watched the woman and the noisome creature which seemed to have no shape or form.

Suddenly, there was a greater writhing. The *thing* there was moving, going backwards, going out of the door. It disappeared, *in flight*. Isabella dropped her hand and went to the door, Palfrey saw her turn into the passage. Botticelli broke his long silence and called:

"Come back, Isabella, come back!"

She didn't answer.

There was a flash and a sharp explosion; the room seemed to shake, a gust of wind came into the room, eddied about the corner and then died away.

Palfrey saw Bruton gazing fearfully at the door; and Botticelli, his face flushed slightly, his eyes half-closed, lowering himself gradually until he was sitting at the desk.

Voices were raised at the far end of the passage, and one of them was Isabella's.

Botticelli said quietly: "Occasionally one of them revolts, but not often enough to worry me. Professor Rebonne, who was in charge of our research, was himself killed in this way, happily when his work was nearly finished. Palfrey—your answer, please. Will you take the message?"

Palfrey said: "What do you want me to say?"

Bruton turned away.

"That is more reasonable," Botticelli said briskly. "Bruton and Forrester will stay here. You will go back to McCall, and if necessary to London. You will tell them how impossible the fight is. You will tell them that with your own eyes you have seen that I am indestructible. They must know the truth, Palfrey, that once they acknowledge me . . ."

Me . . .

Me!

". . . they will have no difficulty," Botticelli went on. "To show that I *have* this power, I shall incite *elementa* to further attack just before your return.

"Now——"

PART FOUR

BOTTICELLI

23

SENATOR SAMUEL McCALL walked slowly towards Fifth Avenue, facing the setting sun, which cast a golden light upon the great buildings towering above the heads of the masses of people on the sidewalks.

It was nearly six o'clock.

McCall turned into 42nd Street, glanced across to the library and the trees around it, with their buds beginning to shoot green, then headed for Broadway. He was one of a jostling, bustling mob. Everyone seemed to be going somewhere with a purpose in mind, all seemed to know what they were doing. The white-skinned and the dark; people from Southern Europe and from the north; the Negroes, the Costa Ricans, the French, the Dutch, the British and the German —these and all their brothers were citizens of a common country here, and all were going about their evening task or pleasure with eager intentness.

None thought of disaster.

Above the RKO building at the Rockefeller Centre, which McCall could see from a corner, wisps of greyish cloud were gathered; grey, not white. McCall saw these, and shrugged himself more tightly into his big coat. The evening was not cold, but he felt cold and lost and lonely.

People streamed into the cinemas, the theatres, the night-clubs, the clip-joints, the restaurants and the bars. At 42nd Street and Broadway up to 48th Street the crowds were so thick that people had to shoulder their way through. Throngs surged across the streets when the lights turned against the traffic, and almost everywhere it would have been possible to cross Broadway or the intersecting streets by walking across the roofs of the taxis and cars.

In the half-light here the electric advertising signs flashed

on and off with a brilliance and a speed which bewildered
the few who were seeing it for the first time; who felt as if
they were engulfed in a sea of light and a sea of human
bodies. On, off, on, off—every colour man could devise,
masses of electric lamps in one single sign, signs going round,
signs racing, signs smoking, signs sneezing, signs coughing,
signs laughing, signs jigging and signs dancing—and the
indifferent thousands passed these by, while the strangers
gaped but did not quite believe.

Above them all, the grey clouds grew thicker, and seemed
to fall lower.

McCall, with two F.B.I. men behind him, although they
were not conspicuous, walked towards the Hudson River.
He stopped suddenly and took a taxi.

"Riverside Drive at 89th Street," he said.

"Okay."

"Just wait a moment," McCall said, and made a fuss of
getting in, enabling the two detectives to get another cab.
They knew that he was going to the apartment which he had
on Riverside Drive, overlooking the Hudson River, New
Jersey and, if only one could see, the land mass of the United
States across to the Pacific coast.

There was comparatively little traffic on Tenth Avenue,
still less on Riverside Drive. Here, the houses were not
abnormally high. Lights were glowing at the windows,
curtains were being drawn, television aerials poked skywards
towards those darkening patches of mist, like the antennæ
of strange creatures unknown to man.

The taxi put McCall down at the corner.

He paid the man, the other taxi stopped and the F.B.I.
men got out. They didn't follow him at first. Another F.B.I.
man was at the door of the house, and saluted him.

"How'd it go, Mr. McCall?"

"Not very well," McCall said sadly. "Is M. Andromovitch in?"

"No, sir, but he'll be back."

The F.B.I. man pressed the elevator button, and when
McCall was in the elevator car, pressed for the fourth floor,
then walked away.

McCall looked very, very old, the only part of him
which seemed to have resisted the struggle of the past

few weeks were his eyes, and even their courage was
dimmed.

Downstairs in the hall an F.B.I. man from the taxi said:
"One day he'll just fall down and die. I'm sorry about the
way he's gone." He tapped his forehead. "He was a good
guy."

The other man shifted his cigar from one side of his mouth
to the other.

"You want to know something," he said. "I think he still
is a good guy."

"Oh, sure. But batty."

"Sometimes I wonder if he's so crazy." The cigar made
the return journey, under an expert twist of the full lips.
"There was a sky pilot who talked the way he did, out in the
Pacific. You remember Yippee Atoll? Sure you do, who'd
forget Yippee? That sky pilot was with us. He didn't go
behind us, no, sir, he went way in front. And he talked the
way old Sam McCall's always talking."

"Did anyone wait to pick up the pieces?"

The cigar started on its journey again.

"It was a funny thing," he said, "he got killed in an
accident, after coming home. Some crazy driver got him.
You know the way it is. But I often think of that padre when
I hear old Sam McCall. Or read about him. You've got to
hand it to old Sam, he gets the air, he gets the video and he
gets the newsprint. You know what Jeff Cardell is calling
him?"

"My wife reads the *Mirror*."

"Who was asking about your wife? The new Uncle Sam,
that's Cardell on video and in the *Times*. They support
McCall. You want to know something else? No one ever
says that Sam's wrong. They just don't do what he wants
them to!"

"It's all too high-hat," the first man said. "Just get ready
to fight—with what?" He held out his hands. "These?
Show me a man with a gun, and I'll tell you what I want to
fight him with." He tapped his pocket. "A gun."

The cigar started another return journey, rather sadly,
rather slowly.

"Maybe you're right," said the man who liked McCall.

McCall stepped out of the elevator car at the fourth floor.

Someone had dropped a newspaper, and it was on the chair of the tiny hall. He stopped to look at the front-page headlines. He had a single column to himself, with the headline reading:

UNCLE SAM
McCALL . . .

"Haranguing the special session of the United Nations Session in New York today, Senator Samuel McCall called for a new assessment of the balance of power, based on what he called 'the defence by will'. He declares that a new religious despot has cells not only in every village and town and big city in the United States, but everywhere in the world.

"He claims that this religious leader, Botticelli, lived in The House of the Angels, the very name of which is significant to Sam McCall, anyway.

"He goes further and says that Botticelli has created a creature which can defy atomic and hydrogen bombs—a creature which can't lose. And, thinks Sam McCall, we can't do a deal with the Devil, so we've got to get down on our knees and pray right hard.

"Maybe he's right about that. Maybe he's exaggerating about some things also. Whether he's right or wrong, tiny Benigua was the only state to support Uncle by putting forward a practical proposition—that a special committee be set up to investigate the situation in the light of known events in Chicago.

"The representatives of Great Britain, the other representatives of the United States, those of Russia, Belgium and Pakistan, all told the Assembly that if more people would think like Senator McCall the world would be a better place. Some of them even sounded as if they meant it.

"The committee of physicists, biologists and newsreel men who made exhaustive investigations after the disaster at Chicago two weeks ago have now made reports which have been accepted by the Emergency Session, which met for the last time today. These reports make the assertion that the disaster at Chicago was the result of freak weather conditions, and claim the explosion of the atomic bombs is not held responsible even in part. 'There was no evidence whatsoever', said the reports, 'to suggest that the freak storm was essentially different from others, except in the degree of violence. There is also some evidence that there was an underground explosion which caused a slight earth tremor. The boiling mud proved to be almost identical with the mud springs of the Yellowstone National Park, in Naples, Italy, and in Rotorua, New Zealand. The springs in these places have been boiling for centuries, causing no known harm to man.'

"Before it committed *hari-kari* the emergency session appointed a Watch Committee, with Uncle Sam McCall as its chairman, to study events and to report any further manifestations of storms of similar violence. There is little likelihood, said the final report, of any serious repetition in the near future, if at all."

McCall dropped the newspaper.

He let himself in with a key, and an F.B.I. man who was watching him from the door of another apartment nodded with satisfaction. Uncle Sam seldom went out at night, he was safe enough.

Another newspaper, the *Journal American*, lay open by the side of the chair which Stefan Andromovitch usually used. A note on the television in the corner said: "I will be back by seven o'clock. S. A."

It was now about half-past six.

McCall dropped into a chair and picked up the *Journal American*. The first thing he saw was a caricature of himself, brilliantly drawn, giving him a goatee beard, a top-hat with the stars and stripes round the crown, and his hands raised in an attitude of benediction. The caption read:

The new Uncle Sam

Beneath this was a brief paragraph.

"Sam McCall's mighty effort to lead the United Nations on a straight and narrow path seen, if the truth be told, only by the new Uncle Sam and a few worthy but not very practical idealists, came to an end today. The new Uncle Sam has made a lot of new friends, and if he ever wants to campaign for a good cause, he will get plenty of support. America hasn't known preaching like it for generations.

"Now that cheeky little Benigua's motion has been thrown

out; the United Nations can go back for its seasonal sleep, and wake up in May to compete with the pressure of world events, and to take practical measures to combat growing tensions in Asia, and to smooth the new difficulties in Europe.

"The Chicago disaster will never be forgotten. The United Nations as well as Washington are to be congratulated for refusing to believe that this was any kind of special visitation. Nature is still a power to be reckoned with, but who is going to try to fight a meteor? Maybe it was a good thing that among the homes to suffer was the house of Botticelli and his modern angels—if angels is the word.

"If ever a man was dead, it's Botticelli."

McCall closed his eyes.

Suddenly, wearily, he got up and went to the television, switched it on and then stood back to watch. It was the end of a musical-comedy review; he saw a flurry of shapely legs and a few pretty faces, and then an ardent young man had something to say about the charm-developing power of a certain perfume. Next the station gave its signal and promised the news.

Cardell, one of the few men who had come down on McCall's side in the past week, appeared on the screen.

Cardell was part of America. He had a big, round, happy face and a confidential fireside manner. When you listened to Cardell giving the news you felt that every word was true; and he was said to have the biggest audience in the world. He deserved it. He had taken every opportunity to publicise Sam McCall, who had been in front of the cameras twice. Cardell always made much of what McCall said at UNO, too.

Cardell waved a hand, smiled, looked round as if he were making sure that he could see every one of his audience of millions. That was the Cardell secret; he talked to each individual, he looked into the eyes of each viewer.

He gave the familiar little preliminary chuckle, a kind of nervous cough, and then said:

"Tonight, folk, we are starting off with a sensation and just to make sure that every one of you knows I'm not kidding, I've brought the sensation right along with me. I hope that my old friend Sam McCall is with us tonight—are you listening, Uncle Sam?—because a friend of his is going to shake a lot of good folk out of a heap of bad complacency. When a man comes back from the dead, or what we thought was death, that's sensational. Anybody say 'no'? Well, we didn't have any hard evidence, but a lot of brilliant scientists who spent some time in Chicago recently gave it as their opinion that anyone buried beneath the ruins of The House of the Angels couldn't survive.

"Well, one of them did survive.

"In fact, several survived," Cardwell went on, "and I've brought two of them along tonight. Come on in, Dr. Palfrey, don't hang back there—about twenty million people want a good look at you."

McCall staggered away from the screen, dropped into his chair and held the arms as if only they could save him. Into his eyes there sprang a glow of hope, and his breast was rising and falling under the great emotion which was shaking him.

Palfrey appeared; the diffident-looking, smiling, un-mistakable Palfrey, with the thin, silky hair and the nose with a high bridge and the chin which looked as if it were a little weak. Here was Palfrey in the flesh, shaking hands with Cardell, sitting down.

"Now, Doctor, we hope you're going to tell us plenty," said Cardell, "but if you've a special message for anyone, this is the time to give it."

McCall was gripping the arms of his chair so tightly that his fingers hurt.

Palfrey smiled; and seemed to smile straight into McCall's eyes. In that moment the Englishman looked astonishingly like Stefan Andromovitch, too. It was nothing to do with the features, only in the expression. Palfrey had always been calm and dispassionate, but this was a serenity which came from the heart, not a calm imposed by a dispassionate mind.

"Thank you, Mr. Cardell," he said. "I'm not going to take up much of anyone's time, but I would like to say 'hallo' to the man you've dubbed the new Uncle Sam. I've been reading some of Sam McCall's speeches again, and a strange thing occurred to me. The burden of what he says is very like the burden of the things that both George Washington and Abraham Lincoln said! After all"—Palfrey smiled, and McCall knew that everyone watching would be attracted by that smile, by the slight shrug of his shoulders, the self-deprecating way in which he went on—"it isn't for an Englishman to remind you that George Washington had a liking for the truth! And that you'd have a job to find any president of the United States who didn't express belief in the highest idealism.

"If it comes to that, there are a lot of idealists all over the world. Practical people, too—you wouldn't call Pandit Nehru exactly impracticable, would you, after the way in which he so politely wished us British farewell from India. And while a lot of people didn't like Mahatma Gandhi, who died of violence, they admired him; and if ever a man won practical results by using the idealist weapon of non-violence, it was Gandhi.

"He wasn't advocating anything very different from Sam McCall.

"The big thing about Uncle Sam's advice just now is that it's based on truth. He told you that he believed that Botticelli caused these storms, including the one here in Chicago.

"That's right.

"Botticelli did.

"Botticelli is alive today. I've seen him, talked to him. Perhaps he's mad, perhaps he's just bad. Whatever it is, he has discovered a new kind of power, and he'll use it if he's not obeyed."

Palfrey paused; and it seemed as if that pause was meant for Sam McCall alone.

Then Palfrey went on:

"The difficulty is, how can a Government give way to one man, no matter how strong? Here's a man claiming to be a great religious leader. He claims——"

There was a moment's pause, a shift of the camera, and Cardell appeared not Palfrey.

Cardell was smiling his usual easy smile.

"That's right, folk," he said, "except that Botticelli is a great religious leader. He's the man the world's been waiting for. I've doubted for a long time, but I've seen and talked to a woman who's made me see it her way. Now I'm wholly persuaded that Botticelli's right, and should be given full freedom.

"That's my opinion, anyway.

"If he is allowed to preach, to convert the world, why, we'll go on living in the normal way, except that thanks to Botticelli we'll stand a better chance of getting a better deal.

"If he isn't allowed absolute freedom, well—he'll call on the friends Sam McCall's warned you about.

"Isn't that so, Dr. Palfrey?"

The camera switched back to Palfrey. For a moment of utter despair, Sam McCall thought that Palfrey had joined Botticelli, that he was a renegade.

For Palfrey was smiling quite freely.

"It's anyone's guess who's right," he said. "Cardell believes in Botticelli. I don't. I think we'll have to fight him——"

"You can't fight the elements," Cardell said, "and these are *elementa*. Botticelli's got nature on his side—doesn't that prove anything? Could an ordinary man control nature?"

There was a pause. McCall longed for Palfrey again, but he wasn't brought back, he was faded out and kept out. In his place came a woman; Isabella Melado.

It was as if a continent gasped at her beauty.

24

McCALL sat tensely, fearfully in front of the screen. He heard the door open, but he did not look round. He heard footsteps, and still did not trouble to turn.

The newcomer was Andromovitch.

The Russian drew close to McCall's side, and Isabella might have been looking straight at him from the screen; at McCall, too; at every man and woman who was sitting in front of the screen.

"All I can say," said Isabella, "is that I am quite sure that Botticelli can lead us to a better world, a happier world, to plenty for everyone. Good men refuse to believe this. They talk of principles, and urge you to fight—but how can you fight the elemental things which obey Botticelli? Answer me that. This isn't another Korea, this isn't another Europe, this is a war in your own home, over your own heads. Just to show you what he can do, Botticelli has planned a demonstration over Lake Michigan and over Long Island Sound which will convince all doubters of his power. He——"

The screen went dead, the woman's voice stopped abruptly.

McCall stood up, slowly, and Andromovitch said between clenched teeth:

"Palfrey's free, understand, he's free."

"With men like Cardell on his side, Botticelli will sweep the country," said Senator McCall.

.   .   .   .   .

From the moment Isabella's pictures vanished, the telephones began to ring at the broadcasting station, newspapers rushed their ace men to see Cardell. It seemed as if one mighty movement started up and down the country. Cardell fed the hungry machines of press, radio and television across the continent.

Palfrey's men, held on a leash, moved out among the people in the United States and Canada, and began to talk Botticelli down. They found some support, but quickening interest in Botticelli. And, not overnight, but in the hour, pictures of Botticelli appeared in shop windows, in drugstores, in houses, in newspapers, on the streets, on buses and trains, on aircraft, in city, town and village. They were small cards, small enough to go into cigarette packets.

They came like snow, and covered the nation.

Meanwhile, a hundred and fifty million people waited with growing tension for the news from Chicago.

Would there be a storm?

.   .   .   .   .

In the apartment on 89th Street, McCall sat very still, quite oblivious of the programme which followed. For nearly an hour Andromovitch was with him, as tense as the old man; then the Russian heard a sound in the passage, and went to open the door.

Palfrey and a tall, handsome woman came in.

"Drusilla!" Andromovitch exclaimed, and the eagerness in his voice made McCall start, forced him out of his stupor.

He stood up and waited for Palfrey. Palfrey looked very pale and strained, moving with a kind of restrained fury.

"I can guess what you're feeling like," he said. "It was planned down to the last detail. With men like Cardell against us——" He broke off. "At least the station he was broadcasting from didn't play, they blacked him out at last. But Botticelli's followers are mushrooming everywhere. If we do get a storm——"

"We shall get a storm," McCall said. "He can make sure, can't he?" He forced himself to look at the woman, who was tall, slender, high-breasted in a suit of smooth-textured navy blue. "You are Mrs. Palfrey?"

"Good Lord!" Palfrey exclaimed. "Forgot you hadn't met. Yes—together for the end."

"It mustn't end like this!" cried McCall.

Drusilla Palfrey said: "It can't end like this."

"Facts are here to be faced," Palfrey said, in a steely voice. "The fact is that Botticelli has cells everywhere, in this country, in England, all over Europe, everywhere. The followers have been waiting for a signal to come into the open. Here we have an overnight conversion campaign, with miracle workers leading it, a supreme leader who can bring thunder and lightning, and men in high places, in the churches, in the Governments, in industry, the schools everywhere, already converted.

"And if we do get a storm——"

A gust of wind came out of the silent night, struck the windows, rattled noisily and howled away in the distance towards the Hudson River.

At the sound of the first gust McCall flinched, Drusilla Palfrey closed her eyes and Palfrey turned sharply towards the windows.

He looked out.

The stars were hidden, the few wisps of grey cloud had become a dark pall. Across the Hudson, lights showed in buildings; a few showed on the river, too. The lamps of the Hudson River Parkway, with the headlights of cars streaking along, showed vividly in the darkness. There was a mist at ground level; and mist at eye level, too.

Another gust struck the building, and the walls seemed to shake.

"Sap, come away," said Drusilla sharply.

She was just behind him.

He didn't move.

"Please come away," she pleaded.

Instead, McCall and Andromovitch joined him, and Palfrey slid his arms through hers and drew her nearer to the window. It shook and rattled violently, and in the distance a flash of lightning lit up the sky.

And distant thunder rolled.

Above and below them the fog thickened. High in the sky the flashes were more vivid, the lightning seemed nearer, and thunder began to roar and roll overhead.

Down below in the streets people looked up apprehensively, and hurried for shelter.

The wind blustered and howled.

Out on the Hudson and the East Rivers along the Sound and out to the Atlantic, a warning was radioed to shipping. Reluctant officials in Washington gave emergency orders, the Civil Defence forces were alerted, fire brigades, police and troops all stood by.

The telephone bell rang. Andromovitch went to answer, listened and then said heavily:

"Yes, it is happening here too."

Palfrey swung round.

"That from Chicago?"

"Yes," said the Russian. "A storm is raging over the lake, exactly as Isabella said it would."

.   .   .   .   .

Downstairs at the main entrance the F.B.I. man rolled his cigar from one side of his mouth to the other and said:

"Bad storm over New Jersey, I guess."

"Looks like Long Island to me."

"Could be both sides."

"Could be all round."

"Oh, sure." The cigar began its unending journey back again. "You reckon that little guy who came and told us about Botticelli was sane, after all?"

"How'd I know?"

"I know this," said the other, "any guy who can make a storm like this can have my vote."

.   .   .   .   .

The network which had banned Cardell the previous night withdrew the ban next morning. Palfrey and the others were waiting when the programme started with news.

"At about ten o'clock last night," said Cardell, looking rotund, ruddy-faced and absolutely sure of himself, "storms of unusual ferocity raged in the neighbourhood of New York City, Long Island, New Jersey and the Atlantic. Meteorological experts are puzzled, as it appeared to encircle New York. Manhattan was threatened with one of the great storms in history.

"It did not come.

"Sailors coming up the East River and along Long Island Sound declared that they have never known such gigantic seas, and but for an urgent gale warning broadcast some while before the storm, there would have been many more casualties.

"Now I'm no expert on storms, folk, and I don't want to claim to be, but I don't think there is much doubt that the kind of storm we nearly had right here in New York last night was the kind that they really had in Chicago not so long ago. But it didn't get this far. I'm just an ordinary newspaperman, and I've had some lucky breaks on video, but I just can't help accepting the truth of this—the way I wondered about Uncle Sam McCall and his new kind of sky piloting. The thing I'm wondering about just now is whether that storm would have hit New York real hard if it hadn't been meant as a warning."

Cardell gave his quick, boyish grin, and pushed back a lock of hair. The cameras glinted on a gold-capped tooth. He glanced down at his papers, then looked back at the viewers, still smiling.

"Now let me tell you some more good news, folk. All over the world there are great demonstrations in favour of Botticelli, the world's Holy Man. I'm not joking. In Pekin and in Moscow, London and Paris, Saigon and Sydney, Quebec and Buenos Aires, Botticelli's disciples are winning converts by tens of thousands.

"This is the great day, folk.

"Get on the Botticelli band-wagon, and you can't lose. Of course, the established Churches won't like it, but where

have they led us to in the past? Any place you want to go?
"If they haven't, here's your chance to say where you *do*
want to go!"
He stopped.

Palfrey turned away from the screen, as a sharp knock
came at the door. It was a cable for Palfrey, and a Western
Union boy waited as he read it:
"Return to London at once, orders from No. 10. Kennedy."

.   .   .   .   .

Palfrey looked down at the troubled surface of the Atlantic
as the aircraft flew towards the British Isles, straight and
steady as a bird. They were nearly across. Nearer New
York they had seen some wreckage of small ships and at least
two rubber dinghies and several rafts, holding sailors ship-
wrecked by the night's storm.

Drusilla sat across the gangway, looking out of another
window. They turned, caught each other's eye and moved
together.

"You stay where you are," Palfrey said. He dropped into
the seat beside her, slid his arm about her waist, squeezed
and said: "I wonder what the Old Man wants."

"The Prime Minister," Drusilla said slowly.

"The Prime Minister in person," Palfrey confirmed. He
wasn't as relaxed as he tried to sound; and Drusilla knew it.
"Emergency in London, too. Kind of thing that no one's
had to face before. Accept me as your god, and all will be
well! The new anti-Christ. Had something not unlike it
once before, but not stage-managed like this. The organisation's superb."

He almost choked.

Drusilla said: "It's—devilish."

"Oh, yes." Palfrey forced himself to grin. "This is the
kind of thing that makes one take the Devil as literally as we
took Hitler. A man sets himself up as the Supreme Being.
He says to every man, woman and child of every religion:
'You've been waiting for me, come and worship, and all will
be well.' The fact is that practically every man, woman and
child of every religion has been waiting for *someone* to take
on the mantle of a dreamed-of deity. They were never sure
how he would come. Jew and Christian, Hindu and Mahom-

medan, in fact all of them. They're all anti-communist, and
here's the one unifying force needed throughout the world
against communism. What a gift for the world's red-baiters!
And study the kind of people who have swung over to Botticelli. Cardell was always suspected of being a believer in
McCarthy-ism plus. All the disappointed little politicians
who see themselves as dictators are in this. It could sweep
the world."

"And if it did——" began Drusilla, and stopped when he
looked into her eyes.

He did not smile, and was silent for a long time. Then
he began to speak, very slowly, very carefully.

"I know what you mean, 'Silla, and what you feel. Would
it be such a bad thing? Can we prove that it would be?
That's the secret of Botticelli's potential strength—the
doubts already in the minds of everyone, the dissatisfaction
of millions with things as they are. He's cashing in on the
normal man's groping after a god one can understand."

"I know, my darling, I wasn't—serious."

Palfrey seemed to ignore her.

"I've seen Botticelli, remember. I've seen him control the
elementa. I've seen him kill and maim, ruthlessly, cold-
bloodedly. He loosed a hideous attack at Chicago, chiefly to
terrify first people and then statesmen into accepting him.
You know and I know: and that's the answer. Take any
religion and any sect, any believer anywhere, and there's
one common factor in belief—only one, but it exists in all
religions. *God is good*. Botticelli is evil. Simple facts. But
in face of fear the people might force the hands of Governments, might begin an age too hideous to think of, an age
when all pogroms of the past will have been Sunday Afternoon Concerts compared with this."

The aircraft droned on.

Drusilla didn't answer, for a long time. Then it wasn't
really an answer.

"Can you see any hope?"

"Just one, only one," said Palfrey. "Forrester. Has he
fought and won, or have they beaten him? I think he's a
kind of test case. He's desperately in love with Isabella,
she has him body and perhaps soul. That's the crucial test—
soul? She's worked hard on him. Can a man who is so

bitterly opposed to everything Botticelli stands for be converted to his side? Forrester's fight has been with everything he's got, subconscious as well as conscious. If we've a chance, it's through him—and he's got to deny himself Isabella. If she were just an ordinary woman, beautiful as she is, it would be hard enough—but touched with Botticelli's magic, trained to absolute perfection, it won't just be hard, it'll be——"

He didn't finish.

Drusilla said: "You don't think he can do it, do you?"

"I daren't refuse to think he has a chance," Palfrey said. "If he could find a way to kill Botticelli, it would be over. The worst of it would be, anyhow—you don't worship a dead man who was going to prove himself immortal only the day before he died."

Palfrey broke off.

Grey cloud floated very close to the window. Palfrey noticed it for the first time, was glad that Drusilla didn't see the way he looked. The sky was darkening; it was no longer a question of low cloud, but a pall as of fog. Now he found his heart beating uncomfortably fast, his pulse quickening.

There was no need for either him or Drusilla to speak.

The flight deck door opened, and a uniformed man came hurrying along the gangway. He approached Palfrey as if he couldn't get to him quickly enough.

Drusilla clutched Palfrey's hand.

"Just had a flash from London, sir," the officer said. "Very bad storms over south-west and west London, we're being diverted to Shannon. From all accounts it's a poor show. The Met. bloke got quite excited, says he's never known such lightning, it can be seen hundreds of miles. And the fog's so thick that everything's at a standstill. The Chief would like to know if you've any message to send back."

. . . . .

Beneath the ruins of The House of the Angels, quite assured of safety from any form of attack, Botticelli collected reports which were coming in from all over the world. Mathilde and the other angels took messages, drew diagrams, marked places on a huge world map with reports of conversions and great demonstrations for the divinity of Botticelli coming in. The atmosphere was brittle with excitement.

Forrester and Bruton knew only a little of what was happening, but guessed most of the rest. Now and again one of the radiant girls would say something that would make the picture clearer.

The two men knew that Botticelli sat in a room as if he sat on a throne, accepting the submission of his followers throughout the world.

No one watched Forrester or Bruton; they were neglected in the excitement which touched everyone.

Each fought a battle which had to be fought alone, and it was Forrester who broke a long, hurtful silence.

"I think he's going to win. I don't think there's a chance of beating him. When you see how the reports are coming in, how•the people are turning to him, the Governments won't have a chance, just won't have a chance. If Palfrey were here, that's what he'd say."

Bruton said: "He mustn't be allowed to win."

"There isn't a way to stop him."

"There is, and you know it."

Forrester's eyes were burning.

"There is, and you know it, and you've got to use it," Bruton went on harshly. "You've a chance, but I haven't. They won't let me get near him. In any case I can't fight the —the *things*." His eyes were glittering, his voice was pitched on a savage key. "I haven't a chance, but you have. This is what you've been building up for. This is why Palfrey sent you to Spain. You're the hope of the world. Don't forget it."

Forrester was sweating.

Bruton said: "If you won't try, I will. After that maybe you'll see what you have to do."

Forrester didn't answer.

"What the hell's keeping you back?" cried Bruton, and then checked his voice and looked round fearfully, lest he had been overheard.

No one seemed near.

"Well, what's keeping you back?" he repeated roughly. "Love for Botticelli? Don't tell me you *believe* in him."

Forrester said slowly: "No, I don't believe, I've seen too much of the other side. But if I kill him, even if I try to kill him——"

He broke off.

Bruton prodded harshly: "Well, what's holding you back?"

Forrester sat in his chair, with the sweat beading his forehead, his hands clenched so that the nails made ridges in his palms. His own body was rigid. His eyes were narrowed and rimmed with sweat; he looked as a man might look if he were staring into the depths of hell itself.

Bruton rasped: "*What's holding you back?*"

Forrester didn't speak.

Then, Isabella came in, so beautiful and radiant, enough to steal the soul of any man.

. . . . .

They knew that she had been to New York, and had appeared on the television screen, but they had seen her only for a few seconds. She came in quickly, her eyes alive with excitement and radiance that made her beauty glow. Bruton sensed the truth; she was exalted.

She *believed.*

"It won't be much longer, Jim," she said, "there is a tremendous enthusiasm everywhere. Quite unbelievable!" She drew nearer, her hands outstretched, and seemed oblivious of Forrester's expression, of the sweat on his forehead.

He stood up slowly.

She glanced at Bruton, but obviously didn't think that Bruton mattered.

She took Forrester's hands.

"It will be over before long," she said. "He'll be accepted, he's bound to be. Won't that *prove* who he is, what power he has? The perfection of the planning, the willingness of the disciples to rise now, the way people are flocking to him——"

"Everywhere?" rasped Bruton.

She glanced at him sharply. "What do you mean?"

"*Are* they flocking everywhere? All Christians, Mohammedans, Hindus——?"

"Oh, there are pockets of resistance," Isabella conceded. "That is unfortunate but not surprising. They won't last for long." She gripped Forrester's hands. "Jim, he wants to see you. Come along. He wants to show you how complete it is, how absolute his power will be soon."

She led the way towards the door.

Over her shoulder, she said to Bruton: "He will not see you yet, but if you stand by that wall you may see him."

He caught his breath.

Then he saw that there was a window in the wall, revealed by the moving of shutters he hadn't known were there. He saw into the room beyond, a small room where Botticelli sat in the pale toga, a picture painted by the original Botticelli behind him, showing Botticelli's angels; and, nearer, angels were waiting upon him like acolytes.

The door of the room closed.

Bruton saw Forrester and Isabella go in, and approach the throne; saw Isabella prostrate herself, saw Forrester stare at Botticelli, teeth clamped together, agony showing in his expression.

Bruton knew why.

Bruton knew, now, that the thing which kept Forrester from trying was his love for Isabella.

He worshipped her beauty.

He was the only man who could hope to prevent the hideous era which Botticelli could launch upon the world.

Then he heard Botticelli say slowly:

"The most powerful opposition is now coming from the Christian Churches, particularly in Rome, in London and in Washington. Religious leaders have sent orders to their followers to resist our advance, and the British Government has given full support to the Church of England's directive.

"When we have crushed opposition in London I do not think we shall have more serious trouble. I have already given orders."

.   .   .   .   .

White-faced, shaken passengers climbed out of aircraft which had come in from London and the other airports of southern England. Shannon Airport was so crowded that it might have been a big city. Cars were bringing emergency supplies by the narrowish roads, a bright sun shone on the islands and the river near by.

Palfrey and Drusilla stood watching as passengers climbed down from a Constellation which had just come in. Palfrey moved when he saw Kennedy, the Z 5 chief in London, here under special orders. Kennedy hurried towards Palfrey and Drusilla, no one else took any notice of them. In the eyes of the man from London there was some indication of the ordeal he had passed through. His hand-clasp was quick and nervous.

"How bad?" asked Palfrey sharply.

"Where it's struck, it couldn't be worse," Kennedy said. "It's dreadful near the cathedrals everywhere. Dreadful! Bomb damage just isn't in it." His voice was clipped, and now that he was close to them they could see that he hadn't slept for a long time. "St. Paul's had it badly, too, like Westminster—both buildings stood up, though—thank God. Some churches have just disappeared. The Thames flooded part of the upper reaches when a tidal wave just swamped the ramparts. Some fires are still burning. I don't know what would have happened if we hadn't been warned."

"Authorities take notice in time?"

"You know how it is. Once the Old Man gave the word, they got ready. Full-dress rehearsal of atomic bombardment defence, and thank the Lord, it worked. Most people were under cover when the storm really reached its height. I don't think I'll ever forget that screaming fury, those flashes, those explosions. If they hadn't done an iota of damage, they'd still live with me. What *is* it, Sap?"

"Botticelli's *elementa*," Palfrey said, "as if you didn't know. Creatures made in the image of man! Let's have a look at the plans."

They went into an office which had been set aside for Palfrey. Two Z 5 men, from Cork, were at the door.

"All okay," one said.

"Get Kennedy something to eat and a drink, will you?" Palfrey asked.

"Why, sure and I will."

Kennedy opened his brief-case and took out folded maps which covered all districts of London. Spread out on a large deal-topped table, they showed the whole of the metropolitan area and the dormitory suburbs. Spread about this were numbers of blue dots and red crosses. The dots showed places where Botticelli's "converts" met; in groups. The crosses showed the places where the worst damage had been.

"Noticed anything even uglier about these?" Palfrey asked.

"Can't say I have. I grabbed them and rushed for the

'plane. We were tossed about so much at first that I couldn't concentrate. What is it?"

Palfrey traced the crosses and the dots with the point of a pencil. Drusilla and Kennedy followed the movements closely. The man from Cork came in with a tray of sandwiches, coffee, and some Irish whiskey and three glasses. None of the others looked round at him. He put the tray down and went out.

Outside, he said: "You'd think they'd seen the Devil himself, ye would."

Kennedy said in an awed voice: "Wherever a group of Botticelli's agents met, there was no damage."

"They can protect themselves," Drusilla said chokily.

"That's it," agreed Palfrey, and drew circle after circle. "What's the scale? Half a mile to an inch. Right—there isn't any sign of storm damage within two hundred yards of any of Botticelli's groups. Count them, 'Silla—the top half. Bottom half, Ken." He kept ringing the blue dots, Drusilla and Kennedy counted—Drusilla in a whisper, Kennedy silently.

Palfrey finished.

". . . nineteen," Drusilla said.

". . . twenty-four," said Kennedy.

"Forty-three Botticelli groups, and no serious damage anywhere near them," Palfrey said stonily. "The biggest damage was caused near churches and cathedrals. That's the size of it."

25

THE storm over London was dying out when Palfrey's aircraft crossed the coast of England, but the air was filled with radio messages being flashed to other aircraft. Storms had gathered or were gathering over many big cities. The Champs-Élysées vicinity of Paris had suffered badly, districts near the cathedrals in Berlin, Vienna, Rome, Milan, Zurich, Moscow and Brussels and Amsterdam had been severely damaged. Civil Defence precautions in most of the cities had saved many casualties, but the full extent of the loss of life would never be known.

It was half-past four when Palfrey's car turned into Downing Street. There had been little damage in Whitehall, although in several side streets buildings had been brought down in ruins, and there were several huge craters in Hyde Park.

The usual guard of two policemen had been doubled; four of these checked Palfrey and Drusilla before the door was opened.

Soon, with half a dozen leading members of the Government, leaders of the Opposition Shadow Cabinet and some members of the House of Lords—all Lords spiritual—the Prime Minister sat round a table traditionally clear of papers, and said in his deep, familiar voice:

"Glad you have arrived, Dr. Palfrey, we are grateful to you again. But you won't want to lose time." He smiled at Drusilla in that way he had of making everyone whom he liked feel at ease, and went on: "I don't know how much you have been told. It cannot be as much as I know." He put a big, wrinkled hand on a sheaf of papers. "These are from your men and from M.I. 5, as well as from consuls, embassies and news agencies." He gave a little, droll smile. "These— ah—severe storms have been world wide. Perhaps the most— ah—elemental was in Sydney, but a great deal of damage was also done in Tokyo. The attacks did not reach the centre of Calcutta, although some mosques in Bombay suffered very badly. There has been no time to assess the situation fully, and there is no evidence that we should be given much rest. Now, will you tell us more about these discoveries you have been making?"

Palfrey said: "Gladly, sir, but you won't like it."

"We shall brace ourselves," said the Old Man dryly.

"I don't know what physical, moral or spiritual resources Botticelli can call on," Palfrey said, "but I do know that he has found a supernatural force which he controls absolutely. Professor Rebonne was working with him when the discovery was made. Rebonne has been working on his own for years, and there is nothing to give our physicists any idea what the supernatural or physical force is, nor how it can be met. In the light of our present knowledge I don't think it can be, physically, and I doubt whether a spiritual answer will greatly help to lessen the material and physical damage of attack." He said that very quietly. "In short, I don't think there is anything we can do to prevent Botticelli from doing what he likes—while he lives."

Palfrey stopped.

No one, not even the Old Man, made any comment.

Palfrey said quietly: "I feel sure that unless something very like a miracle happens soon, we shall be at the beginning of a new Dark Age. If Botticelli wins absolute power he'll start using it wildly, and we've seen what happens when he uses it. I think that the known religions will probably be forced underground—as they have been in plenty of countries before, of course. This time I think it will be world wide."

He paused, as if to make the next sentences very clear.

"I do not think that in any country in the world religious faith is strong enough, among the people, to enable Governments to resist Botticelli. It may be, but I've seen no evidence of it. If Botticelli can crush the first revolt of the churches, and that's what he's set out to do, he'll crush the Governments—or the people will, for him."

He stopped, and for a long time there was silence.

The Old Man broke it: "And you can offer no hope that we cannot see for ourselves?"

Palfrey said slowly: "There is one hope, on one man——"

"You will forgive me," an old man interrupted, in a gentle voice. The Lord Bishop of Llansed did not stand up as he spoke. His lined face showed less tension than that of anyone else in the room, and his mellow voice was soothing. "I think there is more than one hope, Mr. Prime Minister. There is the one that Dr. Palfrey is about to report, and there is the faith of many millions of people. I really cannot allow it to be thought that we are powerless against physical attack, even of this kind. In fact, I am going to make a suggestion, my dear Prime Minister, if I may."

The Old Man said: "I've never been more ready to take advice from you, my lord Bishop."

Even then, he smiled.

Palfrey stared at the face which looked so peaceful, wondered if the old prelate dreamed of the forces lined up against him; and Palfrey felt a hopelessness even greater than he had before.

"I am going to suggest," said the Bishop of Llansed, "that Christians everywhere—in fact I would gladly extend that to invite all who share a belief in God, whatever their means of approach to him—should gather together in one place, and challenge the—ah—forces of the supernatural or the elemental, as they have been called."

Two other Lords spiritual exclaimed: "God leading us, you're right!"

The Old Man's eyes began to glow.

Palfrey felt a sharp, stabbing pain, of *hope*; incredulous but indestructible hope.

The frail old Bishop went on: "We should be failing our Master if we did not try, and I feel convinced that the leaders of other Churches, in this country and throughout the world, would support us in the first act of religious unity that the world has ever seen. Indeed," he repeated, very gently, "this crisis might bring us to an end of the strife between religions, might give us an opportunity for understanding which we have never had before." He fell silent for a few seconds, but no one interrupted. At last, he smiled; it was the smile of a man who had great confidence and faith. "Let us invite the leaders of the Churches and all who will come with us to some remote place where we can challenge Botticelli and his *elementa* and"—Llansed gave a little dry smile—"and his angels. Do you think that is a good idea, Dr. Palfrey?"

Palfrey said softly: "Andromovitch taught himself to overcome the *elementa*, so it can be done." He felt a fierce rising of excitement. "Some place away from big cities, in America perhaps, or Africa—why not the Kalahari Desert?" His mind was racing. "We could get church leaders there in forty-eight hours, could tell Botticelli what we planned to do and defy him to wipe us out. The world would watch. If he failed——"

A short, dark man interrupted harshly: "Supposing he didn't fail?"

"We cannot command success," murmured the Bishop of Llansed, "that is out of our hands. We can strive to achieve it. We will so strive."

The Old Man rumbled: "We most certainly will. I'll send messages to our embassies and consulates, instructing them to get in touch with religious leaders. Your Eminence," he added to a younger prelate who had kept silent, "may I ask you to get in touch with Rome? Perhaps it would be wise to talk to Delhi at once, and approach the Kaliph——"

He paused.

Palfrey saw his eyes glinting, guessed how his mind was racing ahead, knew that he felt this new and exciting hope; a desperate hope which raised them up.

"Palfrey," said the Old Man, "I would like you to tell your agents to watch and report the reaction among Botticelli's—ah—followers. You know many of them, we don't forget that you first warned us of the possibility of grave danger from—but we'll give you a medal if we survive! Now we must select a spot." He swung round on another bishop. "My lord, will you spread word among your church members to talk about this freely, to let the people know that the challenge is accepted? Thank you, thank you. We shall use the radio, of course, the television, h'm, yes. Yes. You know, gentlemen," he added, in a voice which suddenly boomed out above every other sound, "I think this is going to be the fight of our lives."

. . . . .

The news of the challenge reached Botticelli later in the day through a broadcast which was heard by Mathilde, who went to tell him. For the first time since Cardell's confession of allegiance there was less excitement than anxiety in the rooms below the house of the Angels.

Forrester and Bruton were watching through the window. Isabella was with her master, Mathilde, and two of the other girls.

Botticelli studied the report, and called for others. They came swiftly, saying that messages to the masses were broadcast or soon to be broadcast from Canterbury, from Rome, from Mecca, from Benares; from all the holy places of the world.

With them, Botticelli seemed to gain a stature which frightened Bruton as much as anything else.

Botticelli did not rage.

He showed no anger or displeasure or fear.

When it was apparent that the religious world would unite against him, he spoke quietly to Isabella in a voice which came clearly through the loud-speakers into the room where Forrester and Bruton said:

"Of course we shall accept the challenge. It will prove once and for all the truth of all we say. In attempting to discredit us, they will assure universal conversion. What could we want more?" He looked calm, dispassionate, almost inhuman as he sat there. "I shall call upon the *elementa* to gather in that one spot and to wipe out the leaders of all other religions. How *can* that fail?"

In the quiet of their room Bruton said in a strangled voice:

"Well? Will you do it now, or will you wait and let him massacre the—the only men who might beat him?"

Forrester didn't answer.

Forrester was in hell.

Isabella knew it, Bruton was sure, Isabella knew that fight that Forrester was making, and was leaving him to fight it alone; or nearly alone.

Her beauty exerted itself to influence him; her beauty struggled for his mind, his body and his soul.

.   .   .   .   .

Cardell's face appeared on the television screens right across America. He was not smiling. Everyone could see that he had been through a period of great strain; he looked ill. His voice lacked its usual geniality, but one trick remained; he seemed to be looking straight into the eyes of every viewer, speaking to the mind of the heart of each one.

"I'm very glad to be here tonight," he said, "because before I go away, I want to leave a special message with you. With *you*, you understand. And I'm not alone. Throughout the world, on video and on radio, in the newspapers, by every means known to science and used by man, the story that I am going to tell you is being told to others.

"It is very simple.

"You know of Sandro Botticelli, and his priestess Isabella, you know what they claimed; and you know what has happened. The damage and destruction caused by the *elementa* which raged over the whole world, was as great as the destruction by a hundred atom bombs. And many thousands died. To try to settle this issue for all time, the

religious leaders of the world will submit themselves, un-
armed, to a struggle with the supernatural forces which
Botticelli controls. All those leaders who deny the claims of
Botticelli and Isabella—all of them, remember—are now
gathered on a small oasis in the centre of the great Kalahari
Desert. This spot was selected because it is believed that
the terrible storms which will rage about these martyrs—
and whatever else one believes, men and women who are
prepared to die for their beliefs are martyrs—will do less
damage on the Kalahari than anywhere else in the world.
Certainly it will not greatly affect the oceans, and all main air
routes should be safe.

"You see how well everything has been planned," went on
Cardell. His voice became suddenly bitter, his hands
clenched before the unseen multitude. "The life of the
nations shall be disturbed as little as possible, while this
battle is fought out.

"Will it *be* fought?

"I can hear the sceptics, clearly. I can hear their sneering
and see their derisive smiles. Well, maybe they are right,
but I don't think so. I'm going to find out. With a number
of other newspapermen and newsmen, I am going to the
Kalahari. I don't know whether I shall ever come back. If I
do, then maybe I'll have some *real* news for you. If I
don't——

"You'll remember me, folk, won't you?"

   .   .   .   .   .

"You shouldn't go," Kennedy said to Palfrey savagely.
"To leave Drusilla and the children—it's crazy, it's criminal.
If you'll tell me what good you think you can do, I'll listen.
But what difference will one person make?"

Palfrey said: "That's just it. I don't know."

Andromovitch said: "If everyone said that, how many
would go?"

"I know that I can't stop you," Kennedy said brusquely.
"I think I ought to be able to stop Sap. Sap, listen. I think
you're betraying Drusilla. Understand? I think you're
walking out on your son, on Alexander the Second and on
Marion. I think you're robbing a woman of the one man she
cares for, and two fine children of their father. I call that
betrayal."

"Yes," agreed Palfrey. "That's what you would call it."

"You can still change your mind," Kennedy said. "Stefan, why don't you get on board?"

Andromovitch looked into Palfrey's pale, distressed face, then nodded, gripped Kennedy's shoulder and turned towards the waiting aircraft, a four-engined machine with the engines already warming out, the ground staff standing about, the chocks ready to be moved.

A great crowd, thousands upon thousands of silent people, were within sight, watching.

In the aircraft, Sam McCall was looking out of the window. Cardell was also there. The Bishop of Llansed was looking by a window, next to him although he was not visible, was the older, ascetic man, the hostile Bishop of Chenny, compelled by a force he could not resist.

"Don't go, Sap," Kennedy begged. "Drusilla's over there, watching. Just think what she'll feel like when you take off. Hasn't she suffered enough in the past? And isn't there plenty for you to do down here? You can help them, if they've really convinced you, you'll do more good alive than dead. Don't go."

His voice broke.

Palfrey said: "I believe I'll be back."

He turned and mounted the steps, and disappeared into the aircraft. The door was closed, the chocks freed, the engine roared and the machine began to taxi ready for the take-off.

Palfrey sat down beside Sam McCall.

The aircraft began to move.

.   .   .   .   .

"Every possible means of observation is being used in the neighbourhood of the Kalahari," the radio broadcasts claimed. "Preparations have been made in their way as thorough as those made for the trial explosions of the atom and hydrogen bombs in Nevada, Woomera and in the Monte Bella Islands. Aircraft, viewpoints, bomb-shelters, all these will be ready. Cameras with tremendous speeds will operate once the storms start. A report will be broadcast every hour from midnight tonight, and more often if circumstances appear to warrant it."

.   .   .   .   .

An F.B.I. man said: "If Botticelli wipes that lot out——"
Another rolled his cigar slowly along his lips. "I wouldn't like to be on that desert myself, Jo, not for a hundred grand."

.   .   .   .   .

"If you take a concensus of the editorial opinion of the Press of the United States you find that no more than one in thirty refuses to believe that this is the day of great decision," said Cardell's stand-in. "Some don't believe there will be any storms, and the simplest comment has come from the *Sentinel*, Dyoma, Wisconsin. 'Since the world began we've had storms,' it says, 'and since we've had storms we've lived through them. Any man, woman or child who loses sleep over the storms that might happen in a desert six thousand miles away is crazy as a coon.'
"Well, that's the *Sentinel*, Dyoma. But there is the other point of view, the Christian, if you like, although it's shared by people of all religions. Perhaps this can best be expressed in the words of the Nicota *Times-News*, Alabama. 'Every day until the news comes,' says the editorial, 'this newspaper will keep its front page empty, except for one sentence: *No News Yet*. And it's my bet that we won't have an empty front page for long.' "

.   .   .   .   .

"Gee, pop!" exclaimed a lad in Miami, "just you look at that dark cloud. Ain't it moving fast? Gee, pop, it'll hide the sun, won't it?"

.   .   .   .   .

"Look, darling, there's a great bank of fog up there, moving so fast. It's terrifying. It—it must stretch from here to London! Darling, we must—we *must* go to church."

.   .   .   .   .

"And the cloud was as dark as the darkest night and as thick as the thickest fog, may Allah be my judge."

.   .   .   .   .

"So Botticelli is doing what he boasted he could do," said the Old Man, very quietly.

.   .   .   .   .

The British Broadcasting Corporation's news service said: "It is now indisputable that a phenomenal number of moving patches of fog have been seen drifting from all parts of the world towards the African continent. Shipping around the African coast has been warned to change course and make for the nearest harbour.

"A news-flash just received from a French aircraft patrolling the desert area from Dakar reports that lightning of unusual brilliance has been observed in the Kalahari Desert area. Visibility has been reduced practically to nil, and places as far apart as Accra, on the Gold Coast, and Mombasa, on the East Coast of Africa, are blanketed by fog. Reports say that a number of violent explosions had rocked native villages in the Sudan and in Nyasaland."

.   .   .   .   .

The front page of the Nicota *Times-News* had been empty for three editions, covering twenty-four hours. On the morning of the next day, twenty-four hours after Palfrey's aircraft had landed in the Kalahari, it contained one small box, bearing a single paragraph of small type, reading:

"Though they walk through the valley of the shadow . . ."

26

CARDELL, Palfrey, Andromovitch and McCall were standing near the aircraft which had just brought them to the desert when the first wisps of cloud appeared high in the tropical heavens. It was already so hot that the men were sweating. Some of the pilgrims had set up small tables, where water, brought by special transport aircraft, was being dispensed. Thousands of religious leaders were in small groups about the stretch of sandy waste. Hundreds of tents had been erected, and aircraft, mostly obsolete, had been left for their use. Many of the men and women were young, but the elder prelates were in a large majority. Bishops in their robes, *mullahs* in their simple gowns, Sikh priests in their almost primitive array, Hindus naked to the waist and simple men in black, quiet, confident and unafraid, all these people waited to justify their faith.

Another aircraft flew through the darkness which was gathering fast, smaller than most, watched by all. None of the correspondents expected another, the leaders were believed to be here, ready and waiting.

The aircraft touched down.

After a moment, the door opened, the steps were put into position and Botticelli appeared.

A great stillness fell upon the multitude.

Botticelli waited at the foot of the steps, while Isabella followed him, then Mathilde, then others of the angels; twelve in all.

They moved towards the multitude.

With them, close to Isabella, was Forrester. Palfrey saw the way his face was set, saw the rigidity of his movements. He looked like a man remote from the world, from all that went on about him.

Then Bruton climbed from the aircraft and walked towards Palfrey; he looked an old, old man.

He muttered: "Botticelli says they can't hurt him. He'll prove that he is indestructible. Hear that? He says he'll *prove* it. And he can make the *elementa* do what he likes, understand? He can do it!"

"He'll try," said Palfrey gently.

"I tried to kill him, I couldn't get near him," Bruton went on, in a cracked voice. "I couldn't get near him, it's as if he's surrounded by an invisible wall."

Palfrey said: "I think I know."

"I am going to join them, Sap. Are you coming?" Andromovitch said calmly.

Bruton screeched: "You can't go out there!"

"I'm coming with you," said Senator McCall.

Palfrey said to Bruton: "Take it easy, Corny, when it's all over we'll feel better. Take it easy." He moved towards the multitude, watched by Cardell, the newspapermen, the cameramen, the world.

Bruton was quivering.

Andromovitch and McCall went with Palfrey, and all three approached the centre of the host.

Botticelli, his angels and Forrester had neared the centre, and waited. Botticelli was surrounded by his angels, and Forrester was by Isabella's side.

.   .   .   .   .

The fog hung in a great pall, stretching to the horizons, north, east, south and west. It was getting thicker, darker. What little light there was had a yellow tinge, familiar and menacing to those who had been through one of the attacks before. No thunder rumbled and no lightning flashed, but remorselessly the fog closed in.

The Bishop of Llansed, with a Cardinal from Rome, with the world's leaders, stood together, and Botticelli was near them.

Palfrey was close to them, also.

The wind, unheralded, sprang suddenly out of the fog, and as it came the multitude began to pray, and among them were many who were chanting:

"Though we walk through the valley of the shadow . . ."

The wind grew fiercer.

Then out of it tore the *elementa*, screeching and writhing, filling the air with their awful noises, striking at the still and quiet people, striking at the old and the young alike.

Man after man fell.

Leader after leader died.

The others stood fast, while the *elementa* struck and twisted, screeched and killed, the wind howled, the thunder rolled, lightning brighter than man had ever known lit up every face, shone upon every eye, touched every head. More and more of the host fell, suddenly and silently, quite surely dead.

Botticelli and the angels did not move.

An *elementa* struck savagely at the Bishop of Llansed, who stood near Isabella, and he fell without a sound. One struck at McCall, those writhing tentacles of mist carrying death.

McCall fell.

Palfrey felt mist clutch at his throat.

He saw Andromovitch move, heard the gasping, saw the *elementa* try to strangle the Russian: saw the *elementa* vanish in an explosive mist.

He saw Forrester thrust Isabella aside, and stride towards Botticelli. Isabella grasped his hand. Forrester shouted, but what he said was swallowed up in the turmoil. There was exaltation on his face as he struck at Botticelli; as if the faith of so many people spurred him to strike. Isabella pulled at him desperately, Mathilde and others rushed at him, there was a struggling group within the group of men upon whom the *elementa* fell with unrelenting fury.

Botticelli staggered, and suddenly *elementa* turned on him. He *fell*.

And as he dropped there and lay still, the *elementa* seemed to rage only at him, ignoring those of the multitude who were now still standing. Botticelli and Isabella, Forrester and the angels were hidden from the others in a swirling cloud of mist.

Gradually, it began to thin out.

The wind, the lightning and the thunder seemed to meet in a single blasting onslaught; a thousand more believers fell, but as many stayed upright.

Palfrey felt a dreadful coldness . . . the end was close, only seconds were left.

Suddenly, there was an end to horror.

The *elementa* seemed to lose their power, as if the one final effort had been too much for them. There was only the writhing mist. There was tumult in the sand. There were faint patches of an oily substance, pink in colour, a dozen, a hundred, a thousand. There were hundreds upon hundreds of dead believers, but many thousands were still alive.

In the midst of these, quite dead, were Botticelli and his angels.

Near Isabella, was Forrester—also dead, but with a strange smile on his lips.

.   .   .   .   .

The fog cleared.
The sun shone.
The wind ceased.

.   .   .   .   .

As Palfrey walked quietly along the streets of London, a few days later, there was a hint of mist in the air. He could look upon it without fear or anxiety. He could not know for certain that no one would ever create *elementa* again, but he felt a relief from dread which he believed would never come back.

Drusilla was waiting for him.

So was Andromovitch.

Bruton was in a nursing-home, sick in mind, but the reports of his progress were good.

Palfrey was thinking of all that had followed the miracle in the desert, going through the countless things that had been said of it. Cardell had retracted every word. The followers of Botticelli in their hundreds of thousands had turned away from the man who could not be killed, yet who was dead.

There were millions who declared that it was a miracle, inspired only by faith.

There were, perhaps, a few who doubted this.

There was talk of new understanding among the different Churches, even of a kind of union among the great religions. The talk might fade, and hope die. Unity might still be a thousand years away, but in all people there was a capacity for a deeper faith, a greater readiness to believe.

Palfrey knew this.

The Old Man knew.

Did Forrester know?

Palfrey found himself thinking more of Forrester than of anyone else—even than of the Bishop of Llansed. He could picture the smile on Forrester's face. He knew from Bruton what conflict had been in Forrester's mind. He did not know who had broken Botticelli's neck—whether an *elementa* had turned upon him, or whether Forrester had been given superhuman strength. The certain thing was that Botticelli had known fear; with fear, weakness had come, and he had died.

The world was not only free from the threat, but had glimpsed itself as it might one day be.